I Can
See You

Michael Leese

To Maureen Leese
thanks mum…

Michael Leese is a national newspaper journalist who worked in Fleet Street for over 25 years, including 17 years at The London Evening Standard. He had always wanted to write a book, especially a crime or science fiction novel, but with work, family life, and lots of other excuses, he never seemed to get around to it. Then in 2007 Michael went freelance and finally had time to sit down and write. Born in Birmingham, his family moved to London where he spent his formative years: he and his wife now live in Dorset close to their adult autistic son. He is a volunteer trustee for the charity Autism Wessex.

Maidstone, Kent

Details, details, details; it was always about the details. Tom Bennett had thought he was a master of details: now he knew better. The thought had been hammered home as he sat in this strange room. Everything was painted a brilliant white, the colour dazzling in the harsh light produced by the industrial sized, clear-glass bulb hanging from the centre of the ceiling. It was directly overhead, throwing out waves of heat he could feel on his face, head and hands. Just a few moments ago Bennett had been unable to stop himself looking at it. Strange shapes were still dancing around his retinas.

The man who'd brought him here had introduced himself as Mr. Roberts, no first name. He was dressed as though he were on the way to a board meeting. A dark-blue, pin-striped suit, white shirt and pale-pink tie, with chunky gold cufflinks on display. It was his eyes that struck you. They were a bright, almost electric blue. When those eyes turned on him he felt as though all his secrets were being stripped away. There was nothing he could hide from this man.

He had rapidly discovered that Mr. Roberts did know all about him. He knew the medication he was on for blood pressure; he knew that the doctor had recently agreed to prescribe a drug to help him get an erection; he even knew that his wife wished he had never been given it since her own sex drive had faded after giving birth to their second child.

As Mr. Roberts had talked so Bennett could see his life reduced to a series of cold facts. His height, five feet and eighth inches; his shoe size, left-foot size seven, right-foot size seven-and-a-half; his weight, thirteen stones and ten pounds; how many fillings he had, five; how much he'd told the doctor he drank, twenty-one units a week, and how much he really drank, 25 units so far, this week, 30 units the week before. He even knew how often he got up in the night to use the toilet.

On and on it had streamed. At first, he had been puzzled, then alarmed as the story of his life was put on display. How many underpants he had, twelve apparently; what his inside leg measured, twenty-seven inches; the prescription he needed to correct his short sight. By the time Mr. Roberts had worked his way round to his finances he had accepted there was no point in denying anything. Being presented with the details of his Swiss bank account - he thought no one knew about that - turned him into a true believer. Now he was beginning to think of Mr. Roberts as part mentor, part inquisitor and part shaman.

Bennett was a small man, a bit weedy, with thinning hair and glasses that never sat properly. He had numerous physical tics; scratching at his head, arms, face, neck and shoulders. Colleagues said you could gauge the state of his mind by the rate of his movements. Slow for relaxed; fast when firing on all cylinders. Right now, he was showing none of those signs. Instead he was listening attentively to Mr. Roberts's voice. He found his deep voice compelling. He would probably do anything that voice told him.

Something was wrong - he had missed his cue to respond to a question. What was it? Ah, yes, now he had it. Mr. Roberts had just explained how careful observation told you everything you needed to know about a person. That had explained how he had known to be waiting on the common yesterday morning - and it was only yesterday.

Mr. Roberts wanted to know that he had understood. He went to nod his head but he couldn't move. He was bound so tightly with masking tape that even breathing was hard, although he had been rewarded for 'good behaviour' by being given a slightly bigger breathing hole around his nose and mouth. He looked at his captor and managed a hoarse 'yes'.

The answer seemed to please Mr. Roberts because he sat back in his chair and gave Bennett a nod. He even lent forward to pat his right hand, before reaching into his jacket and producing two aluminium knitting needles. They were the larger variety, ten millimetres in diameter. Mr. Roberts stood up and walked round the table so that he could carefully cut a small hole in the tape around both ears. Satisfied with his work he partially inserted the needles until they were pressed up against the ear drums.

All Bennett could focus on was the contrast between the radiated heat from the bulb burning the top of his head, and the cold sensation of the knitting needles in his ears. Those blue eyes locked on his. He stopped breathing. Mr. Roberts smiled and slammed each needle deep into his victim's brain. Bennett couldn't even manage a scream before his body thrashed against the restraints. He was dead instantly.

Mr. Roberts watched impassively as he waited for the corpse to complete its death dance. Once the body was quite still he produced a surgical scalpel from his jacket and placed it on the table. Unwrapping the head, he picked up the blade, worked it into the skin behind the left ear, and skilfully filleted the dead man's face. Finished, he held it up for inspection. He liked the way the light from the bulb shone through the gaps for the eyes and the mouth. As soon as it had dried out a little he would try it on for size. Perhaps this one would work.

1

It wasn't how he'd expected it to be. So far, he'd spotted several Star Wars, an Avengers and a couple of t-shirts bearing the names of what he presumed were rock bands; just none he recognised. The casual dress, and it didn't apply to everyone, did nothing to disguise the intensity. Everyone at GCHQ seemed to be in a hurry to get where they were headed and he noted that few were saying hello to their colleagues.

Just getting in had been complex, but this was Britain's super-sensitive listening post in Gloucestershire, where thousands of analysts worked at deciphering information snatched from the digital world. The Doughnut, as it was universally known, had its own restaurants staffed by waiters and waitresses who'd been security vetted, shops with assistant's subject to background checks and even the Cappuccino was made by baristas given personal clearance to get past the gate-guards provided by a special contingent of MoD police.

All this was new to Brian Hooley, a veteran Detective Chief Inspector with Scotland Yard's Special Investigation Unit. He had been driven down from London after receiving an urgent summons. He hadn't even had time to tell his boss. He was told there was a car waiting outside, they wanted him to hurry. Within minutes he was in the back of a black Jaguar saloon heading out to Hammersmith and then the M4, past Heathrow, and picking up the ever-crowded M5. The driver, a rugged looking man with a military style close-cropped hair cut and dressed in a dark-grey suit, white shirt and no tie, told him roadworks elsewhere made this the only route.

He settled back in the rear seat, glancing in the rear-view mirror to check his hair; he thought his recent trip to the barber had highlighted how grey he was becoming. It didn't feel that long ago when it was mostly dark. Studying the reflection of his eyes he noticed his crows' feet were more prominent than ever. He looked away, the rest of him was in decent shape, he'd even managed to recently shrink his stomach a little. Not bad for an 'ordinary middle-aged bloke' suddenly jettisoned from settled family life to the dubious pleasures of bachelorhood.

As they sped out of London he tried to keep his mind clear. It was pointless to speculate about this summons. In his limited experience of getting close to the security services it could feel like being at the centre of a whirlwind. A short while later, and to his immense surprise, he was woken from a dreamless sleep when a young woman opened the rear door, giving him an appraising look in the process: he had the unsettling impression she was less than impressed. He climbed out, thanked the driver and attempted to surreptitiously wipe his mouth in case he had been drooling. On the day of his departing home, many barbs were thrown his way, including the accusation that he slobbered worse than the dog when taking a nap on the sofa.

His greeter had a pale face, made paler by her jet-black hair and her choice of glasses; they were thick-framed, black and too big for her long face. The look reminded him of someone but he couldn't place it. She handed him a security pass with his picture on it, which got him through one set of barriers and she pointed him at a scanner to have his retinas checked against a data base. As he waited he recalled that the original imprint had been taken at around the time Jonathan Roper was transferred out of the Special Investigations Unit. This was the first time it had been put to the test.

As the lights turned green his companion took off into the building. He barely had time to take in his surroundings before they were rushing along a brightly lit corridor which seemed to cover the length of the building.

As he trotted to keep up, he heard her speak for the first time as she turned and told him he was being taken to meet the "neurodivergence" team. She made a fast right off the corridor and into a more dimly lit aisle of different sized cubicles with people working away. She stopped at a larger cubicle and indicated with a nod of her head that they had arrived. She took off, paying him no more attention. He was finding the initial experience slightly unnerving but as he stepped into the space he was immediately reassured to see the sole occupant was also wearing a shirt and tie.

"I was beginning to feel a little over-dressed," said Hooley, as he made a gesture that took in his dark grey suit and blue shirt with navy-blue tie. The DCI wasn't a fan of suits but had learned early in his career that it made life easier to wear one. To that end he owned four suits, two dark-grey and two dark-blue, and a couple of decent jackets to be worn with black trousers.

To Hooley's relief the man laughed, making him look very young as he did so. The DCI guessed he was probably the same age as the woman: which also made him the same age as Jonathan Roper. He wondered if he was going to be the oldest person in the building. He was also assuming it was because of Roper that he was here today. His former colleague had been working at the spy-centre for the past six months, his work as a police analyst earning him widespread praise.

Roper's talent had blossomed during a complex and highly sensitive case the pair had worked on in the previous year. While the credit for bringing a brutal gang to justice had rightly gone to Roper, it had emerged that Hooley had played a vital role. Roper had a form of autism that made it difficult for him to make friends. In fact, quite the reverse. But with Hooley's support he had worked wonders.

The DCI decided to take the initiative. Holding out his hand he said, "Brian Hooley, I got the call to get my arse down here and I'm guessing that it's to do with Jonathan?" The other man accepted the outstretched hand with a firm grip of his own.

"Good to meet you Brian, and thanks for getting down here so quickly. I'm David Cotter, part of the neuro-diversity team here - and you're right about Roper. My boss, Helen Sharples, had wanted to meet you but she's been called off to something, so you've got me." He pointed at a couple of sofa-style chairs. "They're pretty comfortable so grab a seat, but first, can I get you anything to drink?"

Hooley shook his head. He was trying to cut down on his fluids since he spent a lot of time getting up in the night urgently needing to empty his bladder. What he would never admit was that he liked to keep something back to allow for alcohol, although nowadays that tended to be a couple of glasses of wine or a pint or two of lager. As they sat down Cotter leaned forward, his expression earnest.

"Please indulge me as I give you a little context. Here at GCHQ we employ a lot of people with far from conventional thinking, dyslexia and autism to name a couple. They are the reason why we came up with the "neurodiversity" programme. Basically, a systematic way of saying people are different and need different things to allow them to work effectively."

He paused and then that smile appeared again. "Forgive me. You don't need to be a body language expert to see that you are not entirely happy with the way this conversation is going. Let me assure you that I am not about to produce lots of acronyms to explain some behavioural theory."

Realising he was making things worse, Cotter quickly added, "I'll cut to the point. We've been working with Jonathan since he got here and devised a programme to make him feel secure and able to perform to do his best work.

"Once we identified him as being a potential benefit, it was decided to make the system work for Roper, not the other way around. He has a unique position here because he almost works off-grid. He chooses what he wants to focus on from an initial information dump provided by us."

He glanced up at Hooley. "I don't know if you're a football man, but he's like the really skilful one who scores goals and doesn't have to worry about tackling. The problem is we haven't done a great coaching job because he has been struggling recently.

"I've been working closely with him to see what extra we can do and in the last few days something occurred to me that I hadn't considered because it so rarely applies to people like Roper. I think he's missing company: specifically, there is something about his relationship with you that allows him to do his best work. Something we haven't been able to replicate here at GCHQ."

Hooley was genuinely taken-aback. He was having trouble with the concept of Roper needing his company, but also secretly pleased. He was one of the few people at Scotland Yard who had backed him when his idiosyncratic behaviour intruded on to his colleagues; in some cases, generating ill-feeling.

To Hooley's surprise Cotter jumped to his feet. "Would you mind if I took you to meet him now? I think just watching how he acts when he sees you will confirm, or disprove, my theory."

2

David Cotter quickly opened up a gap as he surged ahead, leaving Hooley to think that a couple of weeks here would make him fitter. They were back in the main corridor, before reaching an area where the cubicles were separated from each other by dividers about five feet high. Cotter had stopped a few yards ahead and was waiting for Hooley to catch-up. The DCI arrived and turned to see Ropers's familiar face sitting at one of a pair of facing desks. His former colleague was working with two large screens directly in front of him and another large screen fixed at right angles to give both desks the ability to see what was running; in this case a French rolling news programme.

Thus far it was, to Hooley's eye, all very high-tech and very Roper, but then realised what was wrong with this scene. Roper was not wearing what amounted to his uniform - and protective armour against the world - his skinny-fit black suit, white shirt and narrow black tie. At Scotland Yard he had never seen him wearing anything else. Here he was sporting what even Hooley would describe as a middle-aged combo of trousers and button-down shirt.

What hadn't changed was his posture, sitting in the characteristic hunched position he favoured as he stared at his monitors. Seeing him like that always made Hooley wince as he thought of the strain it would put on his own back. He waited patiently for Roper to make some sort of acknowledgement that he was standing there. Eventually, he did look up from whatever had been holding his attention; his brown eyes flicking around the room before coming to rest on the DCI. "Oh, hello Brian." His tone was neutral and there was no hint of a welcoming smile; he looked back at the screens and was instantly enveloped in a cloud of concentration.

Hooley felt a sense of dislocation. Roper was famously undemonstrative but given this was the first time they had met in months - he would doubtless know how long down to the very second - surely a little enthusiasm was called for? Instead his former colleague seemed to be ignoring him, and he wasn't sure how to deal with it.

After what felt like a long moment of foot-shuffling uncertainty, at least as far as Hooley was concerned, Cotter broke the silence. "It looks like I was right." Before a puzzled DCI could ask him anything he sped off, if anything moving even faster than before.

The DCI was unsure what to do next, and decided that if Roper was going to carry on ignoring him he might as well make himself comfortable by sitting down at the empty desk: at least he could take the weight off his feet while he tried to work out why he had been rushed down here.

He was easing himself into the seat when Roper spoke. "I'd say you've lost about eight pounds since I last saw you. I'm glad you've decided to do something about being so fat." He hadn't looked away from his screens.

"It's eight-and-a-half pounds actually," responded Hooley, feeling a hot rush of anger. "And thanks very much for taking an interest." He might have tried injecting a note of sarcasm but knew that was pointless. The last time he had met up with Roper after a lengthy absence, the analyst had also told him he was overweight: no change there.

With nervous energy to burn he idly tapped at the keyboard on his desk, making his screen light up with a prompt asking for his password. It took a moment to register but then he performed a double take. The user name, BHOOLEY, was pre-loaded. He looked at Roper who had stopped staring at his own system and was now staring at him.

"When you've entered your password, you will get the same access to the system as me. I thought that would be best. I hope you don't mind but they won't accept the kind of passwords you normally use so I've written one out for you."

He passed Hooley a long list of numbers and letters that was indeed more complex than the name of his favourite pet dog, his usual choice. As he looked at the password he heard Roper say. "Don't worry about remembering it. I have got it stored in my head and you aren't likely to be here without me."

The policeman took a deep breath, he'd only been with Roper for a few moments and already he was experiencing the sensation that events were moving outside his control. Of the many questions tumbling around his mind he decided to pick the most obvious.

"Why would it be best for me to have the same level of clearance as you? Don't you need to be working here for that?"

Roper blinked rapidly: usually this indicated he thought someone had made a statement of the blindingly obvious. Despite having terrible trouble reading other people's expressions, or emotions, it was always a simple exercise to tell what was going through Roper's mind. Hooley waited for more information but the younger man had clearly exhausted his current line of conversation.

"Are you saying that I work here now? What about my other job at Scotland Yard, for the very unit you yourself were working for not that long ago?"

Now it was Roper's turn to look quizzical.

"But how can I do my work without you to help me?"

This strange day was starting to affect his grip on reality. Slumping back in his chair he tried to gather his thoughts. Not only did he have no idea what Roper was talking about; he had just heard the man say he needed his help, something that had never happened before. In situations like this Hooley usually liked to wait for Roper to fill him in on what was going through his mind. His thought processes were so unlike those of anyone else that it sometimes took him a while to explain things. He had long had the impression that Roper held conversations in his own head and then assumed everyone else had heard them.

This time Hooley had a powerful need to get up to speed with everyone else, so he decided to ignore his usual tactic and move directly to asking what was going on.

"OK Jonathan, from the beginning, what are you talking about?"

The reason he tended to avoid this approach was because asking Roper to fill in the details could lead to him presenting a smorgasbord of the tiniest facts, all delivered on an accurate timeline. For people without perfect recall - which Hooley didn't possess - it could turn into a grueling test of concentration, but he figured it was the only way forward.

It took about 20 minutes but eventually the mists cleared. It turned out that, as David Cotter suggested, Roper had, at first, been made to feel at home, working on topics that appealed to him and with Cotter as his main point of contact.

But things had steadily unraveled, which made Roper unsettled. This had led to lengthy discussions and they had tried many different solutions before realising the only answer was to get Hooley. Adding real urgency was Roper's belief that as his problems mounted, a major act of terrorism was imminent. It had been decided, at a senior level, to second the DCI. It seemed that without him being told he was now an honorary Spook. A situation which made him smile as he recalled that his father, who had also been a policeman, had once worked for Special Branch, and often joked to his son that if he had told him anything about it he would be obliged to kill him.

Hooley understood there was little point in making a fuss. A naturally phlegmatic man, he assumed that someone would eventually get around to telling him officially. If they'd assigned his clearance level it must be a done deal. A mischievous thought struck him. His divorce had come through a while back and his former wife was now seeing a teacher. Hooley wondered if his GCHQ access would allow him to dig into the man's background. They had met briefly on the doorstep of his former marital home and it was clear to both men that they would never be friends.

This idea sidled into his mind and despite his attempts to dismiss it he knew it was going to stick around for a while; he really did dislike the teacher. Trying to distract himself he checked his watch. To his surprise it was time to think about lunch. "Where do we go to get a cup of coffee and a sandwich round here?"

Roper leapt up, reminding him of a jack in the box. "Good idea. I was so busy talking to you that I hadn't realised how hungry I was." He rushed out of the door, moving quickly. He'd always been fast but GCHQ seemed to have turbo-charged him. "When we get back here I want to tell you about what I've been working on. I think there is a plot to kill a lot of world leaders."

3

Assistant Deputy Commissioner Julie Mayweather was waiting for a call after the sudden departure of Brian Hooley. He'd gone so quickly he'd only had time to send her the briefest of emails. An hour later and she was sitting in a meeting with the Commissioner, the newly-appointed Sir George Tarrant. Also present was the GCHQ Head of Analysis, Sam Brady, a man she had heard of but never met. To her surprise the head of MI5, Jennifer Cameron, was also present. She said very little, other than to acknowledge her colleagues.

The conversation was led by Brady, who turned out to be a decent sort, apologising for the short notice but stressing it was vital. He said. "I wouldn't have taken this action unless I could see no other alternative. Your man Roper has made quite an impression and trust me, GCHQ is not filled with people who are easily won over. It's that remarkable Rainbow Spectrum of his. Since he arrived he's been helping others try and construct their own versions, but his is still first and best."

Roper had revealed his extraordinary new way of analysing information during an investigation into murder and people trafficking that was linked to a secret attempt to create a cure for cancer by taking stem cells from young women. The investigation proved so complex he had developed a method of assigning principal colours of the rainbow to individual parcels of information. In turn, this enabled him to make new connections to all the different pieces of information. It was rather like solving a jigsaw puzzle by producing the key shape that no one else had seen.

Mayweather had long ago given up trying to fully understand what he had created. But there was no denying it worked.

Brady accurately read her expression. "He's explained it to me three times now and I still haven't got a clue what he's talking about, but plenty of others do. He's created something of a storm and was making a difference."

"Was making a difference?" She instantly picked up on the past tense.

The MI5 man nodded and spread his hands apologetically. "I don't want to exaggerate but we think there is a problem. Not with his ideas - they're still perfectly sound - but he just seems to have lost his way. It took us a while to pinpoint what was wrong, but we eventually concluded that Roper is lonely. Perhaps not lonely as you and I might see it, but he was missing interaction with one man: Brian Hooley."

She knew what was coming but wanted Brady to spell it out. He did. "The thing is, I know you've already loaned us Roper, now I'm afraid we need your deputy as well. It's vital we get Roper back on track.

"One of my senior team has likened what's going on to some sort of fog descending, making him lose his way. What's making us anxious is that a few weeks ago he was suggesting that some sort of unprecedented collaboration between very different terror groups was taking place. He hadn't got in to details before the fog descended. I've diverted senior analysts to it, but they can't see anything.

"As you can imagine the fact that we can't take the initial information forward has sent blood pressures rocketing. Not just here either. We share intelligence with countries all over the world so it's created issues in

Washington, Tel Aviv, Sydney and Paris - to name a few. All are aware of his unique abilities. That's why we need your help."

Even before he'd started name-checking world capitals she'd known this wasn't a request that she would be turning down. She said: "If anyone can get him back on track it's Brian Hooley. In some respects, they are like chalk and cheese, but in others they seem to bring the best out of each other. I would have been happy to deal with this over the phone, so thank you for taking the time to tell me yourself. I appreciate it."

"I wouldn't have it any other way," he replied. "If it hadn't been for you giving Roper a chance in the first place, well we'd never have known what a brilliant analyst he is. I know both you, and Brian Hooley, went out on a limb over him. It's important people remember that."

The meeting broke up and she made her way back to the Special Investigations Unit, an elite team of detectives housed in a secure building in Victoria, just a short walk from the main rail terminal.

On the journey back to the office her mind was already turning to the practical steps she needed to take; crucially, who was going to step into Brian Hooley's shoes? He was a formidable, vastly experienced senior officer, and would be missed. He'd recently suffered a spectacularly difficult marriage break-down, but it had never once impacted on his work.

Back in her own office she was assessing the current case load when Detective Inspector Norman Cleverly appeared in her doorway, an expectant look on his face.

"Tell me," she said, fearing the worst.

"We've had a second attack. This time the victim was snatched in Clapham and his body left in a disused warehouse in Kent, on the fringes of Maidstone. His face had been removed; exactly like the first one."

Her heart sank. "You say we know he was taken in Clapham. I presume that means we know who he is?"

The Inspector nodded. "The killer left the wallet and driving licence with the body. Because his wife reported him missing straight away local police were able to get confirmation from an unusual birthmark on his right forearm; it looks like a strawberry, only pale brown.

Cleverly shook his head. "The new victim is Tom Bennett; he had a wife and two kids, lived in a very nice house on Clapham Common and was a big player in the telecommunications business."

She quickly gathered her thoughts, her decision about who would be her acting deputy already decided. "Brian Hooley has been seconded to other duties for a while. Between you and me he's at GCHQ. I'd like you to take over his role with immediate effect. The first thing you can do is assemble the beginnings of the team to take this investigation on. Are the local police aware yet that this is almost certainly a serial killer at work?"

He shrugged. "We haven't made contact but I wouldn't be at all surprised if they were wondering. Although the first case was up in Yorkshire, just outside Leeds. It made huge waves because of the way the face was mutilated."

Her mouth formed a moue of disappointment. "I'm sure you're right. The best we can hope for is that this stays out of the media as long as possible. Can you get me the contact details for the locals down in Kent and make sure you brief the Press Bureau? I don't want them to lie, but if any journalists start fishing around they can try and point them in other directions."

She watched him head-off, impressed that he had taken the promotion in his stride and not wasted time asking questions. For now, it was obviously temporary, but who knew what would happen in the future. She walked to her personal bathroom. The building had once been a Corporate

HQ and she was lucky enough to have one for her exclusive use. She wanted to take the chance to freshen up while she could.

Locking the door behind her she pulled out a clean white blouse and bra. She splashed water around before checking herself in the mirror. She was always relieved to find that her face was managing to stay one step ahead of the wrinkles that had engulfed her mother. She put that down to plenty of exercise, good food, no alcohol and the fish oils she had been taking for twenty years. Staring back at her was a woman she liked the look of; fit and slim, short brown hair, expressive brown eyes and looking, in her opinion, pretty good for her fifties. After applying deodorant, she put her fresh clothes on and went back to face the world.

Waiting for Cleverly to finish up his preparations before they left, she couldn't help but think that things would probably be easier if she had her two top men with her. But that negative thought was pushed aside as she recalled Hooley's recent words.

"We've got a good team here who don't need us to tell them what to do."

4

The young guy at the counter glanced up as Roper walked in, then he reached down and held up a brown paper bag.

"Lunch order completed by us at 12.31pm then handed to you at..." He checked his watch. "12.34pm and 21 seconds."

Hooley was both amused and impressed. "I see the service around here is right on the money."

Counter guy, wearing a name badge that said "Nigel", jumped in. "We're right on the time, rather than the money. But I guess you being neurotypical explains why you're more interested in the cash."

The DCI caught himself before he could reply. Nigel was likely going to be similar to Roper, so anything he said might be examined intently. He went for a safer option. "Could I have a smoked salmon on brown bread, just a little butter, pepper and no cream cheese?"

Nigel handed him another bag. "Order completed by us at 12.25pm, collected by you at." Another check of the watch. "12.35pm and 42 seconds."

Hooley was already aware that he was in a unique environment, now he was beginning to understand quite how different it was.

"I take it Jonathan placed the order?"
Nigel, looking impatiently at the queue building behind the DCI, nodded his head.

"Of course he did. We're not mind readers. He told me last week that you would be here today and that would be the order I needed to prepare. Unless you need anything else, your coffee is ready at the other end of the counter." This was followed by an emphatic glance at the next person waiting in line.

Hooley moved away and watched Roper collect two take-away cups. As they headed back to the office he reflected he was obviously rather more predictable than he had thought. "Maybe here I am just a number," he muttered.

Roper pulled a large amount of food out of his bag. "Two chicken and bacon sandwiches on brown bread, two blueberry muffins and two bananas in case I still feel hungry." It sounded like he was ticking off a check-list.

Hooley studied the younger man for a moment. Despite his eating habits, it was clear that he hadn't put on any weight since he had last seen him six months ago. With his dark eyes and prominent cheekbones, he was a striking looking man with a semi-detached manner that gave him an enigmatic, almost mysterious air. At least that's what Hooley thought, although he was well aware that Roper's former colleagues found him rather more challenging.

Oblivious to this inspection Roper was demolishing his food: both sandwiches had disappeared before Hooley had managed to extract his from its cardboard packaging, something he was embarrassingly bad at. Sandwich finally freed, he couldn't help being envious of Roper's prodigious consumption making no difference to his weight. He was still skinny, his six-feet-two-inch frame never filling out. He was tempted to ask where the black suit was but decided that would emerge in the course of events. Roper always had a reason if he suddenly changed his habits.

He was just about to eat when David Cotter walked back in and gave Hooley a rueful smile. "I guess you may have realised that we were much further along than I let on." He glanced over at Roper. "Jonathan, is this a good time for me to run Brian through the security protocols? It won't take long then you can get on when he comes back."

Roper had just taken a huge bite out of his first muffin and sprayed food on his desk when he tried to answer. He started an ineffectual attempt to use his hand to sweep up the crumbs.

Cotter grinned at him. "I'll take that as yes then. If you need us we'll be in my office."

As they made their way along the corridor Hooley remembered he hadn't done so much walking since the time Jonathan had come to stay with him at his flat in Pimlico.

He followed Cotter into his office and they sat down facing each other over a low table. The man held his hands up in apology. "I should have been honest from the start, but your transfer here was sanctioned at a very high level so I wasn't sure how much I was supposed to say. I think all of us here were caught up in the urgency and focussed on the logistics rather than the person."

Hooley had suspected this was the case. In his experience people in organisations often became entangled in events; there was no need for him to take things personally. It wasn't as if he had much choice anyway, and if they thought Roper needed his support, then he was glad to help.

As he mulled this over he lapsed into silence, which Cotter attempted to fill. "Let me try to give you all the details. Right from the moment he joined us it was clear that Roper had an emotional connection to you that he doesn't have with anyone else. This was something we were interested in because Roper has a simple technique when it comes to other people: he tends to shut them out.

"He has developed a pretty decent working relationship with myself and others on the team, but that's it. Apart from the guy in the coffee shop. Like Roper he struggles with emotion. This seems to be enough for them to build a relationship on."

He took a drink of water from a bottle on his desk. "I'm getting off topic. The point is that we worked with Roper to create an environment that we thought would allow him to work to his maximum potential, and at first it did. But he has been slowly losing his way. This problem manifested itself just as he started talking about evidence of some sort of global terrorist action, so now we were getting really worried.

The psychologist stared at a point on his desk for a while, gathering himself, then asked. "Has anything like this happened before? Something you have witnessed?"

Hooley nodded. "There was; quite different to what you have just described, but it is worth me telling you. It goes back to the point where he was suspended briefly; something I have always blamed myself for.

"I'm not sure what happened but I do know that in the build up to the crisis I had taken my eye off him and didn't notice how hard he was working, or just how seriously he was taking things. I think he got to the point where he had taken all the responsibility on himself.

"But this was a three-year investigation with dozens of officers and support staff. In fact, he had only started working with us in the previous 12 months, so there was no way he should have thought it was all down to him - but he did."

Cotter had been listening with rapt intention. "So, what did you do about it?"

Hooley looked abashed. "While he was off on his silly suspension I had a chance to do a bit of thinking. I took the view that so long as he wasn't left to his own devices he would be fine. I don't mean babysit him, just keep an eye open.

"I put him in a desk right next to me. That way I could see him all the time."

He leaned back in his chair and grinned.

"No one can argue against what I did because that's when he came up with his Rainbow Spectrum and smashed that gang of mercenaries trafficking women into London for use in medical research."

"I don't think I am giving away any secrets when I say that many people understand that it was you who played such a key role," said Cotter. "Great credit to Julie Mayweather for backing you, but you put your neck on the line. The point is that once we established that you were the missing link - I mean that in a very good way - steps were taken to get you down here.

"I discussed it with Jonathan and he seemed enthusiastic, and after that the powers that be got involved to clear it for you. Your boss has just been told and, as you know, we have given you access to the system here. So welcome to the team."

Hooley smiled his acknowledgement. "It never hurts to try something new, even for old dinosaurs like me." Before Cotter could say anything, he added. "Your position here sounds like you have more authority than just being part of the support team."

Cotter tipped his head to one side to acknowledge a point well made. "I have very high clearance, and need it, because of the people I work with. All the members of the team here do. I need to know what all the people I work with are doing so I can make proper assessments, so yes, we do things differently here.

"Talking of doing things differently reminds me, we have someone outside your flat and if you give us permission they can go inside and get anything you want to see you through the next few days. If you need any medication we have our own doctors here so they can prescribe what you need."

Hooley gave him a knowing look. "Won't your man require a key to get in?" He got the answer he expected when Cotter almost squirmed with embarrassment.

They stood up. "I guess you have everything covered. Tell me though, why did you need me to come down here first? Why not just come and see me at Victoria?"

"I wanted to be certain that I was right and that meant seeing how you and Jonathan interacted."

"But he barely looked up when I saw him; how did that help you?"

"It was his hair. After he had been here for a while I realised you can tell when he's relaxed or not by looking at his hair. If it's standing up you know he's feeling tense. When he saw you it was…"

"Looking nice and flat," Hooley interrupted. "Of course, how could I have missed that? Roper has always been the man who put the 'bad' in 'having a bad hair day.'"

5

He'd forgotten what a prodigious amount of information Roper could work through. By contrast, and after several hours of intense effort, he had barely scratched the surface. Some of the material he was reading was recorded as highly classified. Taking notes was forbidden; memory only. He sat up and eased his neck. Doing this sort of intensive screen work nearly always made his back ache. He was sure he would pay a price later, if not today then tomorrow.

What he needed was a break - yet another short walk would do it - but Roper had disappeared while he was absorbed in his task. Rather than sit there waiting for his return he decided he could at least head to the canteen - the GCHQ trot, as he thought of it.

He returned to find Roper in situ. This time the younger man did more than give him a brief nod of recognition. He was looking positively expectant.

"Did you pick anything up from that material I gave you?"

Hooley took his time, walking round to sit down at his desk and taking a sip of coffee before placing it next to his keyboard.

"If the answer to your question is: did I read a lot of frankly terrifying material about the links between different terrorist groups? Then the answer is a firm yes.

"If the answer is: did I spot any of the links you would like me to see? Then sorry, the answer is no."

Roper's face fell. While he had been working at Scotland Yard this inability to hide his emotions had been the cause of intense debate. The more cynical argued no one could be that open. For Hooley, the real point was that, had Roper been looking at himself, he would have struggled to interpret his own expression.

The younger man said: "I was really hoping you might be able to help me find my way back."

Hooley knew he needed to make sure Roper stayed on an even keel. A lot of people were worried about what he might have discovered, or been on the brink of discovering, so that would create pressure. The trouble is that he didn't do simple. It was likely whatever he had pieced together would have come from multiple strands of information. That was the thing about Roper, he read everything and saw what others missed.

Fortunately, the DCI felt fresh and ready for the battle. He was determined to be positive.

"Let's try coming at this another way? Maybe that will help you get back on track." Roper's expression was neutral, he wanted to hear what Hooley had in mind. The DCI closed his eyes for a moment as he paused to gather his thoughts. "From what you've shown me you clearly think this is terror related."

Roper looked impatient.

"Of course it's terror related. That's one of the big things we do down here. Try and catch terrorists by intercepting their secret messaging."

The DCI wasn't in the least perturbed by this abrupt treatment. From anyone else he would have found it rude, but with Roper he knew it was just the man being honest, a bit close to the bone maybe, but that's how he rolled. He held up both hands in mock surrender.

"Of course, Jonathan, no one is trying to tell you how to do your job; I'm just trying to do things the old-fashioned way and build up some sort of overview of how you got to the point where things suddenly got confusing." He pressed on. "Looking at the timestamps on the intelligence reports, your concerns were triggered by news that Somali pirates got their hands on a new and more powerful boat. Am I right in thinking they have been using it to carry out new attacks on shipping that comes near their stretch of coast? Are we saying that this new vessel gives them new opportunities for piracy?"

Roper had been sitting quite still but now he stood up.

"No, no, no. You can't assume that's the point at all. The only thing we know is that they got it 18 months ago and since then we have heard nothing. It could be they are holding it back, or there's something I haven't thought of yet."

When he sat down Hooley noted that Roper's hair was standing up. This issue with the pirates was clearly important. He made a mental note and moved on.

"The next thing you've flagged up is a report by the Australian Security Intelligence Organisation some thirteen months ago. I've had limited dealings with them but am I right in saying they are like our MI5?" There was no dissent from Roper so he pressed on. "The report is about an upsurge of super-strength cocaine being trafficked in from Bali, although the people behind this are said to be Australian criminals. Nothing to do with Somali pirates who are - and I looked this up on Google - some six thousand miles away across the Indian Ocean."

He stopped to see if Roper noticed his little bit of research but there was no response. He shrugged: he might have impressed himself with his use of Google but clearly the master thought this was elementary stuff.

"Moving on: the next piece of data concerns a meeting eight months ago that was monitored by a joint FBI/Homeland Security task-force trying to infiltrate some sort of pow-wow between three of the biggest white supremacist groups in America."

A thought struck him and he searched for the right piece of paper before realising the report he was looking for was on screen. He found it and quickly scanned it.

"Is this right? It says here that they met up in New York. I thought those sorts of people stayed down in the Deep South?"

Roper raised an eyebrow as he said. "Not everyone spots that straight off, well done." Once again Hooley kept his smile to himself, there was no point in complaining that he had just been patronised.

Roper carried on. "It turns out they may have known they were under observation. They were due to meet in New Mexico but suddenly changed plans and that's how they ended up in New York. By the time anyone found out they'd been and gone. The FBI and CIA are still blaming each other."

The silence went on long enough for Hooley to realise Roper wasn't going to add anything.

"OK. Let me start with the obvious. Are you thinking that this lot are working together, which seems a bit of a stretch, if you don't mind me saying?

"The only thing I can imagine these groups doing is fighting each other. Nothing seems to link them, certainly not geography, and there is no suggestion that any of these groups has worked together before. I'll admit it, I cannot see any circumstance which would make these people act together. The thought of them making common cause is terrifying."

He checked Roper to make sure he wasn't about to speak then added. "The only thing I can give you, and that grudgingly, is they are all criminals. But who believes there is honour among thieves? This lot hate each other's guts."

Now Roper was up and pacing. "If you look at it that way you're right. I'm trying to recall the way I was looking at it, but it's like things have gone all misty. I must have seen something, or made a connection with the Rainbow Spectrum, but I can't remember the detail.

"I can't be sure, but I think I was looking at links between one group and another. Not all three together, but I may just be mixing it up with other information.

"Being here at GCHQ is like nowhere else. The amount of information is just amazing and it keeps piling in. My job is to look at what interests me and see if I can pick out major shifts in what is going on. When I started here that seemed to work well.

"But now that is working against me and that's really worrying me. I have this sense that something terrible is going to happen and I may be the only one who can stop it, if I could just remember what it was."

Hooley was fascinated by this. "Are you saying that the Rainbow Spectrum is letting you down in some way?"

The question produced a huge sigh from Roper. "It's sort of complicated and easy. I know I've been calling it the Rainbow Spectrum, but in some ways, you could call it the Roper Spectrum. It's about the way that I work and think.

"It was helpful to give the process a name because it felt quite separate from me. I still think it will work properly again but now it is causing a problem, a bit like I can't feed in the right information.

"To answer your question, something is going wrong with the Rainbow Spectrum, but I don't know how. I am sure the concept still works, so, maybe I am looking at the information I feed into it the wrong way. That's why I need your help going through it."

As intrigued as he was by this, Hooley felt out of his depth. He moved to safer ground with some light self-mockery. "Now that I'm here you've got someone who can share the blame. Trust me, I've taken plenty of blame over the years." He fixed Roper with a direct look. "I tell you what though, my ex-wife's mother had a thing about threes. 'Bad things always come in threes,' she said."

There wasn't much to say after that and they lapsed into silence. After a few minutes Hooley sat up straighter, he had remembered something that might give a new perspective.

"Much as I hate to admit this, I may have been wrong about something. A couple of months ago there was a restricted briefing note from the Met counter terror unit. I don't recall all of it, but I think it was suggested that, in certain circumstances right-wing groups might be willing to support jihadi terror gangs.

"If I'm honest I dismissed the idea as nonsense. It sounded like someone was being too clever by half, but what if there is something to it?"

At first Roper said nothing but it was clear he was thinking very hard. He finally spoke to say: "That might be very important."

6

Julie Mayweather stepped through the gap in the chain-link fence which enclosed the expanse of crumbling tarmac. It was all that was left of a car-park that had served the warehouse. She was heading towards DI Cleverly who was waiting by an open side-door; from this distance it looked like a black hole in the grey metal cladding of the building.

The DI was a short, stocky man, with a bull neck and heavy features set in a permanent glower, quite at odds with his personality. A fast-track graduate entrant, he had an inquisitive mind coupled with a light touch personality that earned him the respect, even affection, of his colleagues. But as she got closer she could see that today his habitual expression was an accurate barometer of his mood: he was as grim as the early summer weather, which being Britain included threatening clouds, cold wind and rain.

"Looks like you'd better talk me through what we're going to find in there," she said.

"Yes, Ma'am," said Cleverly, his unusually formal manner a further reminder of what to expect. "The scenes of crime people have just finished so we can go inside. He's where local police found him following an anonymous tip-off.

"Inside it's basically one huge open-plan space which was used to store furniture. But it gets weird. Someone has gone to the trouble of building a small cabin right in the centre of the building. They've even hooked a power supply to it.

"Inside this cabin is the body. Mr. Bennett has been bound very tightly with masking tape and is sitting in front of a table. As you know his face has been removed. In front of him someone has left his wallet on the table which is where we found his ID.

"He also has that distinctive strawberry birthmark and someone has helpfully rolled his sleeve up so that we can clearly see it."

The DI paused as he looked at the floor and took several deep breaths. He'd been on a couple of basic psychology courses and thought it was entirely possible the killer - he was sure it was one person - was taunting them. He knew it was never good when sadistic murderers sought to send messages to the police; it suggested they thought themselves quite superior.

Cleverly went on. "Sticking out of each ear are what we think are knitting needles. The doctor will remove them when he gets back to the morgue, but it's got to be a certainty that he died after the attacker slammed them into his brain."

From time to time police officers must see things the rest of us don't. As far as Julie Mayweather was concerned this was going to be one of those moments. She was surprised by an intense longing to have Brian Hooley at her side: his unflappable manner would have helped her stay calm. Then she looked at Cleverly; his determination to do a professional job was clear. She felt guilty for doubting him, even indirectly.

"Right then," she said, mustering a modicum of bravado. "Lead the way." Knowing what was inside the cabin made her suppress a desire to shiver. There was a horribly theatrical element to this. She almost turned to look as she had the sensation that someone was watching from the shadows. She sensed there would be more victims unless the killer was caught soon.

Gesturing at the wooden cabin she asked. "Why do you think someone went to all the trouble of building this? Once they'd got him inside this place they had all the privacy they would need." She stopped and noticed for the first time that the cabin was expertly constructed. The thought was incongruous, conjuring up images of a DIY killer.

She shook off the idea. "Do we know yet if this is one person or several people? Have the soccos picked up anything this time?"

Cleverly shook his head. "No clues so far. The anonymous caller was a male and spoke in a Yorkshire accent, not that I'm paying too much attention to that. Plenty of people can mimic different ways of talking. For what it's worth, my guess is that this is just one person. I'm hoping the scenes of crime team can confirm that."

Mayweather realised she was asking questions to put off having to go inside. She steeled herself. "Right, let's get this over with."

They walked over to the cabin door and she looked inside as the last of the forensic people stepped out.

"We can move the body when you're ready, Ma'am." said a woman, who stood to one side to allow her to go in.

She looked through the door and what she saw immediately went to the top of a private list of things she would recall for the rest of her life. Where the face should have been was a bloody mask with two blue eyes in the middle; even the eyelids were gone. She prayed the victim had been dead before this mutilation took place. The knitting needles added to the grotesque nature of what she was looking at.

Although the overall impression was revoltingly gory, there was little blood pooled around the body and she hoped this indicated he had been killed first. The facial wounds looked clean, not all ragged. She wondered at the skill needed to do such a thing. The team would have to find out; maybe they should ask a surgeon. In fact, they should check with facial replacement surgeons generally. She was prepared to bet it was a small field.

She looked around and saw the cabin appeared to be made out of wood and painted white including the floor and ceiling. As the DI had said, someone had even fitted a light.

Turning back to Cleverly she indicated she had seen enough and allowed in the ambulance crew, who started to gently cut away the tape to release the body. After a few minutes, they had freed his arms and body, one of the men supporting the body, trying to maintain some dignity for the corpse.

She turned away. There was detective work to do. So far, the first murder had been left to the locals but now they would need to travel to Yorkshire to see the murder scene and sign off a transfer of the remains to London.

This was the sort of thing that she would normally have left for Hooley, but in the circumstances, she decided it would be fairer on Cleverly to leave him to supervise the operation here and travel North herself. But first there was one more duty.

"I think the birth mark makes it clear we have the identity of the victim. You and I need to go and see his wife. Let's see if she has any idea about who might have done this to her husband."

7

Lisa Bennett was a small woman and her grief was acting like a sponge; sucking the life out of her and making her draw in on herself. She was sitting on a huge striped settee in the front room of her Clapham Common home. She'd pulled her legs under her and wrapped her arms tightly around her knees.

Talking to her was difficult. She was wracked with sobs, her eyes red and her skin blotchy. Offering comfort in such circumstances was not one of her strong points and Julie Mayweather was privately grateful there was a young woman officer there who had received the appropriate training. She would discover later that it was Cleverly's initiative to have the WPC present.

It wasn't that she found the emotion uncomfortable: she was driven by an urge to get as much information as quickly as possible. While part of her was deeply empathetic another part was restless and impatient, worried that they were moving too slowly in finding vital clues. She needed to know if this grieving widow could throw any light on why her husband had been singled out for such gruesome treatment. The first time she asked had set off a heart-rending outburst.

Now she and the DI were sitting quietly while the WPC, Jenny Green, went off to make a cup of tea. For some odd reason Mayweather experienced a compulsion to say something and had to force herself to be quiet. She decided to go and find the WPC, walking out of the room and along a corridor to a huge kitchen with bi-fold doors that opened onto an immaculately landscaped garden. The poignancy was clear: this was a home designed for a happy family. This one had just been destroyed.

The woman officer was standing to one side staring at a kettle.

"A watched pot never boils, at least that's what my mum always told me," said Mayweather.

The officer, who couldn't have been much older than twenty and had her dyed blonde hair tied back in a bun, smiled gratefully at this attempt to lighten the mood.

"This kitchen is so big it took me ages to find the tea and now this kettle seems to be working at a snail's pace." As she spoke it rocked briefly as steam came out of the spout and then shut itself off. She grabbed it and poured water into the jug, accidentally tipping some on to the marble work-top.

"Damn," she muttered and then snatched at some kitchen roll and started trying to wipe up the water.

Mayweather moved closer. "You concentrate on the tea; I'll tidy up afterwards. You're doing a good job with her, you know. Stick to your training, and that is really all you can do."

A few minutes later the widow was sitting holding the tea in trembling hands. Although she hadn't touched a drop the simple act seemed to bring her some solace and she was doing her best to answer questions.

"Tom is a good man." She was unable to truly absorb his death. "He looks after his staff and he isn't a ruthless businessman getting into fights with his rivals. In fact, he got on well with them, too well according to Fred: he teases him about it."

"Who is Fred?"

"Sorry. Fred Wilson. He's the Chief Financial Officer. He and Tom are great friends and he was often here to talk about the company and how well things were going." This thought clearly upset her as it triggered another bout of sobbing.

Mayweather felt hopeless and was beginning to wonder about being here at all. This was taking too much time; one of the sergeants was more than capable of coaxing information from the broken woman. She decided to focus on this Fred Wilson. If he and Bennett were close then perhaps he could provide some answers.

She waited while the sobbing subsided and then spoke. "Mrs. Bennett, you've got enough to cope with so we will leave you alone. But Jenny will be staying with you for now. I will also have a couple of officers placed outside to keep you safe."

At this statement Mrs. Bennett looked alarmed. "Do you think we are in danger? My mum came to collect the boys this morning but they are asking to come back home."

Mayweather put on her most reassuring manner.

"This is just routine. Having a couple of uniformed officers outside is intended to give you some security and keep any unwelcome attention away - from the press and the like."

The idea that she might be newsworthy seemed to worry her all the more.

"I couldn't stand it if reporters turned up here. Tom being murdered is terrible enough as it is."

Mayweather stood up. "That's why I want a couple of officers outside and Jenny here in the house. If there is anything you want, just ask her. Or if you think of something, anything, that you believe might help us, just tell Jenny and she can get in touch with me."

Moments later she and Cleverly were getting into the back of the police Range Rover that had managed to park right outside the house.

"Do you think she might be in danger?" asked Cleverly.

"I honestly don't know. In the circumstances, I want a couple of armed officers outside. I don't want to take any chances."

At the mention of armed officers, the DI had looked surprised and was about to question the need, but Mayweather was pressing on.

"I want to get over to Bennett's workplace. I think I'm right in saying his company is based down near Leatherhead in Surrey, so we can just head off down the A3. Can you get someone to track down this Fred Wilson, I want to talk to him?"

*

Fred Wilson turned out to be the most unlikely looking accountant. He was huge, with rolls of fat like a sumo wrestler. But his size did nothing to protect him from the shock of the murder. His eyes looked raw from crying.

"I can't believe anyone would kill him, he was the gentlest of men. He couldn't even bring himself to shout at people. All the staff here loved him, you can ask anyone."

They were sitting in a small office in a large building, close to the M25 and nearby Leatherhead.

"Could you talk me through what it is this company actually does?" asked the DI.

Wilson nodded. "Bennett Communications is one of the companies at the forefront of the next generation of telecoms: we are working on projects that will allow instant communication to take place anywhere in the world. That's down to our proprietary equipment, which Tom was the brains behind, and the new generation of satellites currently being launched by companies like Google.

"The big difference was that Tom was combining aspects of our communication technology with aspects of artificial intelligence. I don't know all the details, but I do

40

know it meant that the communications equipment could solve problems without intervention from a human operator. It is designed to make sure that signals don't suddenly cut out. He was also developing security systems that could operate without people controlling them."

"Like I say, don't ask me the 'how' word, but the commercial potential was awesome, and we had just received a private equity proposal that would have provided up to £300 million in research and development funding. I wondered about us exploring the value of the company and put together a proposal to launch on the stock market.

"But Tom was adamant that we should stay private for now, so that's how things stayed. He said this was only going to get bigger and waiting would make us even more money. He also asked me to draw up a proposal that would ensure the staff shared in the benefits; that's the kind of man he was."

Mayweather interrupted. "Forgive me asking this, but did that lead to any conflict between you? I mean just how much money are we talking about here?"

"As the man with the biggest stake in the company his share would have been worth at least £50 million. My share could have been as high as £10 million. But there was no issue between us. All he was doing was delaying things to make the pot bigger."

"I nearly forgot," he said, snapping his fingers. "I need to mention the military angle. He was developing this new communication system directly with the MoD. He'd been down to Dorset recently. And before you ask - no idea. That part was strictly classified, and I think Tom was the only one here who knew anything about it."

"Do you know who his MoD contact was?" asked Mayweather.

"No, as I say, I had to be kept at one removed from that. But his Personal Assistant might be able to help. She had to be security vetted a while back and emerged with flying colours. He could be quite absent minded and needed her to keep track of his day, who he was meeting and any phone calls."

"Is she here now?" asked the DI.

"Her name is Sandra Hall and normally she'd be in the office right outside, but she called in sick. Quite unlike her, actually. I've never known her to be ill in the eight years she's been here."

Mayweather had a question. "Do you know who she spoke to?"

"It was me," he said. "I didn't actually speak to her, she sent an email. It might have been the day before, now I think about it."

8

Sandra Hall's home address was in nearby Ashtead, a commuter town on the inside edge of the M25, or London Orbital. According to the details provided by Wilson she had recently moved to a detached, four-bedroom house, close to the railway station, with its direct services to Waterloo, London Bridge and Victoria. Until the move she had been living in a one bedroom flat above a shop in Dorking high street.

Her new home was an attractive property, thought Mayweather; solid looking with bay windows either side of a front door topped with a red-brick design in the Arts and Craft style, it was a classic suburban home for this part of Surrey, one of London's more affluent counties. But while it may have appeared unthreatening - they had seen no sign of activity inside - she insisted on waiting until they had an armed team in place before entering. "I'm not taking any chances on this." She offered as an explanation, "I don't like it that this woman goes off sick just as Bennett is snatched from Clapham Common."

Cleverly was in total agreement, half-nodding to himself as he too studied the location. Thirty minutes later and a squad of officers in protective gear had smashed their way through the front door and checked the property before announcing it was clear of any threats. Stepping inside for the first time Mayweather noted that it was immaculately tidy. The DI smiled wistfully as he thought of his own home, dominated by young children and a chocolate-brown

Labrador which acted like a slightly deranged child. Not that he would have swapped places.

As to the owner; there was no sign of her at all and nothing to suggest she had been taken against her will. Instead, her scrubbed and polished home might have been prepared for a photoshoot. The only possible clue was the faintest layer of dust that suggested it must have been a few days since the clean-up had taken place.

The DI moved around as little as possible as he made a slow visual inspection of the ground floor, before concentrating his attention on a large wooden dining table at one end of the full-length living room. It was manufactured from pine with the legs painted a matt blue. On the table top was a large Apple monitor with four document boxes stacked up on the right. He tapped the keyboard but it wanted a username and password so he looked through the boxes instead. Beyond the obvious bank and utility letters nothing stood out, apart from the quality of her computer gear.

With a sweep of his hand he gestured at the set-up. "This little lot will have set her back at least £2,000, probably twice that if she's gone for all the extras. I looked at something very similar myself until my wife caught on to how much it would cost. I was quickly downgraded to a laptop."

Mayweather was looking thoughtful. "It doesn't look as though she has spared any expense. The house has been decorated and furnished very recently. That kitchen is full of expensive appliances, and the fridge wouldn't look out of place in a professional kitchen, the sort of thing that is supposed to keep everything at a perfect temperature no matter how many times you open the door. I know they cost thousands. And did you notice the 'climate-controlled' wine cellar?"

Cleverly laughed. "I did notice that. I'm not much of a one for kitchens, but wine drinking? Now that, I could take seriously, especially a cheeky little Chardonnay served at the perfect temperature."

His boss walked through to the living room turned and looked at the sleek black television mounted on the wall. "That's one of the latest 4K TVs; they cost quite a bit as well. So, as well as finding her, we need to dig into where she got all the money from. Wilson reckons she lived alone so she must have paid for it herself."

She stepped out of the front door to remove her protective gloves and overshoes, Cleverly in her wake. For a moment, she couldn't help but think of Roper. She hadn't seen him for six months but this was his territory. A potential crime scene with no obvious clues, it was entirely possible that he would have spotted something useful. But he wasn't here and she was just going to have to get on with it.

She watched as more members of the scenes of crime team turned up, noticing they were attracting the attention of neighbours, a couple of whom were standing outside to get a clear look. One woman appeared to be filming the scene on her phone. She shrugged, this was not the sort of area where they would be used to seeing scenes of crime officers in full protective gear.

"I want to find out everything we can about this Sandra Hall and until we know otherwise I think we should consider that she may well have been taken by the same person, or persons, who grabbed her boss. Or maybe she's part of it."

She left Cleverly to sort out talking to the neighbours. She wanted to get back to London and start speaking to her contacts. If this case was going to take her into the top-secret world, she wanted to get as much inside information as she could.

9

"Lamb bhuna."

Roper looked at him but said nothing. Hooley tried again, unconsciously trying to give his voice the sort of natural authority possessed by actors and TV newsreaders.

"Lamb bhuna, your favourite."

A deep frown appeared in the middle of Roper's forehead. "But I like lamb rogan josh - it's what I always order."

The DCI thumped his desk in irritation. Getting that wrong was a schoolboy error.

"My apologies, but I remember you once said that eating curry was something you associated with work, I messed up by getting the wrong dish."

Roper hadn't quite lost the frown but at least it had faded a little.

"You're trying to see if you can jolt my mind into remembering what I saw in the intelligence data. David Cotter tried something similar and it didn't work. But you know different things about me and maybe that will do it. Actually, you might have come up with a very good idea."

Hooley thought it was just as well he was sitting down. Roper congratulating him was a unique, and slightly disturbing, experience. He decided he quite liked this new sensation, although he doubted it would last.

Roper quickly proved him right to be cautious when he said. "It would be best if you stuck to one thing at a time. It isn't just about having good ideas you know, you need to do things properly."

Before Hooley could think of something to say to that, Roper went on. "I've got an idea. Let's go and have a curry this evening and I'll see if ordering a lamb rogan josh makes things any clearer. I haven't actually been out to an Indian restaurant since I stayed with you."

Hooley whistled in surprise. "That must be six months. I could never last that long without a curry and a pint."

"It's 149 days, to be exact."

"You know what I mean. It's a long time."

"Actually, you need to define what you mean by a long time. I don't think 149 days is a long time at all."

Hooley held up his hand. It was a combination gesture that said he both surrendered and wanted to move the conversation along. It was something they had agreed upon last year. Roper was quick off the draw when it came to having an argument and this tended to bog him down in a determination to prove he was right, regardless of whether it was an important issue or not. Hooley had discovered, by accident, that the physical act of holding his hand up, palm outwards, gave Roper a powerful visual cue to stop what he was doing. Roper simply went back to looking at his screen and a short while later the DCI decided it should be safe to start a conversation again.

He said. "So, it's curry tonight - that sounds like a great plan. Do you actually know where to go if you haven't been since moving up here?"

"Oh yes. There's the Cheltenham Tandoori, not far from my flat so it should be fine. I have heard people talking about it very positively."

"Sounds good," said Hooley. "Perhaps we should book it now. Talking about your flat, that reminds me, I have no idea where I am going to stay tonight and my clothes haven't turned up yet."

Roper beamed at him. "Don't worry about that. Your stuff arrived at reception an hour ago and I told them to keep it there since we will be leaving together. I get the chance to repay you for when I stayed at your place.

"I've been given a very nice flat in town. It's got three bedrooms and you will have your own bathroom. You can stay in a hotel if you prefer but I thought it would be good to repeat what we did in the last case. I'm hoping it might even help me to remember what it was I detected." Hooley didn't have to give it a moment's thought. In many ways Roper was the perfect flatmate. He could be fascinating to spend time with, yet never took the slightest offence if you went off on your own.

Hooley rubbed his hands together. "Is it OK with you if we eat early? It feels like it's been a long day already. By the way, how are we getting into town? I was driven down here so my car's up in London. You were talking about taking your driving test when you left to join GCHQ. How did you get on with that?"

Roper managed to look both sad and cross. "I keep getting sacked by the driving schools."

It took a moment for this to make sense.

"What do you mean, 'sacked?'"

"You probably won't understand, but nowadays you have to take a big theory test as part of your driving examination."

This casual insult made Hooley flush. "Of course, I know about that," he said forcibly. "My kids had to do it for their tests. My boy failed it a couple of times."

Roper shrugged. "Most people do. I passed it straight away and scored one hundred per cent; I didn't make a single mistake."

"Are you saying that after doing so well in your theory test, the driving schools refused to give you any more lessons?"

"That's right."

The DCI could tell there was more to come and he started to get a shrewd idea of what it was.

"Did you end up having arguments with them?"

Roper became quite animated. "Well they did accuse me of arguing with them, but all I was doing was giving them the benefit of my advice."

"Could you give me a little more detail?"

"I realised that I was even better at the theory than the driving instructors so when they made mistakes I told them where they had gone wrong. But the instructor at the first school got very nasty and it was no better at the second school. They both said they never wanted to see me again so I've given up for now."

Hooley was doing a manful job of not laughing. He said. "Well I do have luggage to bring with me, so perhaps we should organise a taxi."

"I'd already fixed that," said Roper. "The cab will be here at 4.45pm. It's about the same distance as between your place in Pimlico and central Victoria. If it's not raining I usually walk home."

A couple of hours later and they were in Roper's new place. Hooley looked around. There was nothing to indicate that anyone lived there. He'd forgotten how the younger man rarely left a trace of himself where he lived or worked.

Unpacking finished, Hooley went in search of Roper.

10

Roper turned down the offer of a menu. "I know what I want: a lamb rogan josh, a double portion of pilau rice, one sag bhaji, one onion bhaji and a Peshwari naan."

The waiter scribbled the order down and then looked at him. "The kitchen does pretty generous portions. It's up to you but I don't think you will need two portions of rice. Why not order one and if you still want more, well no problem, just ask."

Roper looked doubtful. "I think I'll stick to the double portion. I've got a very high metabolism so I need to eat a lot."

The waiter shrugged; he'd been taking in Roper's beanpole physique. "No problem, mate. You certainly don't look like someone who ate all the pies."

Hooley jumped in before this last comment could somehow turn into an argument about Roper not eating any pies.

"Can I have the masala chicken, one portion of rice and a plain naan bread? And can I have a pint of lager?"

Although it was only just 6pm, Cheltenham was clearly a place where people liked to eat early and there were more diners present than he had expected. Despite that they were seated at the back with their nearest neighbours a few tables away. It meant they could talk openly, if they were cautious.

As Hooley watched the waiter heading towards the kitchen, Roper leaned forward.

"I'm surprised at you remembering what you ordered the last time we had an Indian meal. I thought your memory started going once you get older?"

Hooley, who had lately found himself forgetting where he'd left things like the car keys, refused to dignify this remark with a reply, settling instead for an enigmatic shrug. Like Roper he'd gone for a tried and trusted order. He saw another waiter approaching with his beer, the glass pleasingly frosted, and waited until the drink had been delivered before saying anything.

"I don't want to push you at all, but has this triggered any connections for you?"

Roper shook his head. "Smell is a powerful stimulus for memory. Perhaps when they bring the food that will make a difference. I really hope something does come back to me because I really can't see how those three things go together."

Hooley took a sip of his pint. "Let's try to be as patient as we can. The one thing I do know is that there is no point in allowing you to become stressed about what is going on. You work much better when you have time and space to think about things."

Hooley finished off his pint and managed to get a second ordered and delivered just as two waiters arrived with their food. Roper looked on approvingly as he was surrounded by steaming platefuls. Hooley was pleased that his own meal seemed quite small in comparison. He watched Roper carefully. It was fanciful to think this could be the breakthrough moment, but it would be good if it was. "Anything?" he asked hopefully. Roper shook his head again. After that they ate in silence, Roper finishing first as well as winning the admiration of the waiter for easting all his rice.

Hooley mopped up a puddle of sauce with a portion of bread and then pushed his plate away with a satisfied sigh.

"Every bit as nice as Pimlico." He washed the food down with a mouthful of lager and declined the offer of a third pint.

"I want to get home, watch a bit of telly, and then off to bed. Let's hope a good night's sleep will start to make things look a bit clearer in the morning."

He placed his elbows on the edge of the table and rested his chin on his hands. "I keep meaning to ask you. Why aren't you wearing your suit and tie? I thought you said you needed to wear the same thing every day to help keep you in balance."

Roper fidgeted in his chair. "I did wear it when I first came down here but a lot of people dress very casually, I thought maybe I should change."

"I think it's entirely up to you. Some people like to wear t-shirts, others like to wear a suit and tie. I reckon you are definitely a suit and tie guy. Did you ever discuss this with Cotter?"

Roper shook his head. "Are you thinking that changing my routine might have had an impact on the way I work?" Hooley's natural caution kicked in. He didn't think it was likely that a change of clothes was going to be the answer. But maybe it was going to be part of the solution.

He said: "Whatever is causing you to struggle at the moment will be down to more than one thing. So something like wearing, or not wearing, your suit and tie is up to you. I have always known you dressed that way so I certainly can't see it doing any harm. I expect you are going to have to try all sorts of things to try and get back to where you were."

Hooley laughed as a thought struck him. "Perhaps we need to come down here tomorrow with you in your suit and see if that makes any difference."

Even before he'd finished speaking Roper was out of his chair and had walked over to the bar. He came back looking pleased with himself.

"I've booked us in for the same time tomorrow."

The following morning Hooley's alarm dragged him out of a dreamless sleep. As he came to he suffered that momentary sense of panic that can follow waking up in a different place. His heart raced and he took a moment to calm down before heading for the shower. A short while later it was coming up to 6.30am and he was ready to face the world.

His bedroom was at the back of the flat and he had to walk through the living room to get to the kitchen. The first thing he saw was Roper, sitting at the dining table. He was wearing his black suit, white shirt and black tie. With his unruly hair beaten down by a severe brushing, he looked as though he might have got dressed and then pressed himself to ensure he had perfect creases. His heavy black brogues were so highly polished they virtually sparkled.

"You look like you're raring to go."

"I've been up since 4am. I can't wait to get to work and see if this makes a difference."

Hooley quickly produced the hand. "I'm not going anywhere until I've had a decent cup of tea."

11

Roper had insisted on walking to work, setting a brisk pace. The DCI was happy to oblige, it was a nice cool morning and, more importantly, he was going to need the exercise to offset eating a lot of curry. It was entirely possible they could be in for several visits to the restaurant because the younger man would insist on exhausting any possibility that a visit might restore his memory.

They arrived at GCHQ with Roper in a positive mood but an hour later he was looking less enthused. Most worrying of all his hair was starting to spring up and look disheveled. Hooley wasn't entirely sure how to deal with this. He was anxious about Roper becoming withdrawn but couldn't find the right thing to say to him. He was relieved when David Cotter walked in. The psychologist immediately noted the more formal clothes and nodded his approval at both men. He said: "I think it is sensible to try different things."

Roper was not to be comforted. "I really thought wearing the tie would make the difference, but it hasn't. I still can't make out anything that might link those three events. I can't see what it was that made me so interested in them.

"I've thought about your idea, Brian, and you could make it fit. We are talking about the far right and the jihadists, but I can't quite make the mental connections I want."

There was a plaintive tone in his voice. Cotter glanced at Hooley and from his slight frown the policeman wondered if he shared his concerns that Roper would become introspective.

He said. "I don't want to be telling you what to think Jonathan, but you mustn't lose sight of a couple of important issues." He leaned against a wall and crossed his arms. "You'd been here for three months before you made your first breakthrough. But even then, you couldn't say what it was that interested you.

"In fact, if you remember, it took us a while, about a week from memory, to realise that you were talking about potential links. But you couldn't say what they were; just that you were putting all three pieces of information into your Rainbow Spectrum.

"That was it for a while, then you said you thought that more links were forming - but still you couldn't really explain what it was that you were looking at."

Hooley was watching Roper and could see that he was paying very close attention to Cotter's words. The psychologist paused for a moment to give Roper a little more space to take things in. The DCI silently applauded Cotter for backing off. Roper hated being told what he was supposed to be thinking. He had a naturally challenging perspective at the best of times.

After what felt like a couple of minutes of silence, but was probably a few seconds, Roper leaned back in his chair. He said. "You're telling me to take my time. I can see that is the only way to deal with this."

The watching Hooley surprised himself by letting out a breath he hadn't realised he'd been holding. Now all he needed to do was find a way of seizing the initiative that Cotter's intervention had won. A thought hit him and he grinned at Roper.

"I've got an idea. At the moment, you're trying really hard to recreate the environment you were in when you first spotted the links. But why don't we go right back to the beginning when you were first working here?

"I think we should start looking at each case in an individual way, but first can you recall what it was that drew you to them in the first place."

"Actually, that bit is quite easy," said Roper. "It was because all three seemed a bit odd to me and they all happened at about the same time, within a period of a few weeks. I mean, the amount of information that comes through here is amazing; but those three did seem to be worth a closer look."

As he was talking Cotter pushed himself away from the wall he had been leaning on. "Good to see things moving smoothly. You know where I am if you need me."

They spent the rest of the morning looking at the details of the Australian drug case and stayed with it over their lunch break so they could exchange ideas. Getting their food followed the same pattern. Hooley couldn't help wondering what would happen if he opted for something other than a smoked salmon sandwich.

Finishing up he took a moment while he was eating to check the sports headlines on the BBC website and tossed his rubbish in the bin before going to wash his hands to get rid of the smell of fish. Roper had finished much earlier and was impatient to get going again.

Sitting back at his desk Hooley swiped at a few crumbs, even though Roper was staring at him, anxious to get on. He knew that if he gave way to the younger man's unspoken demands he would end up rushing about on Roper time, and that was a fate he was determined to avoid.

Housekeeping over, he looked up. "Shall I go first?"

Roper nodded.

He took a sip of coffee and said. "Looking at it from your perspective, the thing which stood out is why this top-quality drug was suddenly being sold on the streets? Looking at the original intel provided by the Australians, the thing that came to mind was their opinion that this wasn't a mistake, the sort of thing where a powerful version of a drug gets out by accident and kills a load of addicts. How am I doing so far?"

"You're on the money," said Roper. "The pure drug costs five to six times more than normal cocaine. It's the most concentrated form you can buy. No dealer would sell that at anything other than a premium price. That's assuming they could get hold of it. It's the sort of thing that normally only goes to the richest customers and the most discreet dealers."

"Are you agreeing with the Australian view?"

"Not at first. I thought it must have been a mistake. Maybe different grades of cocaine had been bundled together and somehow the best stuff had accidentally been sold at street level. But this went on for a couple of weeks, and over a wide area. If it was a mistake, someone kept making the same one repeatedly. It made me think again.

"The guys at the top of the business are pretty smart. They make a lot of money out of this and you don't do that by being careless. If any of them do take drugs then you can be sure that only the very best will be provided for them. So I decided that making a mistake wasn't the answer.

"I did think about a rival gang moving in and flooding the market to cause problems. I read a while ago about two gangs in London who really hated each other. One of them deliberately released some super strong heroin which killed a lot of addicts. The idea was to cause chaos and move in on the rivals' territory. But that didn't seem to fit either."

Hooley got up to stretch his legs. He said. "So what approach did you take next?"

"I couldn't make any progress after that and went around in circles for a bit. Then I decided there could be only one explanation, but it still didn't explain what had happened.

"I think the gang did it deliberately, but I don't understand why they would do it. It must have cost them a lot of money." He smiled at Hooley. "At the time that made me think of something you like to say. 'If they want to get rid of money that fast they might as well set fire to it.'"

"Why would they do that? Something must be happening behind the scenes. The only thing I could think of was that they were doing something new, something apart from their normal thing of dealing in drugs. Could it be that they were working with fundamentalists in Bali, where they sourced their drug supply, and trafficking weapons, explosives - even people?

"That might explain why they apparently took their eye off the ball over their normal operations. Maybe they are being used as a front for a terror group. To be honest, it wouldn't take much to take over a smaller drug gang. I imagine they would just grab the top people and threaten the rest. By the time I got the first reports this had been going on for 239 days, so it was well established."

Hooley resisted using his fingers as he converted 239 days into the best part of nine months. He would never tire of Roper's grasp of the smallest details, but he wasn't convinced to the analysis attached to the numbers. He said. "That's quite a bold jump you are making there. Isn't it just as likely that the gang's leadership is struggling; perhaps they've been helping themselves to too much of their own product?"

"I did consider that but we know that, in the past, terrorist groups have controlled criminal activity; well, the newer groupings are starting to do the same thing. It certainly makes sense when I update my Rainbow Spectrum."

Roper closed his eyes and stayed very still, clearly deep in thought. More than a minute elapsed before he spoke again. "There is another way of seeing this. If I was coming up with the wrong ideas, could it be the data is at fault, rather than something being wrong with the Rainbow Spectrum?"

12

Hooley had put off considering the implications of Roper's latest theory and was instead thinking about the time he had observed millions of pounds going up in smoke. That image was with him now after Roper's suggestion that the drugs gang might as well set fire to their profits. He knew exactly what a huge pile of flaming cash looked like. He'd once watched as over £20 million in counterfeit, but almost perfect UK bank notes, was reduced to a pile of ash in a special incinerator. The Bank of England had a special facility in Kent which handled the destruction of 'funny money' and required witnesses to ensure all was above board.

He recalled it had been a surreal experience. Even though he had known it was fake, the notes looked so real. It was more money than he had ever seen in one place before, or ever would again. It would have supported not just his wife and children in some style; there would have been something left over for his grandchildren and probably great-grandchildren.

The memory had popped up as he and Roper walked past rows of new build houses as they headed through the suburban streets of Cheltenham towards the centre of town and the flat. It was late afternoon and while the temperature was mild, the sky was becoming dark and threatening. Twice in the last few minutes he had felt fat drops of rain landing on his head. His thinning hair made him especially susceptible, while Roper, with his thick curly mop, seemed oblivious.

Hooley kept an anxious eye on the sky and another on his watch as he noted they had now been walking for twelve minutes, just over half-way, and he started daring to believe they could make it back without getting a soaking. A few moments later and those hopes were dashed as they were caught in a brief, but torrential downpour that dumped what felt like a bath load of water straight onto them. As quickly as it started it was over, leaving Hooley wet and cold.

He rubbed his hand over his head in a pointless attempt to mop up the rainwater that was trickling unpleasantly past his shirt collar and down the back of his neck. He turned to his companion to issue a complaint and saw that Roper, who looked like a drowned rat, was perfectly relaxed.

"My grandmother always used to say it was raining cats and dogs when we got a proper downpour. For a long time, it was something that really worried me. I used to think she meant there really were cats and dogs coming down out of the sky, but I could never see them.

"One of my teachers at school helped me to understand it was just her way of talking. It was an expression rather than a statement of fact. So, when it rains like this, it always reminds me of her, and me looking out for cats or dogs."

Standing dripping wet in the street, this insight was the last thing Hooley expected. Just when you thought you had nailed him down, he came up with something to make you think again.

They carried on back to the flat, with Hooley anxious to get a marker down. "I know how keen you are to get to the Indian restaurant again, but there's no way I'm going until I've changed into something dry and I've warmed up a bit."

To his relief, Roper didn't put up a protest. Once set on something it could be hard to distract him but this wasn't the case today. Instead he said: "I want to make sure that everything is very precise for when we get to the restaurant which means I also want to wear clean, dry clothes. I'm surprised you need to warm up though. I thought the rain was lovely."

Hooley didn't think there was anything remotely pleasant about it and couldn't wait to get out of his wet clothes. His discomfort was being intensified by the way his damp trousers were chafing the insides of his thighs. He was determined to slow the pace down, and when they arrived home he asked Roper to ring the restaurant to warn them they would be late. While he was more than happy to eat there two nights running, he felt like he had been running non-stop since the summons to come down here. It already felt like he'd been in Cheltenham for a week and half, rather than just a day and a half.

He made himself a cup of tea, ran a hot bath, and laid back in the comforting warmth. A couple of paracetamol to nip an incipient headache in the bud and within 30 minutes he was feeling ready to go again; not exactly a new man, but certainly a revived one. A couple of beers would help the process.

He dressed and left his room and straight into deja vu. Roper was sitting in the same place as this morning, wearing a fresh version of his 'uniform'. Knowing his man was ready to go, he sketched a casual wave at the front door. "Lead on, MacDuff."

Roper glanced about the room, apparently checking there was no one else there. "What do you mean by MacDuff?"

"Sorry, Jonathan; like your grandmother, it's just an expression. Don't worry about it for now, I will explain later."

As they walked in to the restaurant, the familiar spice smells made his stomach rumble. They were shown to the same table - Roper had been careful to request it - while the same waiter appeared and took the same food and drinks order, Roper sticking to tap water and Hooley ordering his beer. The DCI was pleased to see his lager arriving. He carefully picked up the pint and drank steadily while they sat in silence.

He ordered a second pint and took the opportunity to look at Roper. From the air of disappointment, he could tell the plan had failed. He decided to wait until the food arrived before asking. Might as well give it every chance.

The delay made no difference other than deepen Roper's misery. To his astonishment it had even stopped him helping himself to the food. The waiter appeared, clearly sensing something was amiss. Hooley waved him away. "Don't worry, it's not the food."

He persuaded Roper to eat. "There's no point in you getting hungry. It was always a long shot that doing this was going to help you to refocus. I bet it takes quite a bit more time, so try not to worry about it tonight. We'll get there, I'm totally confident."

He added: "When we get to work tomorrow, how about looking at the American intel reports? I think there is something fascinating about that."

13

"The Texas Skinheads! I hadn't really thought about that culture appearing in America. I thought it was more of a European thing, or even over here. When I first started as a police officer, back in the late 1970s, there were lots of issues around skinheads. Especially at football matches."

If Roper was interested in this information he was doing a good job of hiding it. They'd been there since just after 5am, walking in while it was still dark. It had been mercifully rain-free, but Hooley had unearthed an umbrella which he intended to keep with him to avoid any more soakings.

He was concentrating on some new intelligence that had been provided by Roper. He'd explained the sudden appearance by claiming that he hadn't finished with it himself. That was why he had left it out of the material Hooley had seen yesterday, he claimed.

He'd only spent an hour on it but he was already wondering what he was missing and why Roper was apparently trying to read so much into it. Taken at face value it was an interesting analysis. As well as learning about the Texas Skinheads, he had also discovered that the Ku Klux Klan were alive and well, acting as an important power broker in the field of the ultra-right. While he was too long in the tooth to think these groups couldn't cause major problems, this all felt like domestic difficulties.

They were also under the close attention of the US law enforcement teams. The new documentation came from a joint FBI/Department of Justice investigation, probing the use of fake news to promote troubling conspiracy theories.

He was so taken with one bit of information he read it out. Waving a printout, he said. "It says there are court cases where people are claiming that if they write out a cheque they don't need funds in the bank to pay for it. That's because banks are some sort of international conspiracy designed to take money off the poor. A thought crossed his mind. "Maybe I could try that as a method of ducking out of my divorce payments?"

He stopped. Talking about the financial settlement for his divorce, and thinking about the hated teacher being in his former home, had the effect of making him angry, as well as making his blood pressure spike.

He needed breakfast to restore his sense of humour. "I don't know about you, but I can't do this stuff on an empty stomach. I think I'm ready to eat now, so is our cafe open?"

Roper had no problem switching seamlessly between terror attacks and sorting out food. "It certainly is. If you give it five minutes Nigel will have three bacon sandwiches ready, white bread, no butter and tomato ketchup on the side, plus a large take-away pot of strong coffee."

The DCI said. "Have you worked out some way of reading my mind? A bacon sandwich is exactly what I want."

The answer turned out to be down to observational skills, rather than anything mystic. "I know how much you love bacon sandwiches, but you only allow yourself one from time to time. I knew this would be a very early start and that is usually when you do decide to have one. It's why I was talking to Nigel yesterday and explained that he should have our food ready for 6.30 am: two for me and one for you. I've got coffee on order as well. At your age, you need all the help you can get with maintaining mental function."

The glare he received was so potent that even Roper realised there might be an issue. "Have I said something wrong?"

*

Twenty minutes later and all was forgiven. The food had been perfect. It was almost worth getting up in the middle of the night to be rewarded with such a treat, and the coffee was precisely what he needed. There was no point hiding from it; a bit of help staying alert never hurts as you got older. Nigel had provided a flask of coffee and Hooley was helping himself as he looked over to Roper. "You look like you have at least one other surprise up your sleeve."

Hooley managed to contain his laughter as Roper checked his sleeve then looked embarrassed. "Just an expression. I was being too literal again. But no, that's it really. No more surprises. What about you; what do you make of it so far?"

"I must admit the main concern I have is that I can't see any big picture here." He held his hands up. "I admit I haven't taken anything like the time you have over this, but it all feels very domestic. I was hoping for more international intrigue."

"It may be you are right," said Roper. "People here did say to me at the start that you get so much information it can be a bit overwhelming, and it is easy to jump to conclusions.

"I am beginning to understand that something is going on here that shouldn't be. After I talked to you yesterday I couldn't get it off my mind, so much so I had very little sleep last night. I am starting to get an idea of what it might be, but I don't want to talk about it until I have thought it through properly. I think I have done quite a bit of guessing lately."

Hooley was stunned into silence. He had never previously heard Roper being so tough on himself. He was almost dreading finding out what the younger man's theory was that had led to this situation.

14

It hadn't taken a great deal of detective work to establish the reason behind Sandra Hall's sudden change of circumstances. Eighteen months ago, she had been the sole beneficiary of a will leaving her a house worth £500,000, her parents turning down their share so that their only daughter could leap straight on to the property ladder. If that wasn't enough, she had also been awarded a year's salary as a bonus - a more modest sum but it helped pay for finishing touches and boost her savings account.

The bad news was that all their inquiries had failed to shed any light on where she might be. Julie Mayweather had reluctantly authorised a missing persons alert. She was anticipating it would trigger a media firestorm once reporters established that Hall was the trusted PA to Tom Bennett. Clearly there would be speculation that she might be the latest victim of a killer being dubbed the 'Face Ripper'.

She need not have worried. Hall was a major story in her own right. Pictures supplied by her worried parents showed a pretty young woman possessed of the 'girl-next-door' look beloved of the tabloids. Her backstory helped. As a student she had devoted time to working on aid projects all over the world. After taking up full-time work she had done what she could.

Her parents were also an appealing pair. Both retired academics who came across as kind, if slightly otherworldly. It all added to an irresistible package that was soon featuring the word 'Angel' in headlines.

*

Mayweather had returned to the Victoria HQ to prepare for her trip north when she was interrupted by Cleverly. He looked grey and unwell. Mayweather was shocked; what could have happened?

"What is it? You look like you're just received terrible news."

He didn't wait for an invite but sat down heavily in one of the two seats in front of her desk. He'd chosen the one where Hooley normally sat, although she was sure he wasn't trying to make a statement. He needed to sit down. She noted his eyes seemed bright, almost feverish, and he was swallowing hard as he tried to compose himself.

Finally, he pulled himself together. "You haven't opened your email, I take it." Her mystified expression confirmed he had guessed right.

"We've both been sent a message with a video clip in it. Quite terrible. The video is so awful you keep thinking it must be some sort of sick joke, brutally realistic, but a bad taste prank and at the end everyone will get up and go home."

He rubbed his thumbs into his temples, trying to erase what he had just seen. With a cold feeling descending on her she fired up her computer screen to look for messages. She was startled to see that an email had been sent to an internal address that was not widely known. In fact, she was pretty sure only her husband, outside her professional circle, was aware of it.

She went to click it open then stopped, her finger tips hovering above the keyboard.

"Do you think we should get the IT people in here? Might this be some sort of attempt at hitting us with a virus?"

The DI managed to look even greyer.

"I should have thought of that, but look at the subject line. You might forgive me for opening it straight away." He picked up the phone while she looked at the header and caught her breath. The subject line read "Tom comes out to play."

About thirty seconds later an IT man with a frantic manner, and wearing a crumpled shirt that had clearly started out as white but many trips to the washing machine had given it a light grey tinge. Ignoring the two detectives, he carefully checked the whole room then fixed on Mayweather's screen. The only computer in sight.

Wrapped in his own bubble, he studied it closely, plugged in a small device which he attached to a laptop. He said. "Use this thing for now, it should be secure, but to be honest if there is anything nasty then you may already have let it in. I've ordered a check so will be able to let you know. What is worrying is how someone found their way into the system in the first place."

He left, leaving them the laptop, and Cleverly saw it was primed for his boss so he handed it to her to enter her details. She called up the rogue email. Just as she hit the enter key she saw Cleverly was bracing himself in his chair, clearly hoping it would ward off what was coming.

Moments later a video was playing. The picture was clear and horribly in focus. It started a few seconds before the knitting needles were smashed into Bennett's brain.

The video looked as though it had been shot from in front of the victim and offered a very good close-up of the moment the knife appeared and filleted - there was no other word - the victim's face. The screen went black for a moment then the film restarted.

This time it lingered on a figure, probably a man, wearing the face of his victim and offering a thumbs up to the camera. It shut down and for a moment Mayweather wondered if she might throw up. She hoped not, but she turned to look for the waste paper bin just in case the feeling in the pit of her stomach got any worse. It was strange: she'd not been so badly affected seeing the body in situ, but seeing that film, with the killer obviously relishing what he'd done, made it so much worse. To her relief the feeling of nausea faded, leaving her feeling washed out and exhausted.

She suspected she now looked as ashen as Cleverly, who started to apologise. She took a steadying breath and rubbed her hands, noting that her palms were clammy. "Don't apologise. Nothing could prepare you for that and having it arrive by email seems to make it more personal somehow.

"What I'd like to know is how did the sender know to direct that at you and me? It's not been announced we're on the case, at least not officially, so how did our names come up?"

Cleverly shrugged. "It could have come from the local boys in either Clapham or Leatherhead. Maybe someone was annoyed at us muscling in, or maybe even just mouthing off because they were relieved to escape a nasty case. But I'm willing to bet though that we won't ever know."

"I expect you're right: there's no time to waste on worrying about things we have no control over. It underlines what a clever man it is we are looking for. I take it that scruffy bloke who was here a minute ago was just the advance guard of a tracking operation?"

Cleverly nodded. "I've been promised one of their best people."

Moments later a young woman turned up, introducing herself as Anne James. Mayweather guessed she was in her mid-twenties. She had long brown hair, held in a ponytail, and protruding eyes that gave her the look of being permanently startled. The police woman smiled; she could imagine Roper exchanging shy looks with a young woman like that.

"Sorry about the delay. I launched a tracker analysis before I came down here so we might get something. But I can tell they're using high-level protocols. The sort of stuff you might expect our intelligence services to use. I'm going to be really honest and admit there may not be anything I can do, although you can be sure I will try."

She added. "If you know anyone at GCHQ, for example, now might be the time to call them. They can do far more than we can."

She missed the look that passed between the two officers. "I do know someone who might just be able to help," said Mayweather. "I'll put a call in to find out who can help you."

The young woman explained the video was now contained on the lap top and left them to it. Mayweather hated the idea but knew she was going to have to watch that video again. As she explained to Cleverly, she had been gritting her teeth to get through it last time, meaning she might have missed all sorts of crucial detail.

After a second run the DI was clearly exasperated. "Unless we've got some clever bit of software that can pick up things the human eye misses, I don't think we did miss much the first-time round. The killer is careful to keep his face out of shot, and while I'm no expert, my guess is that the camera was in a fixed position, so there was probably no accomplice."

"I agree with you. I don't think there is anything there," said Mayweather. "Obviously we'll keep our options open until the IT team has been over it." She smiled at the DI. "No reflection on you, but this is where we need Roper. If anyone can work out something from that," she gestured angrily at the laptop, "then he will. It's quite amazing what he picks up on."

The Detective Inspector looked embarrassed. "I have to admit that I was one of those who wondered why you allowed him back but he more than proved himself in the end. I still say he's a bit of a funny bugger, but not everyone can be the life and soul of the party."

Mayweather laughed at that. "No, he's never going to hold court like some do. But letting him rejoin from suspension was quite easy. I just listened carefully to Brian Hooley and did what he asked."

They were interrupted by Anne James. "I've got something for you but it's not very precise at the moment. That email appears to have originated in Russia, most probably in Moscow. I think you will need that friend at GCHQ."

They let her leave before Mayweather picked up. "Moscow and psychopaths ripping people's faces off: why do I feel like we're disappearing down a rabbit hole?"

15

"Our own people are confirming the address belongs to a computer in Moscow, it's coming from somewhere in an apartment block on the outer fringes of the town." Cleverly looked pleased that his team had got in ahead of the GCHQ whiz kids.

"That was quick work," said Mayweather, who hadn't expected a response until much later in the day.

Cleverly's grin disappeared. "There's a reason for that and it doesn't help us. Apparently, it was too easy to find where the message originated from. I'm told that the best hackers would have made life very complicated."

"How does that leave things regarding the Moscow address?"

"The most likely thing was that the victim's computer was accessed remotely."

Mayweather shrugged. "It sounds like you're telling me Moscow is a dead end. I suppose someone wants us to think in terms of Russian hackers when it could be anyone who knows their way around a keyboard."

She didn't need to look at the DI's expression to know she was right. "I'll update my man at GCHQ with what we suspect. We need them to stay on the case. Whoever our killer turns out to be he's not going to be some wide boy. Our man has brains and is following a plan.

"We need to stop him as fast as we can. The fact that he has gone to all the effort of establishing who we are, and then taking the time to taunt us, is depressing enough, but I have no doubt he will kill again.

"I am sure that he has Sandra Hall and I shudder to think what he has in mind for her. Between ourselves I don't think we can expect a positive outcome, but I won't give up on her until we know, one way or the other."

Cleverly puffed out his cheeks. "It's frustrating not having clues to work with. The one bit of good news I have for you is that the profiler will be with us today. It's the one you mentioned you quite liked and as luck would have it she's available."

"I'll take all the positive news I can get. She's a decent sort and she doesn't mind being asked for her first impressions, just as long as we promise not to hold her to it. Anyway, enough of that, grab a seat and give me some old-fashioned details."

The DI took his place and produced a note book which he briefly studied before starting his briefing. "If you don't mind I am going to hold the key bit back until the end, just to give some perspective. I've had a chance to look through the information from the first killing. There are some broad similarities, but I'm not pinning too much on that at the moment. Our first victim was Harry Jordan, he was 41 years old, married with two kids and ran a software company.

"As I understand it he wasn't a technical genius, like our man Bennett, but was brought in as a Chief Executive to run the company. Peter Knight is the brain who developed the software; a youngish guy who has little interest in management, so Jordan took care of all that.

"Jordan disappeared four weeks ago after leaving home in the morning. It was a normal day and his wife said she was unaware of anything out of the ordinary. She said her husband was his usual self.

"That was the last confirmed time he was seen alive. Five days later they found his body, bound to a chair with tape, in the basement of an abandoned farm house outside Leeds. He'd also had his face removed. Obviously, the MO was the same and what clinched the argument is that it was the same brand of tape used, a slightly more expensive version of the standard package tape."

Mayweather had steepled her hands as she listened closely. "I think we need a slight change of plan when the profiler gets here. It seems obvious that the two killings are the work of the same man. Ask her to look at that as her priority. Let's see if she agrees."

"Will do," said Cleverly. "But like I said, I have been saving the most interesting thing until the end. It turns out that the software developed by the young genius has military applications. So, we now have both companies with links to the MoD. Don't ask me what this software does, but I gather it is important."

It took a lot to impress the ADC. This did. "At last, something we can do some real detective work with. Who have you assigned to chasing the lead down?"

"Wendi Smith. She's not only one of the best young sergeants we've got, she's also bright enough to understand computers and totally dogged when it comes to tracking down vital information. We've only just got going but I've assigned it the highest possible priority. We need to find out who at the MoD was dealing with these two men."

"I couldn't agree more. What about this software designer though? Presumably he must know something about it."

The DI looked troubled. "This is one more thing I saved until the end. Peter Knight has disappeared. Leeds police sent a couple of uniforms to his apartment because they had been unable to make any contact with him via email, phone or even social media.

"The uniforms rang the bell to his flat but got no response. Luckily, his place has got a concierge with a spare key. When they got to his front door they tried his mobile again and could hear the ringing.

"They decided he might be in danger and used the key to let themselves in. There was no trace of him. Just his mobile on the kitchen table. According to the company he never goes anywhere without it. He's one of those people who can't stand spending any time disconnected from the Internet."

Mayweather's joy at finding the MoD connection had evaporated. "This is not going to be good news. I think I may need to stay here and monitor things rather than spending time travelling up to Leeds."

"I anticipated that might happen," said Cleverly. "I spoke to the DI on the case and he's got clearance to come and spend a few days with us, maybe longer if necessary."

Mayweather said: "That's a very good call. Have you warned this chap he might be here for a long time if things drag on?"

"I told him and he was fine about it. He's only in his late 20s, sounds pretty bright and is clearly ambitious. I asked about wife and kids and he's a free man. Lucky so and so," he added with a sigh.

16

Mr. Roberts was having a strange day. He knew there was a reason why he had two people tied to the beds - Sandra Hall and Peter Knight - but he was struggling to remember what it was and why he had taken them in the first place.

Now he needed to decide what to do with them. He had been thinking he had better not kill them straight off because he might discover there was a very good reason to keep them alive. But looking after them would prove very time consuming and he didn't know how long he could keep that up for.

For the past few hours he had tried running through different ideas to see if that would help his memory. He was coming around to the idea that perhaps they weren't that important. He just wished his memory wasn't letting him down so badly.

He sat down at the small table in the room and listlessly tapped away at the keyboard of a computer he had bought for sole use here. This particular one would never be connected to the Internet. He wasn't going to risk being caught by some super-smart tracking software. He'd heard that people at GCHQ were even working on Artificial Intelligence to help them search people out online. He suspected that if such technology was in use it was still at an early stage of development. But he didn't know that for sure. He was using it as a word processor, storing documents which he checked for clues.

A frantic grunting noise made him look up. The woman's face had gone a dark purple and sweat was pouring from her head. She was clearly having one of her panic attacks again. He stood up, turned on the TV to generate back-ground noise, went over and partially untied her, placing a warning finger to his lips as he unwound the tape from her mouth. When he'd done this earlier she'd started screaming. He'd needed his lightning reflexes to locate a pressure point at the junction of her neck and shoulder, rendering her unconscious. He doubted that anyone would, have heard her, but he wasn't taking any chances.

They were in a small, two-bedroom penthouse in a newly constructed apartment block very close to Blackfriars Bridge. So far, the rest of the building remained unsold, so it wasn't as if he had neighbours to worry about. This time Sandra Hall remained quiet. He'd hit the pressure point very hard and when she had come around she was in agony. Roberts had told her, in a very matter-of-fact voice, that he could have killed her and she would be foolish to risk being hit there again.

With her head and mouth finally clear, the PA sat panting heavily, but showed some signs of regaining her equilibrium. He went to the kitchen and got two glasses of water. First, he untied the women's left hand and she grabbed one of the offered glasses to quickly down half the contents. She watched as Peter Knight was similarly released so he too could have a drink.

"You don't need to keep us so tied up you know. We've got the message and you're the boss. When you're here you can just let us be free. I'm sorry about earlier, I don't want to get hurt again."

Despite the reasonable tone of her comments, tears were flowing down her face; he found this stress response deeply fascinating. It was not something he would ever do. He ran the request through his mind and decided to untie them: the woman first, then Knight.

"If you start shouting or try to escape I will make it even worse for you. But behave and you can move around and even use the bathroom if you like."

The woman looked eager. "Could I have a shower? I think I must stink. Some fresh clothes would be useful as well, especially underwear. I've been in the same stuff for days now."

Knight, who had been looking on hopefully spoke, his voice was cracked and weak, betraying his recent treatment. "Me too please. I hate not being clean and having to wear the same clothes day after day. It makes me think that I am going to catch some form of virus or bacteria."

For the second time, he found himself in agreement with his captives. There was a store nearby which stocked clothes. He was sure he could get something from there. Half-an-hour later he'd left the pair handcuffed to their chairs. There was no way they could be allowed freedom of movement while he was out.

On his return to the flat he was struck by the stench of unwashed bodies. For some reason, he hadn't really noticed it before. The flat boasted two bathrooms so they had gone off to clean up at the same time.

Knight was out first by quite a margin and then Paul was there as well. He tossed them a leaflet covering a range of local restaurants offering delivery. They both ordered Chinese and when it arrived they devoured it.

As he watched them eat he thought that while it would make no difference to what was going to happen to them, there was no need for them to suffer. He turned his computer off.

"I need to go now and won't be back until the morning. I've decided the best thing is to handcuff you each to a bed, but only on one wrist, so you will have a bit of movement.

Don't try to get out of the restraints. You can't possibly beat them and will only end up hurting yourselves quite badly."

As he was attaching the handcuff to Paul's wrist she looked at him. "Thank you for allowing us some freedom. I can't tell you what a difference it has made." She bit her lower lip and looked worried for a moment. "Have you decided what you are going to do? If you let us go I can promise that I won't tell the police anything about you. You will be quite safe."

He studied her. "I can sense you're telling the truth, but I don't know what to do for the best." He gave her a brief smile, although there was no warmth in it. "I don't want to make things really bad for you so if I do decide to kill you both then I will make it painless."

He stood up and walked out, leaving her lying on the bed, her face white. Even in the context of the last few days his seeming indifference to whether they lived or died had hit her like a hammer blow. She started to cry as she thought of her family and friends and never seeing them again.

Stepping on to the street Mr. Roberts came to a sudden halt, much to the irritation of his fellow pedestrians who had to swerve around him. He'd realised he was going to have to check the other properties he owned, especially nearby Elephant and Castle. He'd need that flat soon so didn't want any surprises.

17

The DCI had drained the last of his water and was looking thoughtfully at Roper. Normally the younger man would be absorbed by intelligence reports. Instead, he was leaning back in his chair his eyes half closed. He'd seen him do this a couple of times before when he was deep in thought.

They'd been over the Australian drugs report again, this time with the DCI deciding it would be best if he took his most skeptical position. After a couple of hours, he was convinced that Roper had read too much into it. The younger man was now thinking about how he could have made the misjudgment.

As tempting as it was to interrupt him, Hooley thought better. From past experience, he knew that pulling Roper out of one his fugue like states would be like expecting to have a coherent conversation with a teenager freshly prodded out of bed. He picked up another report, this one from the CIA, and carried on reading about links between political groups and drug smuggling.

He was interrupted as Roper suddenly sat up and said. "I think it is starting to make sense."

Hooley felt his adrenaline flow. "Are you about to tell me what you think has been going on." If he was hoping to get a positive answer, Roper's abrupt "No." soon put him right.

Before he could say anything, Roper went on. "I need to split this into two things. The first is the analysis. I think I have got that all wrong, and I think I may have almost worked out why, but I need your help to make sure I am wrong."

Hooley shook his head. "You've lost me a bit there. You're wrong and you know you're wrong, now you want me to prove you're wrong? Isn't that a wrong too many?"

Even Roper laughed. "What I'm trying to say is that I need to be totally sure about this. That is the only way I can be just as confident about what has really been going on and causing all the problems."

"Are you saying you need to clear the decks before you can do anything else?" said Hooley. "I get why you want to be totally certain, but if there is something untoward going on, can we afford to delay a moment longer in letting people know?

"I don't want to add to the pressure you're obviously under, but this is national security we're talking about here. Maybe we don't have the luxury of being one hundred per cent sure, maybe we have to settle for something lower; say, seventy per cent."

He could tell his words had struck home because Roper tightened, but then that familiar stubborn look appeared. It always amazed him how he could dig his heels in.

The younger man said. "I know we need to be as quick as possible, but I have to be totally certain that my analysis is wrong before I shut it down. To make it more confusing, not everything I'm saying is wrong. I've read almost half a million words about this so some of it must be OK.

"Not just big reports or news items, but analysis, interpretation and some of it pure speculation. Part of the problem is that we are provided with stuff that may not have been handed over with permission.

"A lot of what I read came from reports put together by the Australian security services, but they don't know we have it and so I haven't been able to ask any questions about the details and have just had to take things at face value."

He had been talking quickly, the words seeming to fight each other on the way out. He added. "I knew you being here would be good. Since I have been able to talk it through with you I have started to see it differently. This is just a domestic incident. I did read too much into it."

The DCI decided that this was the moment for Roper to take a time-out. He had that bright-eyed look that suggested he was in danger of taking things too personally. He stood up. "I could really do with more coffee. How about you?"

Roper muttered he didn't want anything so Hooley stepped into the main corridor, matching pace with a woman who was trotting past, but hanging back far enough she wouldn't think he was a stalker. He was determined to improve his fitness while he was here and was sure fast-walking would do the trick. Nigel looked up as he walked in, an unreadable expression on his face.

"Didn't expect you here just yet: lunch won't be ready for a while."

"That's fine," said Hooley. "After that sandwich, I won't be hungry for a while yet - no, I've come in for a coffee."

A deep frown appeared on Nigel's face.

"I'm not sure that's wise after all the coffee you've already had."

Hooley hid a smile, he'd had the foresight to anticipate this conversation.

"Oh no, it's not for me. It's for David Cotter who's just popped in. I just wanted to stretch my legs after sitting at the desk for hours, so volunteered to come and get it." The lie flowed easily because it had occurred to him while he was heading here that Nigel might well challenge him. Had he looked flustered he knew he would have been sent away empty-handed.

Back at the cubicle he enjoyed a long sip of his drink. For some reason, it tasted all the better and he suspected it was because he had managed to obtain it by subterfuge. Neither spoke. Hooley was thinking of it as a companionable moment; Roper was probably just thinking about something else.

He watched Roper scrunch up a piece of paper and toss it into the rubbish bin. Roper's sensitivity about not being pushed was one thing; this felt like feet dragging. He was determined to keep things moving.

He said. "Well let's plan the rest of the day. I think we've agreed the US side is dead in the water. So, is it too soon to look at the Somali material? We can do this properly, setting up a work schedule. A two-hour burst will take us up to lunch."

He knew Roper loved anything with a suggestion of a timetable so quickly hurried on. "Once lunch is over we can set a deadline of 3pm. We'll have done a full day by then so let's not overdo it. We're both bad at knowing when to stop so setting a target makes sense."

To his surprise Roper readily agreed.

"That sounds great. We can go back to the flat and then I can practise my yoga before we go to the Indian restaurant again."

Hooley did a double-take. "Since when did you start doing yoga, and did you say we're off for another curry tonight?"

"Yes, but that can be the third and last attempt to check if I was on the right track, or, as it seems now, getting it all wrong. I know I keep saying this, but a final visit and I can let it go."

Hooley puffed his cheeks out. He knew he'd been backed into a corner and there was nothing he could do about it. Oh well, if sacrificing himself to another curry was the price for saving the world; he supposed he'd better pay up.

He spoke. "Well, if we're going for a third curry then save the yoga stuff for tonight. In the meantime, do you want to give me what's available on the Somali case?"

To his surprise it turned out to be a relatively thin account, some of it quite skimpy considering what was supposed to be high level intelligence. It was the sort of stuff you might read in serious newspaper coverage of unrest in the region.

As it was he had finished by 2pm and with Roper slowing up, they called it a day, delaying long enough to make a reservation at the restaurant.

18

Mr. Roberts decided to make the most of a warm, sunny evening as he crossed the River Thames and headed for south London. His mind was in turmoil but he hoped the walk would allow his racing thoughts to settle as he made his way to Elephant and Castle. The flat was in a less upmarket part of London, but boasted a significant advantage; it was a busy residential area, so local people were on the move throughout the day and evening. Add in the students from the London College of Printing, and it was a great place to remain anonymous.

Mingling with the crowds around the tube station he enjoyed being among so many people; London really was a great city for disappearing. A trio of young women walked past, their heads close together as they laughed at some shared joke. They didn't spare him a glance as they swerved round him. But he had noticed them, and if they'd spotted his response they would have started running.

His face had taken on a predatory look as he turned to his right, pretending to read a notice in a shop window, but really keeping the three under observation. Without being conscious of it he had switched to hunting mode. His senses heightened and his body preparing for a sudden release of energy. His tongue flicked out as if sensing the air. Would it be greedy to grab all of them? Could he manage that many in one go? Of course he could.

He turned and started to follow them, his mind filling with ideas. He hoped they lived nearby; even better if it was in shared accommodation. The fun he could have then.

Perhaps he could introduce them to his version of Freddy Krueger; something he hadn't done for a couple of months.

His blood was pounding in his ears and he speeded up, closing the gap to just twenty feet. Even though the women were absorbed in each other, he was getting far too close. He slowed down to open up the gap.

They carried on for half a mile; the lurking Mr. Roberts now convinced they were indeed heading home. He felt a sharp tug of disappointment as they suddenly turned into a bar; even from one hundred paces he could hear the music and realised it was a student hang-out.

He scouted for somewhere he could stand and wait for them to come back out; maybe he would be lucky and they would stick together, confident that numbers would keep them safe. On the opposite side of the street was a cafe with a sign claiming it was open until 10pm. Perfect, he could get something to eat and drink while keeping the bar under surveillance.

As he walked in a man sitting in the window seat got up, leaving a copy of the Evening Standard on the table. "Excellent," thought Mr. Roberts. Reading the paper would render him invisible.

His order of tea and a ham on white bread turned up. He was starving and took a huge bite out of the sandwich, swallowing so hard he hurt his throat and made his eyes water. The pain shocked him out of his animal state. He looked around wildly, suddenly aware of what he was doing. There really was something wrong with him. Here he was, off on one of his spontaneous little 'outings', as he liked to think of them, when he had so much to do. He ruthlessly stamped down on a thought that he really was losing his mind. There was no time to deal with that now.

He sat for a moment, regaining control. He felt the urge to get up and run, but that would be a mistake. Never do anything that makes you standout, he reminded himself.

Think, don't panic. Did he need to pay before leaving? Yes. He made his way to the counter and handed over his money, the remains of the sandwich stuffed in his jacket pocket; leaving food behind might get him remembered.

A few seconds later he was outside and retracing his steps. He'd thought his memory loss was alarming enough; now the self-control he took for granted was letting him down. As he trotted back towards the Elephant and Castle he kept a mantra running in his head. "Take your time; check the flat."

Arriving at the building he decided to take the stairs. But around the fifth floor things came back into focus. It was no gradual thing. Where, at the bottom of the steps, had been a big hole in his memory, now everything came back to him.

Four nights ago, he'd accosted a young woman who was looking at job adverts in shop windows around the area. He'd guessed she was East European and it turned out she was from Albania. An instinct had made him realise she was desperate enough to consider anything so he offered her £50 to come with him. She'd been suspicious but doubling the offer was too much for her to turn down.

After that it had been child's play. Once back at the flat, he'd left it until late so it was dark, he'd overpowered her with ease and then gagged and handcuffed her to a bed. He had every intention of practising his knife skills on her; removing human skin was very difficult and he liked to do a neat job, but needed plastic sheeting and towels to soak up the blood. He'd left her there overnight, intending to return in the morning with all his gear. That was the last time he'd thought of her until now.

He opened the front door and was greeted by a strong musty smell. Walking into the bedroom he saw the young woman was lying quite still. He checked and could feel a faint heartbeat but she appeared to be in a coma. She hadn't been in good shape when he'd got her here so he supposed she had little physical resilience. Knowing he couldn't afford any more distractions he carefully lifted her up by her head and savagely twisted her neck. He heard a sharp crack and lay her back down.

Opening the windows to let in some air, he left to go back outside. On the walk here, he'd seen one of the traders in the Elephant and Castle underpass selling a collection of cheap bags. She was only a tiny woman so a large hold-all should do the trick.

Tonight, he'd take the body for a walk along the embankment. It was always quiet later in the evening and he would get a chance to toss the bag into the river when there were no other pedestrians around. He moved quickly to complete his task. He still had the other two to deal with. Their fate was a foregone conclusion, but for some reason he felt the need to try something different.

19

Brian Hooley was a remarkably patient man. Partly by nature and partly by training he had learned to hold his temper and try to see both sides of the argument. It was one of the things that made him a great foil to Roper. But this time he was getting irritated.

He was sitting at his desk, lightly tapping his forehead with a rolled-up print-out of information about the Somali situation. Noticing Roper look up he decided to express his feelings.

"Forgive me Jonathan, but I don't know how you got anything from this. Not only is this stuff clearly unimportant, you've even given me something that says the information may be inaccurate."

He snatched up a document and brandished it at the younger man. "It says here the reports have not been independently verified and it is all based on the word of a third party who had since disappeared, so we can't check back with them. And we can't check with anyone else."

He screwed the document up in an exaggerated fashion before throwing it at the bin, where to his increased annoyance it bounced on the lip and fell on the floor. It triggered another outburst.

"What exactly is this so-called intelligence about? We seem to have a report that says a bunch of pirates have bought a boat. Is it just me or isn't that what pirates do? Otherwise they wouldn't be able to do any pirating, would they?"

Roper surprised him by holding up his hand, palm-outwards. He was instantly mortified. This was supposed to be the other way around. If nothing else, his job was to bring calm and balance to proceedings. The hand was the way he warned Roper his enthusiasm was getting the better of him.

Roper said. "You're right, but I needed to hear you say there was nothing there. It confirms a suspicion I have that I allowed myself to be influenced by reading other material. When I first looked at this intel I made the mistake of thinking the boat was being used to help move money and people linked to jihadi groups. It all made sense at the time."

"Sorry, Jonathan, but this isn't making a lot of sense to me," said Hooley. "I don't recall seeing anything about links to terrorists."

Roper nodded. "OK. I need to go back a bit. You know I've said we get loads of material? Well, very soon after I arrived here I was sent some material that was highly classified that discussed jihadi groups meeting out to sea. This method of linking up was being seen as safer than a land meeting since it would be harder for the West to track them.

"The Americans have been particularly good at targeting traditional meeting places and using missiles to blow up some of the key players. What clinched it for me was reading verified reports describing the movement of militant leaders out of Syria and Iraq towards Somalia, Sri Lanka and on into the Philippines.

"I was very convinced by this so when, months later, I was given the documentation that Somali groups with links to Isis had got their hands on a powerful new boat with the range to travel hundreds of miles; I made the connection."

He stopped and looked at the DCI who had been listening avidly and knew what was coming next. "You added up two and two and made it five."

Hooley suddenly made sense of what Roper was doing. It wasn't that he was deliberately dragging his feet, it was more that he was forcing himself to confront, in excruciating detail, where he had gone wrong. He realised that with the amazing memory he possessed that must be a very painful process.

Roper was at a critical point. He could now see that he was struggling with the thought his trusted methods were letting him down. A memory came back. Even before Roper left for GCHQ he said he was worried he might struggle. At Scotland Yard he had the support and space he needed; it was how he had been able to develop his Rainbow Spectrum.

Hooley had done his best to reassure him. Stick to his methods and all would be well. In private he had been less confident and did what he could to keep tabs on him, with what he heard seeming to suggest all was well.

Maybe Roper had been right to be anxious in advance. But the fact that he was having problems posed a question. Were his amazing skills at analysis breaking up under the pressure of his new, high-powered environment, or was it something else?

The DCI leaned back in his chair. Despite his grizzled appearance he put a lot of thought in to his work and the state of mind of colleagues, not just Roper. He wasn't one for constant hands-on staff management, believing that was a waste of everyone's time, but he knew that sometimes you needed to step in to keep people on track.

He was also aware that sometimes all the skilled management in the world could count for little; especially when people were performing at the very edge of their abilities and under stiff pressure to perform. Even the toughest could waver in those conditions.

That was why he had come up with an alternative theory of the workplace. One he liked to think that only an 'old fart' like himself could have created. He called it, ANCOT, or 'A Nice Cup of Tea.' It might lack the brain power of the Rainbow Spectrum, but it was tried, tested and worked because it focused on the basics - food and drink. That was something he would take every time. And right now, ANCOT was exactly what Roper needed.

He'd come to think of Roper in terms of a piece of crystal that has sprouted in different directions. In one way, it was all hard edges and straight lines, but in another it was brittle and easily broken. Once before he had experienced Roper having problems firsthand. He didn't want to see that again; it had taken far too much out of the younger man.

In the meantime, he needed to play his trump card and he had to find the best way of doing it; one that would benefit them both. It involved his standing order for a lunch-time smoked salmon sandwich. Much as he liked it, and was pleased Roper had picked it for him, there was a bit of him that felt like he was locked in a culinary version of Groundhog Day.

A sly smile appeared on his face. He had just thought of the perfect way to hook Roper and help him take his mind off the pressure he was applying to himself.

"I want to make some changes," he announced in Roper's direction, knowing this would get his attention even if he had to wait a moment. Sure enough, after a slight delay, Roper looked up. "Changes? What sort of changes?"

Hooley was cheating. He knew that mentioning 'change' in Roper's earshot was sure to get his attention. He was always suspicious of change, preferring to keep things as they were.

"Yes. I'd like to make a change to my sandwich order and I'd like to make it now."

Roper came up with three suggestions. "You can pre-order the old-fashioned way by going to the cafe; deciding what you want and leaving the order with Nigel. You can even do an order every day if you want to vary it.

"The most efficient way is to send him an email. I have memorised their menu so you can check with me, or I can make suggestions if you like. Sometimes I like to try different things; I might have chicken and avocado with sliced avocado one day and mashed up the next."

Hooley resisted the urge to make fun of the avocado idea. He really didn't see much difference between sliced and smashed, but what did he know? Roper was being serious and that's where he wanted him. Engaged with anything but work. "You mentioned a third approach."

"Really old school. Just go there whenever you want and place your order. You'll have to queue up. With the pre-ordering system Nigel has it ready at a precise time and you get priority for ordering in advance, so the time savings can really add up over the course of a week, month or year."

20

His plan worked faster than he could have imagined. Shortly after they'd eaten their new lunch orders, using a different ordering system, Roper announced. "I can sense my Rainbow Spectrum starting to work properly again. It's been like everything I was trying to do was getting lost. Normally I can see how anything links to whatever else is in there.

"When I got here I was told it might make a huge difference, especially with so much terrorist activity out there. One slip with looking at the intelligence material could see lives being lost. But when everything started getting confusing, it worried me even more because people could die if I made a mistake."

Despite Roper's obvious anxiety, Hooley felt a lift in spirits. It sounded like he was clearing his mind and could start to sort out what the issues were.

They could talk later about him assuming too much responsibility, for now he wanted to let Roper move along at his own place. "So what are you thinking now?"

"Now that I know there is no doubt I have got it wrong, I can go back to find the answers. As you are aware, I have perfect recall and I am sure they will be in what I have read."

He got up from his chair and came around to sit on the edge of his desk, his face masked in concentration. "I can now see The Rainbow Spectrum wasn't giving me complete answers. It had never done that before and I couldn't understand it."

Hooley realised there was one question he did need an answer to. "Are you still thinking these three things, or any of them on their own, are connected to an attempt on the lives of world leaders?"

Roper didn't hesitate. "No."

After his unequivocal answer Roper had lapsed back into silence, his mind fully engaged on the puzzle. As the evening shift started to arrive the DCI was able to persuade him to head home and so one of them could get some rest.

Hooley had grabbed another early night and was asleep by 10pm. He woke up the next morning just as dawn was breaking. He'd been out for seven hours straight, not something he usually managed. With a definite spring in his step, he headed for the kitchen to set up the first of what would be at least 10 cups of tea or coffee over the course of the day.

The first thing he saw was Roper, in black pyjamas, and performing some sort of exercise. He was bent at the waist, with his hands stretched out in front of him and his palms on the floor to give his body a sort of V-shape.

"Been there long?" he kept his tone nonchalant.

"It's the downward dog. A brilliant stretch technique. It's wonderful for your back and helps me to think. I've been awake most of the night and getting nowhere. I've been doing some yoga exercise for the last half-an-hour and I think I have finally come up with something. Or when I say me, I mean my Rainbow Spectrum."

He said. "You've got my full attention."

With his head down near the floor Roper said. "What if someone was making things happen because they wanted to attract my attention?"

The DCI thought about this for a moment, then thought about it for a lot longer.

"Tell you what. Let me get the kettle on, maybe have some toast and you can have a shower. There's no way I'm thinking about the implications of that until I've had a cup of tea and something to eat."

Roper held his yoga position: he was impressively still. "You think I am going to say something complicated. I can tell by the way you frown, then stop yourself. But your face is so wrinkly that frowns sort of disappear."

Hooley was determined not to let anything spoil his day, like thinking about his face being full of wrinkles. He pointed at himself. "See this? This is my 'I'm off to make tea' face."

The smell of the toast filled the flat, finally luring Roper from his stretches. He polished off four slices, liberally spread with Marmite: with his mouth full he told Roper he couldn't understand why anyone could dislike it. Hooley watched him virtually inhaling the final piece of toast and thought "I can."

Within thirty minutes they were walking towards GCHQ. The DCI attempted to set what he felt was a brisk pace, but his companion showed a disappointing lack of effort as he trotted along.

"I'm ready to go. Tell me about this latest breakthrough. You've got one of those looks that says it's important."

Roper replied. "My yoga session let me see that the three situations we have been looking at are connected by something I hadn't thought about before. Someone was pushing my attention towards them. If the reports I saw were manipulated to attract my attention that would explain a lot.

"If I am right about that, and I think it is at least fifty percent I am, there is a lot more I need to consider. What if it is someone who knows about the Rainbow Spectrum and understands the way I think about things; could they be able to influence what I am doing?"

Hooley slowed down and turned to his companion, his face severe. "Are you suggesting that there might be someone who knows all about you, possibly one of the team at GCHQ? Not only that, you think you might be being targeted in some way? That would be very serious indeed." He looked around searching for words. "This is the home of British intelligence gathering. Are you saying that the centre is compromised?"

Feeling an intense sense of anxiety, he gave Roper a searching look.

Roper nodded. "I am a lot more than fifty percent certain; I think it is ninety per cent. The reason I can't be one hundred per cent is there is a slight chance it could be an outsider: someone in MI5 or MI6, they both know I'm working here. Or it could be the Americans, the French, the Australians or the Canadians. We share a lot of intelligence with lots of people."

Hooley knew the moment he flagged this up it was going to cause an almighty rumpus. He'd been involved in this sort of thing in the past and it often turned into a witch-hunt: colleagues under suspicion and everyone feeling the strain as checks were made.

A problem like this couldn't be sorted out with a couple of phone calls. It needed careful investigation and he could only guess at what sort of disruption an organisation the size of GCHQ that was going to experience. He didn't know how things were set up, but he hoped that some departments could be ruled out through having no contact with Roper.

An unpleasant thought struck him. If he was in charge, one of the people whom he would be looking at very closely would be Brian Hooley - recently called in because he was said to have influence over Jonathan Roper. He wondered if they did brandy to go with the coffee he was having when they arrived.

21

After the debacle which led to him throwing the young woman into the Thames, he was determined to do things differently. That was why he was studying the clear liquid that filled the one hundred millilitre bottle almost to the top. It would be more than enough for what he had in mind. The mix of Rohypnol and ketamine, would do the job. It had taken a moment's research online to work out that it was freely available.

Last night he'd visited a nightclub to get what he needed. He was confident that the raw material was the proper stuff: despite wanting to keep a low profile he couldn't resist letting the dealer know that Mr. Roberts would be back, and not in a good way, if it turned out he was selling fake gear. He felt good to go, mentally refreshed and back on track. So long as he ignored the nagging doubts as to why he had grabbed the pair.

Whatever! He was on his way to put things right. He'd left them handcuffed to the beds for ten hours now so they would be more than grateful for a drink. This one would send them off into a deep sleep. Probably a sleep they wouldn't wake up from.

He hoped that would be the case. He knew from his research that about fifty mills of the mixture would knock them out, it might even slow down their breathing so much they effectively suffocated. The only thing he didn't want to happen was for them to be overcome by nausea. That would just make a mess that would need clearing up. Another distraction he didn't need.

One hour later and he was watching the woman gulp down the water. He left one hand cuffed. He didn't want any last-minute problems. He was learning that no matter how careful you were, some people could sense when they were about to die. They would make desperate attempts to get away and sometimes their panic could give them phenomenal strength. He wasn't going to risk that.

He smiled at Sandra Hall as she handed the glass back. She was one of those who thought acting all defeated and grateful would make a difference. He stopped himself sneering, instead patting her hand. She foolishly interpreted it as a good sign, smiling nervously and making eye contact. Mr. Roberts released one hand for Peter Knight. He too greedily bolted what was likely to be his last drink. Minutes later and both were unconscious. In their already weakened state they had succumbed to the effects in the fastest possible time.

He needed to get them out of the flat and into the van. He'd identified a disposal site at some woods near Dulwich, in south-east London. Not that far from his flat and at this time of night it should be a nice easy journey.

With no other residents in his block he didn't need to be cautious, carrying each victim to the lift and down to the basement car park. He grabbed the woman first and left her lying half-in and half-out of the lift so she could block the door. As they rode down he smirked at the thought of the lift stopping at the ground floor and someone wanting to get in. By 2am he was on his way and hoped to be back within the hour.

He'd checked them both before setting off and their breathing was so slow he was hopeful the drug alone would do it. If not, he had his scalpel with him. A quick incision in an artery and that would be it. They would bleed out, neither of them knowing the slightest thing about it. In the circumstances, he thought he was being as kind as possible.

*

"A dog walker found the bodies at about 6.30am this morning. Quite a nasty way to start the day, but he seems to be holding up OK."

DI Cleverly nodded towards where a grey-haired man, wearing glasses, jeans and a thick jumper against the morning chill, was talking to one of the detectives from the Special Investigations Unit. His dog lying bored at his feet, disgruntled that his morning walk had been ruined.

"The good news is that he is one of those people who likes to keep a close eye on the news. He recognised Sandra Hall from the stories about her going missing and when he called 999 he identified her to the operator. It means there wasn't any wasted time in us getting the call."

This last statement stopped a question from Julie Mayweather who had been about to ask why they had been put on to the case so quickly. Even with an efficient local operation it could take a few hours, or more, for messages to be passed on. She had been called as she was driving into the Victoria office just after 7am.

"Small things; it's always the small things that make a difference," she said, almost to herself, unaware she was echoing the words of the man she was hunting.

Although her team had pulled out all the stops, the lack of progress on the case was starting to weigh heavily: she wished it could be otherwise but at least with the bodies they now had something to work on. She had always feared it would end like this. The nature of the killing on the video clip left no doubt to the kind of person they were dealing with. She wasn't a fanciful woman but there were a few words you could use about such a killer. Evil was one of them.

She studied the two bodies carefully as the scenes of crime investigators went through their painstaking protocols. She thought the two victims looked quite peaceful. At least they hadn't been brutalised like the first two.

"Anything yet?"

"Not a huge amount. Preliminary says they've been dead for a few hours, maybe four or so. But otherwise there are no obvious signs of violence, no obvious signs of what the cause of death is.

"Both have bruising around their wrists and ankles indicating they were restrained, and for some time. That seems to be a thing about our killer, and I am assuming he is responsible for all the deaths: he likes to restrain people. Maybe he gets a kick out of it.

"But the doctor says that, with no physical symptoms, cause of death may be poisoning. At first, she assumed they must have been asphyxiated, but could find nothing to support that idea. She needs to get the bodies into a lab to do a proper check, but preliminary examination hasn't helped."

They were standing to one side of an area of rough ground that looked as though it served as an impromptu parking area for people using the woods. The bodies were just lying behind a large oak tree.

Mayweather pointed to the spot. "I take it this is how they were found?"

"That's right. No attempt to cover them or hide them in any way. If I was to guess I'd say he backed up a vehicle, most likely a van, and pulled the bodies out. He just wanted to make sure he wasn't seen. If the doc's right about time of death then it would have been about 3am, give or take, so not likely that anyone would have been here. To be honest it's a bit spooky here anyway. If I'd been that dog walker this morning I think I might have legged it before calling it in."

Mayweather couldn't help but agree. There was something slightly off about the place. It was strange to come across such an apparently wild area in a suburb that was just a few miles from the city and was home to well paid professionals.

"Another reminder, as if we needed one, that the man we're looking for has an inhuman quality. I should imagine this sort of place would appeal to him."

22

By mid-afternoon the 'rumpus' at GCHQ had enveloped Downing Street - something that comfortably exceeded Hooley's worst fears - and discussions were taking place about informing the Americans. It was times like this that the so-called Special Relationship could be put to the test. US intelligence chiefs never hesitated in putting the boot in when the Brits were having problems. The Cabinet Secretary, Sir Paul Deans, one of a handful of people on a genuine need-to-know, was briefed.

"So, tell me again about this analyst," said Sir Paul. A fit-looking man in his mid-fifties, he favoured well-cut, pin-striped suits. Today this was paired with a blue shirt and pink tie and pocket handkerchief combination. It suited his dark colouring. Despite wielding significant power, he was known for his relaxed manner and courteous behaviour towards colleagues. Now he had pushed his gold rimmed spectacles down his nose and was studying GCHQ deputy director Reginald Green very closely.

Green looked like the sort of nerdy school teacher who appeared in films. His hair was messy, his glasses never sat properly and he had a natural enthusiasm that he couldn't contain. In many respects he resembled a large, boisterous puppy. He was well aware of the impression he gave people and often wished he looked tougher, like Arnold Schwarzenegger. With Sir Paul's bright green eyes fixed on him, he was wishing he could indeed channel the Terminator.

"He's been with us for six months and was transferred from Scotland Yard. We have a lot of unusual people at GCHQ; it's one of the reasons we're so good at what we do, and I think it's fair to say that Mr. Roper fits into that category.

"Admittedly he does have a different approach - some would say unique - so he is not operating according to conventional protocols. He has the freedom to sit above the day to day needs and has been given his head to dip in and out as he sees fit. We also direct his attention to items of interest. We feel this enhances our ability to see the world through a diversity of people."

Even as he spoke he was reflecting that sometimes you just had to take a leap of faith. On paper, what he was talking about, didn't sound hugely promising. Perhaps he could arrange a site visit for Sir Paul, to help reassure him.

As countless politicians could confirm, the Cabinet Secretary was not a man who wore his heart on his sleeve, so could be difficult to read. Not on this occasion: a flash of anger alerted the GCHQ boss that he was not happy with what he had just heard.

"I try not to judge people I have never met," said Sir Paul. "But there is something in the way you described this man that gives me pause for thought, especially when we are on the very cusp of alerting the PM that something has gone wrong with our national security operation.

"It is not inconceivable that the President of the United States will have to be informed. Once that happens we will be instantly cut-off from any new intelligence material and it won't take long for the rest of the world to find out that we have a problem."

He stopped and breathed in hard through his nose before continuing. "Is there anything else you need to tell me about Mr. Roper before we escalate this to the very top?"

While Green was nervous at being in Downing Street, he was far from being overawed. Rather than responding immediately he took a second to really consider his response. In one way, the honest answer to the question was, 'yes and no.' But he knew this was not a moment to hide behind semantics. The man he was talking to had a tough decision to make and he needed a solid response.

He said. "It is fair to say that Roper is not the easiest of people to get on with, but that has never been a serious issue when it comes to the quality of his work. In many ways, he is an enigmatic man who has developed an extraordinarily esoteric way of looking at intelligence gathering."

Sir Paul raised an eyebrow. "Is this the man who came up with the concept of a Rainbow Spectrum? I gather it has created quite a stir."

That question gave Green pause for thought. As usual the Cabinet Secretary was remarkably well informed. The GCHQ man knew he needed to provide a straight answer.

"That is the case. Other analysts at GCHQ are trying to copy his approach, with little luck so far. The point is that he is a genuinely innovative thinker, something that is very rare to find, and his methods have a track record of working. I'm not sure I can explain how, but they do."

Sir Paul's eyes flared slightly. "Do I detect a but?"

Green sighed. The man was a mind-reader. "You may do. Up until a couple of months ago he was doing fine but then he seemed to lose his way. Funnily enough we had anticipated he might have problems and had come up with an option of reintroducing him to a senior Scotland Yard officer who, for want of a better description, has been something of a mentor to him. That happened recently and he does appear to be getting back on track. It is part of that very process that has resulted in you and I having this meeting.

"Mr. Roper was the first to come up with signs that something wasn't right, then he seemed less certain; now he seems more certain. While I have no doubts about his overall capabilities, I suppose that if we were looking at this entirely in the moment, then maybe there is a slight shading of doubt."

Sir Paul walked around behind an ornate office desk and sat down. His fingers drummed gently on the polished wood. He said. "For the time being we keep things as they are. You carry on your checks and I will delay talking to the PM. If you gather new evidence then let me know straight away and I will alert him. But my experience is that these things are best done under the radar, if at all possible.

"Having said that, if nothing has changed in the next forty-eight hours, I think I have no choice but to alert our masters. In the meantime, I leave everything with you. If there is any question over resources tell me now and I will fix it."

Green shook his head. "We have all we need. I wouldn't have brought this to your attention unless I felt there was a significance to it. But I also understand the reasons for your decision."

Moments later the GCHQ man departed for Gloucestershire. He didn't need to be there for this stage of the investigation, but it felt a lot more comfortable to be properly hands on.

Back in Downing Street Sir Paul thought that while many warnings brought to his door were untrue, some happened. He hoped this wasn't going to be one of them. Public confidence in the intelligence service was at a low ebb. The last thing they needed was some sort of hand grenade going off; one that might be thrown by someone on their own team. Any suggestion that there might be a spy in the ranks of the spies would be tough to stomach. It would further undermine the morale of some very good people.

23

"It's not a question of trust. I'm sure of that. When you look at it carefully, they're not even saying they don't agree with you. We've got another 48 hours to try and come up with a bit more - and even if we don't, they still have the option of pressing the button."

Roper was clearly doubtful and Hooley was privately sure there was more to the delay than the way it had been sold to them. But he also took the pragmatic view that it was a done deal and they had to get on with it. His principal concern was in helping Roper stay on track and not get distracted.

"Let's put any worries to one side for a moment and think about what could be done in the next couple of days"

"There's plenty to do, obviously." The reply was snapped back. It would have been terse from anyone else; from Roper, it was just a statement of fact. Hooley was glad he didn't take these things to heart. Even his ex-wife, who liked to complain he was emotionally stunted, had acknowledged it was a useful trait for someone in his line of work. She knew, from talking to others, that some police officers brought their work home with them, or drank heavily. Neither option tended to end well.

He glanced at Roper who had adopted an odd-looking pose, leaning his head back and pinching his nose between the thumb and forefinger of his left hand. It made him look like he was avoiding a bad smell. The DCI felt an urge to check his armpits, despite having showered a few hours ago.

He left Roper to it and quietly re-arranged the documents in front of him, trying, and failing, to find inspiration. While this took very little time at all, Roper never moved a muscle. He started to wonder if the younger man was going into one of his trance-like states. It was something he did when he was absorbing information.

He picked out a coin from his pocket. Heads he would interrupt; tails he would leave him to it. It came down tails. Now what was he going to do? If in doubt, get the coffee in. Perhaps the aroma of a freshly prepared Americano would get through where all else failed. He set off on what he was thinking of as the jog to the cafe. Nigel nodded at him as he came in.

"Bit early for lunch. You should have phoned ahead."

"No worries, anyway, I'm not here for food, just caffeine. Two cups of your finest Java. Can you make them both Americano and I'll take two small pots of cold milk on the side."

This time there was no quiz as to who they were for as the barista busied himself with the machine and handed over the drinks. After grabbing a carrying tray, the DCI made a slower return; he hadn't yet mastered the GCHQ trot while fully laden.

Walking into the cubicle he placed Roper's drink in front of him, receiving zero response. He matched this with his own brand of indifference, utterly pointless since no one saw. Grunting, he sat down wordlessly and grabbed some document about the US militia groups. He had agreed with Roper that he would float between the three topics rather than risk getting bogged down in one.

Faced with a delay they had agreed to keep checking. Roper had won over Hooley by assuring him that his help was invaluable and would make it faster to get the truth. The two men were carefully examining all the reports.

They were no longer looking at them purely from the perspective that they were wrong, instead they were trying to detect how Roper had been drawn into making the wrong conclusions.

"It's at the heart of everything," he told Hooley.

Kicking off his shoes he placed his feet on the desk and began to read. Twenty minutes later he leaned back in his seat and closed his eyes as he went over a key point. He sat up and reached for a pad to jot down a note when he noticed Roper looking at him.

"You've been muttering to yourself for the last couple of minutes."

Hooley suddenly felt bashful. "I think your way of thinking must be rubbing off on me. Before I say any more let me do a quick Google check."

He tapped away and then read the results, nodding to himself as he went on, then he looked up at Roper, tapped his forehead, and said. "The good news is that the little grey cells still seem to be functioning, despite my advancing years, as you keep reminding me.

"That meeting they had in New York. There was freak weather that disrupted flights in the South, but the East Coast remained clear. I remembered it because my son was due to fly out to Texas but had his flight delayed by a few days because the weather was so bad.

"Well it seems to me that our ultra-right groups may have had a practical reason for ending up in New York. It may have been the easiest destination for everyone to get to. I think that is even more likely because of the suggestion that groups from the east of the country also attended.

"It could be they booked a group meeting months ago. Like everyone else they would need to coordinate well in advance. When the weather turned on them it was probably easiest to relocate the meeting."

He half-expected Roper to dismiss the idea, or at best put it to one side, but he surprised the DCI with his response.

"That's very interesting. It makes me realise I made another mistake. If there were any weather details like that, they should have been in the packet. I never saw anything and didn't chase it up, which is bad."

"Hold on before you kick yourself too hard, there is another way of looking at it," said Hooley. "You're already thinking that someone may be interfering with your access to information. Maybe this was held back because they didn't want you to reach the conclusion I just did. That would fit with you saying it feels like you are being manipulated into seeing some special significance, when it was down to fate."

He snapped his fingers as he was hit by a thought.

"How do they normally send you reports to look at?"

"A lot comes via the GCHQ intranet; some are printed out and there are hard copies of various reports."

"And do you get any sort of warning, or a background briefing? I imagine it must be hard to just pick this stuff up and try and make sense of it without some direction, or the chance to ask questions about where it came from.

"Speaking as a policeman, the source of the information is always going to be crucial. Is the source someone who has provided reliable information in the past? If the source wants to be anonymous, what are they hiding?"

Roper responded. "There was a lot of discussion about that with lots of different people. Some of them quite senior, and quite a few analysts, all sorts of people with different ideas. In the end, it was felt it was best for me to get the information unfiltered and as it came in. No briefing and no explanation. Everyone decided that was the best way to work with the Rainbow Spectrum. The idea was to remove any trace of subjectivity and just leave me to deal with hard facts."

Hooley was surprised. "That's quite a big ask. Were you happy with it?"

Roper looked pensive. "I did worry and said maybe we should start more slowly, give me a chance to settle in, but everyone was keen to push on. They said there was too much going on to take it easy. I went along with it."

"I bet you did. And was there any attempt to control the volume of material you were looking at?"

"I don't think so. When it was ready to send to me then off it went. Somedays I would get lots of reports and be here all night, other days it would be much quieter."

"And what about who sent it to you?

Roper looked doubtful. "Everyone here is divided into teams, so say you might have many different sections flagging up whatever they thought might be of interest, as soon as they got it."

Hooley absorbed this. He could think of a lot of things that might be wrong with that system; mostly about swamping Roper with so much intel that it was little wonder he lost track of where everything came from. It also sounded like far too many people were supplying him material so it would be hard, maybe impossible, to single out an individual.

24

Mr. Roberts used to like roaming between his three London homes. But now, they had become a cause of concern instead of pleasure. As well as discovering bodies, he could no longer recall purchasing the properties; only the fact that he had the deeds reassuring him they were his.

This lack of recall, combined with his natural paranoia, made him super-sensitive. From the start his priority was to ensure he never became a familiar a face in any one location. Even in a huge city like London you had to remember that most people stuck to the same patch and visited the same places.

Today, he was sitting in the tiny living room of a flat not that far from the Houses of Parliament. It amused him to be so close to the seat of political power; although he could never imagine being forced to act like one of the many MPs who turned up to toe the party line. He didn't need other people to give him orders.

It particularly amused him that he had been in the flat for the big Royal wedding, when the next in line had married a girl from the Home Counties, albeit one with film star looks. He had grinned at the behaviour of the security teams. Had they known that a dangerous man was a stone's throw away, there would have been panic attacks. Perhaps they had even carried out background checks on the names of the registered owners of these flats. This one was in the name of Tim Broadbent and Tim himself was the tenant: it wasn't let out.

If the time ever came he would have plastic surgery; the surgeon and procedure was already in hand, generous cash deposits keeping the doctor keen. He would dye and restyle his hair, alter the colour of his eyes with contact lenses and wear special shoes that increased his height by almost two inches.

He felt hungry. Living his life this way meant he also needed to stay on top of mundane issues like food shopping because he wanted to avoid being recognised in local outlets. He endured the boredom of a trip to the suburbs to stockpile essential supplies. No one would notice you bulk buying bacon in a Croydon superstore.

The contents of his big shops were distributed around the three individual freezers. Today he picked out a shrink-wrapped packet containing three sausages, and a small portion of butter. The sausages were dunked into a bowl of lukewarm water and were soon ready for cooking. Putting a frying pan on the cooker to warm up, he grabbed two slices of frozen, wholemeal, bread and put them in his toaster.

Not long after that he was taking his first bite of the sandwich, cooked just the way he liked it and slathered in brown sauce. The strong taste made his mouth pucker slightly but he loved the sensation and carefully ate his way through the rest of his meal. It would, most likely, be the only thing he ate that day. If he felt hungry again he would just ignore it. He finished his meal with a cup of strong, black, instant coffee and two heaped spoons of sugar. He never bothered with milk.

He pulled up his laptop and searched various news feeds to see if anyone was carrying information about the bodies he had left in Dulwich. So far there was nothing, which surprised him, but he assumed the police must have some sort of reason for not publicising them. He was trying to work out what that might be when he realised he was guilty of overthinking things. The sitting Prime Minister had announced a general election, the second in 18 months - that was the big story of the day.

But as he sat in his small one-bedroomed flat, he again experienced an unusual feeling. He had the impression he had forgotten something. He had no idea what it was, only that there had been something he knew about and then it was gone. To try and unravel this mystery he was minutely deconstructing what he had done over the last two days. It didn't take him long and it didn't help him find any answers. This led to another unwelcome intrusion: he was worried. Normally he would have congratulated himself that every move he took was minutely planned. Now he wasn't so sure.

It felt like there were a series of black holes in his mind where memories had melted away, leaving no trace of what used to be there. He wasn't even sure when this had started happening but could, at least, pinpoint when he had become aware of it. Ignoring his situation regarding the flats was one thing; finding those two in one of the flats was a nightmare.

It wasn't that he worried about killing them. He was indifferent to their fate. If he'd thought they would cause him no trouble, he might have let them go. Well, maybe. He enjoyed the professionalism called for in killing people; it gave him a sense of purpose.

But with all this confusion a worrying thought emerged. He couldn't help wondering if some sort of dementia was happening. Had he been a normal person he would have gone to a doctor, but that was out of the question. How could he possibly explain it? "Sorry, doctor, I killed two people and the thing that is bothering me is not the murdering; it's because I don't remember kidnapping them in the first place."

He sighed. There was only one thing he could do. Forget about it. Which was not a joke but was quite funny.

He was forgetting to forget. The truth was he did not have much time to invest in self-indulgent retrospection. He had the sense that events were in motion and trying to stop them would have unforeseen consequences. Not good ones.

25

"It was a drug overdose, or perhaps I should say poisoning, that did for our two victims." DI Cleverly had walked round to Julie Mayweather's office with a copy of the initial autopsy details held in his hands. He passed it over as he added. "The doctor says it was a mix of roofies and Special K. Lots and lots of it. The combination slowed down their respiration to the point where they effectively suffocated. Very hard to say at this point if they suffered; there may be some markers in the blood tests but we haven't got those yet - but I wouldn't want to go out that way."

The policewoman flinched slightly. For some reason, she found drug related deaths especially hard to deal with and had done ever since her days as a rookie. Just a few weeks after starting she had been selected to work alongside a more experienced officer as they checked a report that a heroin user had overdosed.

When they had broken into the stinking bedsit the druggie called home, they had also found the body of a tiny, emaciated, three-week-old baby. Time had eventually dimmed the memory of the infant lying there, but the anger never left.

Her fists clenched and unclenched as she said. "To think some clowns refer to those two as party drugs. What sort of party is it where you take stuff that will kill you?"

The DI shared her dislike of drugs and the all the problems associated with them. "I'm going to talk to the drugs squad but I did a bit of online research and people do talk about taking this combination, although I think it is quite unusual."

His own kids were very young but he had started getting nightmares about the day they were old enough to be introduced to the drug scene. He shook himself. "As I say, I need to get a more solid take on it. I've put in a request for a briefing and someone is going to get back to me today, I hope."

He glanced down at his own notes. He'd already passed the report on to his boss but he knew she always liked a verbal report on the key points of interest.

"The doc reckons they were both in a weakened state, partly from being kept in restraints and partly through not really having enough decent food or water. Not enough to kill them outright, but just enough to magnify the effects of the drugs. Again, the doctor is being cautious until the bloods come back, but her guess, maybe her hope, is that they would have been deeply unconscious and known little about it."

"But it's cold comfort to think they may not have suffered. What I don't understand is why our man spared us the really nasty stuff this time?"

He checked to see she was happy to pursue this line and from her expression knew he should carry on. "I think it is worrying that we have a serial killer who is behaving differently with different victims. I thought they were supposed to keep to the same sort of MO. I'm sure I've been told that they like to have a signature statement, or leave their calling card. That is what I thought the face removal was all about."

He was pleased to hear his boss share his concerns. "I don't think you are getting ahead of yourself. It defies belief to think that we are dealing with random events: one killer for the first two and a brand-new killer for the latest pair. I agree with you about serial killers and doing the same thing. That's what we have always been told. I suppose we have to consider the outside possibility that it is two people operating as a team.

The DI let this thought run for a moment. In this job, you had to try and imagine a variety of possibilities; even if only to rule things out.

He said. "Is it beyond the pale to think there might be a man and woman? The bloke does the slicing and dicing and his lady friend is a poisoner. Or am I being sexist? Anyway, we've got no evidence that two people are involved."

Mayweather sat up, clearly having made her mind up about something. "You may be right about a male and female team, but as you say, we only have physical evidence of one person being at both sites.

"We need to get a break on this case. Why don't we get the press team to put out a big number on the drug deaths? The Press is already going mad about both of them. They love it that Sandra Hall is so pretty and Peter Knight is some sort of genius geek.

"If the press team let it be known we are speculating a woman might be the poisoner then the media will probably go mad. I hate playing these sorts of games but we need to focus as much attention on this as we can. The killer's been out there for a while and seems to be several steps ahead of us. Who knows? Maybe there is a woman involved."

"Sounds like a very good plan. The papers have already been all over the links between the various victims. I'm guessing you don't want to add anything to what has already been reported?"

Mayweather said. "Definitely not. I'm just grateful that no one has picked up on the MoD angle yet. How is that going?"

"Quite slowly. But that's not down to the military coming over all secret squirrel. They've introduced us to the main contacts and been pretty open. The trouble is that it is very, very complex. Good for geeks, annoying for detectives hunting a murderer. If you have time I could tell you about miniaturisation techniques, GPS enhancement protocols and Artificial Intelligence applications. I'll keep pushing."

As she watched him walk out Mayweather had a flash of inspiration. Something was telling her that she needed guidance on what sort of technology was made by the two companies that had been targeted.

What she needed was a contact who could help her. Who better than the head of MI5. The woman was already aware of the police investigation, perhaps she, or one of her people, could provide her with an 'idiots' guide' to what was involved. It must be important to have captured her interest in the first place; now it was time to find out what might be behind this.

*

As the two police officers had hoped, the story of the two drug deaths went down well with the media. The big headlines became even bigger. The new story-line was running on websites within minutes of the details being issued by the Press Bureau. News organisations outside the briefing circle simply picked the story up and credited the veracity to those that had been briefed. It was enjoying saturation coverage by the beginning of the peak evening period.

One of those who saw it was a still unnerved drug dealer. When he read the details, he was even more alarmed. He was one of those people who can normally rationalise their criminal behaviour. In his case he was simply an entrepreneur making a living providing people with stuff they wanted. He boasted that his drugs were always of the best possible quality.

In truth, he was a chancer and not a brave one. He was certain it was his drugs that had been used in the deaths, it was too much of a coincidence that a complete stranger had turned up demanding such an unusual combination, and reasoned that it would be best for him if the police arrested the man as quickly as possible. He had read with keen interest the suggestion that officers would be able to overlook potential criminal activity if they got information that led to an arrest. He debated it for a while longer when it occurred to him that there might even be a reward in it. That would be very handy.

He rang the hotline number provided in the story and when the phone was answered began talking. Within an hour he was sitting in the offices of the Special Investigations Unit, recalling his encounter with the man who had bought the drugs. At first, he had tried to portray himself in a positive light, but before long he was admitting that the man had badly frightened him.

"There was something weird about him. He was very cold, if you know what I mean," he said to DI Cleverly. "He told me that if the gear was no good he'd be back and I wouldn't like that. In my line, you get a lot of people talking like that, but this geezer meant it. He wasn't the biggest bloke I've ever seen, but he looked well hard.

"The thing I keep thinking about is when I told him to be careful with the doses. Some people get carried away and take far too much too soon. But he just gave me a funny look and then laughed in a strange way."

An hour later, after Cleverly felt he had extracted every scrap of information from the dealer, he put the man with a police artist and he went off to assign a team of officers to visit the nightclub and check CCTV on the premises. Hopefully, it was on a digital machine and they could get a copy of the night in question emailed and go through it with the dealer. That was assuming they had kept it. He had to hope for the best. Getting a picture would make all the difference.

He sent two of his best people to the club and was glad he had. They reported that on arrival the manager had been very unhelpful, muttering about warrants. His people had suggested to the man that if he refused to help, they would have no choice but to have uniformed officers in the place every night. Their job would be to question every single person trying to get in or out. They would be especially vigilant about searching for drugs, since it was a drugs' tip that had brought them there in the first place.

The manager had quickly caved in and provided a copy of the recording they needed. In the early hours of the following day a very frustrated Cleverly admitted defeat. The dealer had picked the man out easily enough, but somehow all the cameras had of him was the back of his head.

It was like he knew exactly where the lenses were and how to keep out of shot.

26

The Cabinet Secretary might have wanted to slow things down but behind the scenes at GCHQ things were moving at a fast click. What was happening owed less to a security sweep, than it did to an increased drumbeat.

When you ran a secretive organisation dedicated to electronic counter-surveillance, it would be negligent not to think that other organisations, countries and people might be keen to steal your secrets. You also had to consider those working on the inside who might, one day, be working on the outside. Add in those determined to feed disinformation into the machine and you had a heady mix that needed a lot of protection.

GCHQ security took pride in their work, very little of which they could share with the outside world. But you could be certain that it featured a very big firewall, maybe a lot of firewalls, all connected to the digital equivalent of a loud alarm bell. A signal to mount a major counter-offensive was not lightly undertaken. But once started it promised to be far reaching.

As part of the sweep Roper and Hooley were granted new and improved access. The argument being that Roper needed more background information about the material he had seen and his current access didn't allow for that. What Roper had, also went for Hooley, which in his case, the DCI reflected, made no difference at all. Now he just had more complex things to try and decipher.

Analysis was not his forte. Not because he didn't get it, his years as a policeman had taught him to revere cold, hard evidence above all. His idea of an intelligence report was to guess the IQ of those villains who used Facebook to boast about their criminal activity, then wondered why the police turned up to arrest them.

Although he had only been in Cheltenham for a few days he was already yearning for something like a nice simple murder. He knew it wasn't to be. He was just going to have to let Roper take the lead and follow up as best he could.

"What's the biggest difference now that we have been given new access?" he asked.

Roper was so intent on what he was reading that it took three more attempts to get his attention. Hooley had to keep prodding as the younger man kept getting drawn back to the information displayed on his screen.

For some odd reason, this behaviour reminded the DCI of himself when he was handed a nice, cold, pint of lager: a sense that all was well with the world, if only for a few moments. He shook his head to clear the image. How shallow was he to be thinking about booze when they were up against such a tough puzzle?

Planet Roper reported in. "This tells me where all the information I have been working on originated. It turns out we'd just been looking at reports of reports, or even worse, a highlighted summary. Now I know that the information about the militias and the Australian drug situation were lifted from communications that took place on the Internet.

"You'd already highlighted issues with the Somali information. Now I have found out that the core information was drawn up by a CIA operative who was working with a transcript of an interview with an arrested pirate. But the transcript wasn't done at the time; it was weeks later. That tells me it might not be reliable for all sorts of reasons. Maybe the person providing the details was lying. You just can't tell."

Hooley did a double-take. "Is it even legal? I'm no prude, and information is information, but you surely need some legal basis to be operating from. How else can you arrest people and charge them?"

Roper shrugged. "How will anybody know. Officially, GCHQ doesn't take information in that way so logically we can't be breaking any laws. I have spoken to some of the other analysts here and they are cool about it.

"I think it will be fine. Look at the militia situation. The Americans could have obtained that under anti-terror legislation and then shared that with us on national security grounds. Our far-right parties have been showing signs of becoming more organised in recent months and that could have a seriously destabilising effect. Especially if they started working together on both sides of the Atlantic."

Hooley wasn't convinced but also realised he was in danger of creating a red herring. They had to deal with the here and now. He said. "I'm going to park that. From what you just said, you now know that you were never provided with all the information you needed. Instead, you were sent edited versions that sent you off in the wrong direction. I think your theory about being manipulated is looking more and more on the money."

Roper didn't answer. He'd retreated back into his semi-trance state. Hooley wasn't really surprised. Now that the evidence of someone trying to feed him disinformation was mounting, he had a lot to think about.

Ironically, what looked like an attempt to sideline him was actually placing him back on centre stage. He suspected that whatever Roper finally came up with, and he knew he would get to the bottom of this, was going to have a profound impact on the way GCHQ worked.

Just thinking about that made his throat dry. It was time for tea, plus cake for Roper. He didn't bother asking what he wanted. In this mood, he ended up eating and drinking what was placed in front of him.

Walking back with supplies, Hooley was thinking about the differences and similarities between the people at GCHQ and his own unit at Scotland Yard. At first glance, there was little in common. In reality, both were fighting crime and terrorism - they were just using different tools.

He was sitting at his desk mulling this over when Roper interrupted his thoughts by saying very loudly: "I've had sex, you know."

When the DCI was a young boy he was very partial to comic books like the Dandy or Beano, reading them avidly every week. One of the comedic standbys would be the scene where someone was surprised while they were having a bite to eat, or drinking something.

The victim would either receive a powerful slap on the back, or see something that shocked them. Either way the result was the same. The speech bubble would contain the word "gnmph" and the victim would spray the contents out of their mouth. Until this moment Hooley hadn't realised this also happened in real life. Luckily, he managed to hit the carpet rather than his keyboard.

Gingerly wiping his mouth, he looked around furtively to see who was looking at them, relieved when he realised this had apparently gone unnoticed. He glanced at Roper and saw he had returned to his reading after making his unexpected statement.

Hooley began to wonder if he had somehow misheard. At first his inclination was to totally ignore what had been said. He could still recall his excruciating embarrassment after his wife persuaded him to have "that" conversation with his son. The 12-year-old had listened patiently to his fumbling explanations before saying "Our school lessons on sex are much better."

As the afternoon wore on he got over his embarrassment, and started thinking about what this meant to Roper. They'd never really spoken of it, at least not in depth. Hooley was under no illusion that he was a master of relationships and would never tell someone else how to live their own life.

Just before they were due to go home, he decided he couldn't leave it as it was. For Roper to have found someone was a huge thing. He struggled badly with personal relationships, despite being keen to have friends, or even a girlfriend. As one of his few mates he knew he owed him the courtesy of taking an interest.

He tossed a crumpled sheet of paper on to Roper's desk to get his attention. "I know I've been saying no beer until answers, but life is too short. Do you fancy calling in for a drink at the Kings' Head on the way back, then we can go for a curry?"

27

As he downed his pint he admitted to himself that if he was going to talk to Roper about sex he definitely needed a drink. He had hoped the pub would work as a place to discuss the momentous event, but there was a loud, and raucous, hen evening getting under way. Hooley shuddered to think how it would go if the women heard Roper talking about his private life.

Roper was still sipping at his own half-pint of lager so he might as well use the delay to his advantage and order another one. Out into the harsh light of the real world, his plan to talk to Roper was looking less straightforward. He decided it was down to fate. If they got to the restaurant and found it full he would have to leave it for another day: if not, well there was always lager to soothe the way.

Arriving at the curry house the manager welcomed them with a warm smile. It didn't look like he was going to be saved by circumstances.

"It's so good to see you. Most of our regulars are staying at home tonight. I don't know why. We are only normally empty like this in the week before race week when everyone is keen to save up a bit of money.

Since neither Hooley nor Roper was a betting man, they looked blank. Realising they hadn't followed what he was talking about the manager said. "It's the big racing festival. Most of Ireland comes here for it, the Gold Cup is the main race of the event. I'm sure you've heard of that. Even I go and place a bet. Once it gets going we get all sorts in here, especially people from the bigger stables who usually have a tip for us."

He realised what he had said. "A tip and a tip, don't you see?"

Hooley nodded vigorously. He thought he did but also suspected that Roper was a tip short of comprehension and about to start asking questions that no one would be able to answer. He gestured for Roper to sit down and said. "I doubt we're going to need the menus since we both know what we want to eat."

"Of course," said the manager. "I'll bring your order over when it's ready." He stepped back as a waiter glided up with Hooley's beer and a water for Roper. He placed both drinks and left them to it. The DCI took a gulp of his beer and then decided to slow down: he was already two pints in credit, this needed to be his last.

He looked around and saw there was no one nearby. Taking a breath, he asked. "This afternoon, at GCHQ, did you tell me that you've had sex?"

Roper nodded.

"I know these things are private but I wanted to tell someone and you are the only person I can tell. She's a very nice girl and works at GCHQ. She came up one day and told me to look at SpyBook. It's a sort of GCHQ version of Facebook for people like me."

"But I thought you didn't like all the social media stuff?"

Roper nodded. "Not the normal stuff. All people do there is shout. But at GCHQ there are all sorts of versions aimed at people who work there. SpyBook is invitation only and everyone knows that you must be polite and not nasty.

"This girl sent me a link and I was able to join and saw that she had sent me a message. When I read it, it said she liked me and wanted to know if we could meet for coffee. After that we met up loads of times."

Hooley couldn't help smiling. Trust Roper to find himself being asked to join something so that someone could ask him out. But he thought that was probably the ideal way to do it. If the girl had asked directly he would have run a mile.

From what Roper said it seemed they had a lot of interests in common, including finding it hard to make friends. It was the woman, Sam, short for Samantha, who had suggested they had sex.

"We wanted to do it properly so we both read up about it and got help from the advice team. We chose a date and then it happened. I didn't know what to expect but it was brilliant."

Despite himself Hooley couldn't get embarrassed. Although Roper was talking in a very matter of fact tone, it was clear that the pair had made a deep connection. He really hoped something would come of it. It was oddly touching that they had been so careful to get advice and made a detailed plan.

"So why haven't you introduced me to this lady since I came down? She sounds like someone I'd be delighted to meet."

"She's not here and hasn't been for a while."

Hooley feared the worst. Had the relationship foundered already? He hoped not.

Roper hadn't noticed the worried look and carried on. "Sam wants to travel for a while and the chance came up to go and work with intelligence services in Canada and the USA. She left just before you came down and won't be back for two years.

"She says that if we are still together after all that time then we will be together forever. I haven't spoken to her in ages because we agreed she needed time to settle in but I'm hoping to do a video call this weekend and find out how she is getting on."

Hooley took his time in responding. The truth was he was very happy for Roper and hoped it would work out well. For anyone else it might have seemed a strange way to have a relationship, separating immediately after consummating it, but Roper was not normal people. And he was prepared to bet Sam wasn't either. The thought of Roper having little Ropers made him laugh out loud.

He explained it to Roper. "I was thinking that if you had children your house would be full of people asking questions. Lots and lots of questions. It made me laugh to think of you having to answer them. It would certainly make up for some of the stuff you've asked me about in the past."

Roper was having none of this. "It's far too soon to be talking about children. I haven't thought about it and neither has Sam. Perhaps I should ask her on the video call?"

"Perhaps take your time before going down that path," Hooley was careful to keep his voice neutral, he didn't want Roper to think he was laughing at him for being so presumptuous. "From what you're telling me you've found a girl, or she found you, who you can relate to. As you know, I'm no relationship expert, but I would just enjoy what you have for now. There's no need to take it any further just yet."

To his surprise Roper looked relieved. "Thank you; I've been worrying about what to do next. I thought you needed to keep coming up with new ideas. Just the idea of having a girlfriend has been pretty hard to understand."

28

GCHQ was designed with an open plan area containing cubicles broken up by dividers. This was to stop the space feeling overwhelming and create a basic sense of privacy for the staff. Unsurprisingly, there were huge numbers of computer screens being studied night and day. It made the need for air conditioning totally essential. Opening a window was not really an option.

Naturally, there were some areas where the open plan approach was less in evidence. From time to time everyone needed access to some privacy, so rooms were set aside for that. The security team especially tended to favour out-of-the-way spaces when they could.

One of these was currently occupied by the head of security, Alan Smith, a man whose expression made him look as though he was stuck somewhere between anger and disappointment. A thin man, in his mid-50s, colleagues joked that his hair was suspiciously dark and suspected he was guilty of using a hair dye. If this was true, his little vanity sat at odds with his famously fastidious habits. It was even claimed he ate sandwiches with a knife and fork.

Sitting opposite him was his deputy, Georgina Moore, who could not have been more unlike her boss. Today she had a pink fringe in her straw blonde hair. Normally impassive, Smith had once made the mistake of narrowing his eyes when she had first turned blonde. After that she had made a habit of adding new colours at every opportunity. She was only 25 years old, but had risen fast because of her extraordinary expertise with surveillance technology. If there were candidates for the real-life version of Q - the James Bond Quartermaster - then she would have made the final list of candidates.

She found Smith deeply irritating and suspected the feeling was reciprocated. But they worked together well enough, neither willing to sacrifice their work over petty relationship issues, but never missing the chance to engage in a little jousting. Smith's face had remained impassive as he listened to Roper's conversation with Hooley.

Internal security had been stepped up in recent times, making his job more important. It wasn't that they had any particular problems, but the extraordinary breach revealed when a US defense contractor dumped sensitive material on to the internet had made every intelligence service in the world sit-up. After initially laughing at the Americans the penny dropped - this could happen to us.

In the light of the new protocols, Roper had been upgraded to active targeting after he suddenly appeared to lose his way. With no obvious explanation for what was happening, the worry was that he might have been "compromised" in some way. And in the last few hours they had been ordered to include the Scotland Yard man Brian Hooley. There was a big fuss going on.

Smith looked at his younger colleague. Had he let his feelings show it was likely he would be sneering. He was especially drawn to her eyes - they seemed to be very blue today and he wondered if she was using coloured contact lenses. He shrugged. He knew that his approval, or disapproval, meant nothing. She had been marked for promotion by people well above his pay grade so he put the distraction out of his mind. He leaned forward and tapped the compact speaker she had placed on the desk between them.

As she had anticipated he was impressed with the sound quality. "Excellent clarity," he said. He was always impressed with how good modern speakers were and she supposed it had something to do with his growing up in the days of hi-fi and speakers the size of dustbins.

The thought amused her and she was about to say something when he got in first. "You obviously chose the right table to bug. I presume they always like to sit in the same place?"

"Yeah, they do. But I don't like to take chances so I bugged every table in the place. Why risk missing out?"

She noticed a slight tic over his right eye and correctly interpreted the coming question. Reaching into a bag on her lap she placed what looked like a lump of well chewed gum on the desk. She'd been looking forward to this bit and for good measure she prodded at it, making it spread over the desk. This time Smith could not hide his horror. She knew he had a phobia about germs so this would really upset him.

Drawing it out as long as she dared - he might be a knob-head but he wasn't a stupid knob-head - she said. "Looks exactly like a lump of chewing gum, right? Most of the time no one looks at the underside of a table, but say staff were doing a deep clean, this is what they would see. No one likes to handle someone else's used gum, so they just get rid of it as quickly as they can. I'm not saying it would baffle Mossad, but a restaurant in Cheltenham? We should be fine. Once we're done I will get the stuff retrieved. Even if someone found it, it's not as if it says 'Property of GCHQ. Please return.'"

A slight release of tension in his shoulders told her that her boss went along with what she was saying, even if there would be no chance of a pat on the back. They didn't play that well together.

She carried on with her explanation. "We used a Bluetooth signal to activate the monitor once they sat down. It can transmit constantly since we can also recharge the battery through the active signal.

"Retrieving the information is much easier because we can use the other bugs as relays so our man just needed to get within forty metres of the restaurant to pick everything up. I was outside last night and there was nothing untoward said, unless they are using some type of code we have never come across before. I wanted you to hear it today just in case you picked up on something I missed."

Smith shook his head. "All sounds perfectly innocent to me. Although I was surprised to hear Roper talking about a girlfriend. I always thought that would prove beyond him. I suppose we need to remind ourselves that he is capable of many surprises."

Despite herself, Moore agreed with him. "Judging by the way he described things I think the girlfriend was a bit of a surprise to him as well. But yeah, I put her on my list and we're doing a full security shake-down. Don't hold your breath; she looks clean."

Smith didn't respond. He steepled his hands and made a face that she found especially annoying. She called it his 'look at me, I'm thinking,' expression. Oblivious to her thoughts he asked. "Have you run this through the artificial intelligence program yet?"

She'd expected the question and had her answer. "I have and it hasn't come up with anything. But even if it had I would have needed serious convincing. Everything we've seen about Roper suggests he is exactly what he seems: a brilliant analyst and a complicated man to get to know. Difficult company."

She was regretting her comments the moment she finished talking. Smith let the brief triumph show with a little smirk. Moore knew she had just been marked down for allowing her response to be shaped by her view of Roper the man. You could never afford to let your guard down with this man.

Moore couldn't stop herself wondering if he had deliberately blindsided her with that annoying facial expression. He obviously knew she didn't like it. Fortunately, she didn't have time to dwell on her mistake, as he was asking her about her arrangements to monitor the pair in the flat they shared and the bugging of Hooley's Pimlico flat.

"It's in hand but it will take a couple of days." the reply terse enough to hint at rudeness.

"That will have to do," said Smith. He did such a convincing job of looking like he meant it that Moore assumed he had to be faking. He went on. "I do have some news for you. The Home Secretary finally agreed to us listening in on Julie Mayweather's phone and the plod who has stepped up as the replacement for Brian Hooley. There was some concern at your initial request but I managed to persuade them the stakes were high enough to warrant the measure."

Moore had to clamp her jaw shut. The 'bastard' had clearly presented it as all her idea, just in case it was knocked back. She had thought it was being presented as a joint initiative: in fact, he should have taken full responsibility, he was the boss. Instead it sounded like he had done a lot of brown nosing in order to make himself look good.

29

Julie Mayweather was genuinely shocked as she was informed about the surveillance equipment that had been dug out of Tom Bennett's office in Leatherhead. His home in Clapham was currently being inspected and the expectation was that more would be found there.

"Who found this stuff? I thought it had been given the all-clear."

DI Cleverly looked unsure if he was the recipient of a dressing down or his boss was simply telling it like it was. The Special Investigations Unit had missed it altogether. They had only found out when they had been called by a special liaison team at MI5. The grey area between policing and domestic intelligence had led to too many misunderstandings. The liaison team had been set up to bridge the gap and keep everyone informed. It usually worked.

He had spent a frustrating afternoon trying to get information out of the liaison team and it had been heavy going. He had finally made headway when he offered to share every scrap of evidence about the four victims. It gave him just enough leverage.

He said. "I'm not exaggerating when I say that they started out with an 'I could tell you but then I'd have to kill you' attitude, but I have managed to get a bit more from them. But this is where it gets interesting.

"It seems as though the military agency Tom Bennett dealt with decided to double check that his murder wasn't a cover for some sort of industrial espionage. And before you ask, they're not going to go into what was worrying them. It seems they are not being as open as I first thought.

"We only find out the truth when something goes wrong. Talk about 'my enemy is my friend', this lot do your head in. If you tell them the time they check their watches.

"It seems that 'persons unknown'" - he mimed quote marks around the words – "sent a couple of experts to the work place and they are the ones who spotted this stuff.

"They really didn't want to tell me about what they found but I had a shouting match and explained that if it was deemed they were interfering in a murder investigation but in the interests of the country I was willing to share information.

"We're apparently talking miniaturised cameras the size of a fly and listening gear no bigger than a pinhead. It's why we never spotted anything. I know we weren't looking, but even if we had I doubt we would have seen it."

Mayweather had barely moved throughout the briefing. She paused to make some notes, then sat back.

"This is turning into a national security matter? I suppose we might have suspected something because of the nature of Bennett's work but this is like something out of a Le Carre novel. Well, the big question is; who put the bugs there in the first place? Have our friends in security got any thoughts about that?"

Cleverly said. "I asked them exactly that. They said there was a real concern about it because only ourselves, the Americans and the Israelis are supposed to have access to equipment as sophisticated as this. They let slip this was going to cause an almighty row.

"When I asked if that meant we, as in some branch of our own security services, could have been responsible I got the clear impression they really didn't know. I learned this requires very specialised manufacturing skills. You can't just knock it up in any old factory, even if you had the technical specs. You need specialised tools, custom made parts and high-level engineering skills to put it all together. They've promised me an answer in the next 48 hours."

Mayweather leaned back in her seat. "I may be able to get some more information. I've fixed a meeting with the head of MI5. I thought I might need a briefing about what these two companies are involved; seems I was right to wonder.

She was about to say more when her mobile went off. She looked at the screen, saw who it was, apologised to Cleverly and took the call. She stepped across to the far side of the room as she listened to whoever was on the other end of the line.

Phone call over she clicked the red off icon, stared at the device for a moment as if willing it to ring again and then looked at the DI.

"You and I need to be in Downing Street in the next twenty minutes."

*

The meeting lasted a little over half-an-hour. No politicians were present although it was made clear that the Prime Minister, Home Secretary and Foreign Secretary were in the loop. As well as the head of the Civil Service, the spy-chief Jennifer Cameron was present.

The meeting was told that the multiple murders were being regarded as potential threats to national security because of the military equipment made by the companies they worked for. Mayweather waited to see if Cameron would talk about the discovery of high-tech surveillance kit in the boardroom, and private office, at Bennett's company, but the woman kept silent, leaving it to the police officer.

It broke up rapidly as all concerned accepted there were more questions than answers. On their way out, Cameron held Mayweather back and promised to talk to her tomorrow. "I don't have a smoking gun for you, but there are things you need to know. They'll explain why everyone is so worried that our secrets have been compromised."

As she and Cleverly made their return to Victoria she reflected the meeting had gone better than it had looked on first appearance. Mayweather had fought her corner effectively. She pointed out that suddenly taking the Special Investigations Unit off the case could be counter-productive by drawing attention to the change. All her team had signed the Official Secrets Act, and she also offered to restrict those with full access to as few people as possible.

"Everyone who works for my unit has considerable investigative experience before they are considered for a place. They are all used to working with highly sensitive material and understand that sometimes there is a good need to operate on a need-to-know basis."

When this idea was supported by MI5, the relief on the Cabinet Secretary's face was tangible. He had been experiencing a private nightmare in which he imagined that the elite Scotland Yard team and the elite spy chasers would end up in some sort of bitter power struggle for control, which would only lead to recriminations and leaks to the media.

With the car making minimal progress in London's interminable traffic Mayweather turned to the DI; something had been bothering her and she had just realised what it was. She said. "I was looking at Cameron whilst I talked about the surveillance equipment. Even though she obviously knew about it, she still looked shocked, and that is quite telling. It suggests she didn't authorise its use."

Cleverly's face darkened as he absorbed the idea. "If you're right that might suggest there is some sort of rogue operation taking place." He shook his head. "This could turn out to be a can of worms. I've never had any direct dealings with the security services myself, but mates who have say it can be a nightmare."

"I'm afraid that is exactly what I'm thinking," said Mayweather. "I think we need to work on the assumption that we will only receive information that MI5 thinks we need to have, rather than what we really need."

She gazed out of the window as the car inched its way along the road. She could have asked the driver to switch the blue lights on, but she was a stickler for only using those in a genuine emergency: a policy she was regretting. She was itching to get back to the office but in the meantime, she was going to have to get on with it as best she could.

She turned back to Cleverly. "Can you get someone to call Bennett's finance chief? Tell him I would very much appreciate it if Mr. Wilson could come into our office to go over some issues that have been raised. I want to apply some pressure to him because he may well know more about what Bennett was up to than he's letting on."

As her deputy was murmuring into his phone the congestion eased enough for the car to get above walking pace. She sighed. There was a lot to like about London, but travelling around was a pain.

30

Fred Wilson had been 'treated' to a blast of 'blues and twos' as the driver bringing him from Leatherhead had switched on his lights and siren for the last leg of the journey into Victoria. Some people love the experience, some people hate it; Wilson clearly fell into the latter category. It had taken him a good five minutes to settle after being given a cup of coffee and left in the interview room. Julie Mayweather had guessed right. She knew that once he had calmed down he would be in the right mood to share any scraps of information he might have been holding back.

Mayweather didn't normally like leaning on people, but she was sure he knew more than he was letting on. She wanted him to feel the heat of the fire. Now she was standing looking in through the two-way mirror. The finance chief was shifting restlessly in his seat, his large frame meaning he couldn't get as comfortable as he would have liked. Again, this was deliberate. Cleverly had a better chair which would be handed over once they were ready to do the interview.

Deciding now was the time, she walked in with the DI behind her. The accountant jumped to his feet looking flustered but before he could say anything he was treated to Mayweather's biggest smile. "Thank you so much for coming here at such short notice. Sorry for keeping you waiting, partly that was because I remembered how useless the chairs are in here. DI Cleverly here has found something a little more suitable for a man of your size."

Cleverly placed the chair within easy reach of Wilson, who was clearly pleased at having something he could sit on without wondering if it would buckle under his weight. Small advantages could often prove crucial in extracting information from people. She doubted that he would lie to her directly, but might feel conflicted over revealing any confidential information.

She led the interview cautiously, going over previous ground and being careful to thank the accountant for the help he had given them so far. After about five minutes of questions on general finance issues she could see he was relaxing. He'd gone from worrying that he was a suspect to offering insights into the company and Bennett the man.

Finally, she got him on the topic she wanted, deciding to approach the subject directly. Sometimes you could be so cautious you never got to the point. "How did Mr. Bennett tell you he was doing top secret work? That must have been an odd moment for you?"

Wilson nodded his agreement. "It was. The thing about Tom is that he would have made a useless spy, at least in the long term. He was just so passionate about his work and loved talking to people about it. When he told me about his security work he was quite apologetic. We had always known exactly what each other was doing so this was the first time he'd had to keep anything from me.

"It wasn't something that worried me. I knew he would only do that if it was necessary and I imagined that it involved work to keep the country safe from terrorists so, in a way, I felt quite proud that my company was involved in something like that. Even if I didn't know all the details."

Mayweather, listening carefully, noted the way he expressed that. Not knowing all the details meant he did know some. Her reactions now owed a lot to her father. He had taken her on long rambles in the countryside, teaching her the need for patience and quiet if she wanted to catch a glimpse of wild animals. Without meaning to, he had equipped her with valuable tools for being a detective - or a stalker, as she liked to joke.

Now she felt she could afford to push a little as she steered the conversation - this was not an interrogation - to where she wanted it to go.

She said. "My DI and I like to take time out just to get a little perspective over what's going on. Not making a big deal out of it, just 10 minutes over a cup of coffee, usually in my office. It makes sure we know what each other is up to and gives us the chance to review what we are doing. It's surprising how often you spot things that are going wrong."

For the first time, he was clearly relaxed enough to smile. "We used to do the same thing. It was Tom's idea, he called it our 'sort it' time. You know, when we could sort out problems and make sure everything was on track."

"I can imagine that you are going to miss those moments. Just the two of you in the office; I bet you made sure the phones were switched off for a few minutes." He nodded, making Mayweather wonder if she was getting too good at this sort of thing.

She went on. "I know he never told you about his secret work, but is it possible that you were able to surmise things, sort of pick up details? I wouldn't normally pry over sensitive areas, but I still can't find a reason why anyone would want to have killed your boss; your friend, I suppose."

She knew this last comment had grabbed him: shaping her appeal in that way was intended to help him make the right call. He needed to be totally sure he would be helping his friend, not betraying his memory.

He sat still, clearly having an internal conversation and then half-nodded, as if realising he was making the right decision. He said. "Like I said, it's not that he ever told me anything in detail, but he was a man who loved to talk about his work. When we had our 'sort it' time he knew he was safe to say things and that they wouldn't go any further. It meant he didn't have to be on his guard so much. He and I go back a long way.

"One time he was talking about an article that suggested the Americans had produced tiny drones the size of a bee. He was genuinely fascinated by the topic and I got the impression that he felt it was OK to discuss it because it was out there.

"I can't really explain why, but I thought that was exactly the area he was working in with his secret stuff." Taylor looked down at the floor for a moment. "That's all I've got. I'm sorry it's not much and I hadn't wanted to mention it before because it's just what I thought. He never said it in so many words, but I am sure he was talking about making tiny components."

Mayweather stood up. "Actually, Mr. Wilson you have been more helpful than you know. Many thanks again for coming in, and could I remind you that this is an ongoing investigation. So please don't discuss our conversation with anyone else without talking to me or DI Cleverly first."

The two officers watched Wilson being escorted out by one of the uniformed officers then made their way into Mayweather's office.

The DI was the first to speak. "Have we just been told that he was being spied on by top secret equipment that he made himself?"

"That's exactly what I'm thinking. Now all we have to do is find out which bit of the intelligence service he was working for. I'm rather glad I have that appointment with the head of MI5."

31

Sometimes it felt like they were surrounded by an invisible force field. Working in an open plan office meant colleagues could be exaggeratedly respectful of personal space; you could be working physically alongside someone while doing your best to politely ignore them.

This was adding to the sense of isolation afflicting the DCI. Much as he knew he'd helped Roper start to work out what was going on, it was frustrating to have so little to do. Part of him knew that was inevitable from the moment he had been called from London. The younger man needed his support but it didn't alter the fact this wasn't his world.

Had he been working at the Special Investigations Unit he would not be having a problem. There was more than enough to occupy him and he could keep busy and productive while waiting for Roper to find whatever he was looking for.

Thinking about the active cases he had left behind was making him restless. He wasn't designed for this sort of thing. Sitting on his hands and killing time. It was making him feel crabby, but there was nothing he could do about it. Everyone said the case was in the national interest. That made him huffier. Everything here was in the national interest.

He tried to analyse his feelings, attempting to decide if his sense of dislocation was simply down to the inevitable hiatus while Roper tried to make sense of the complex issues he was focusing on.

His mood wasn't being helped because he was concerned about the younger man. On the face of it he appeared calm and in control. But the DCI knew that this could be deceptive. Roper felt tension as much, probably more, than anyone else. Looking at him now, his eyes glued to the screen, he didn't look as though he was coming back to the real world any time soon.

He might as well go to the cafe, he had to do something. He couldn't take much more of sitting at his desk, killing time. With a groan, he heaved himself out of his seat. That was another thing: since coming to Cheltenham he had been missing out on his osteopath sessions. Perhaps a visit to the onsite medical centre would help. If his back got much stiffer he was going to be in difficulties. He knew he was being grumpy but couldn't help it.

When he returned an hour later his posture suggested someone who has been vigorously manipulated - a sort of 'it hurt but it will do me good' approach. To his relief it was helping. He was already feeling better.

He had been lucky to have arrived at the centre just as a patient canceled an appointment. He had been waved straight through. The young osteopath had quickly identified which joints were out of sync and he had been treated to some robust treatment that had left him feeling like he had been run flat by a steam roller before being miraculously re-inflated.

Feeling pleased with himself he had stopped off to collect two coffees and two chocolate muffins. Walking back to their work area he was delighted to see Roper was out of his reverie and had clearly been looking for him. Roper was about to say something when his eyes took in the two cups of coffee and a bag that he clearly hoped was food.

Handing over his prizes, the DCI sat down, took a huge bite of muffin and washed it down with a gulp of

Americano, cold milk added separately. As usual Roper had wolfed his down at such a speed that Hooley was amazed he didn't choke.

"I think I am on the right lines with my distraction theory." This was followed by an intense study of the empty coffee cup before he threw it into the nearest rubbish bin.

The DCI knew full well that there was no point in trying to rush him and was content to sip his coffee. For the first time in a couple of days he was free of back pain. He hadn't realised how much it had been affecting him. He savoured his drink and thought about the upcoming Arsenal game on Saturday. Many of the fans were up in arms with the manager but Hooley was more sanguine. They might not have won the league for a while but they were still a competitive side. Perhaps this year would be the one. His football fantasy was disturbed as Roper finally picked up on his opening comments.

"I now understand how distracted I've been, because that's all I can think about. I've even been wondering if I imagined being distracted. So, this has been a very clever piece of work and it has taught me a lot more about the way my Rainbow Spectrum works."

Hooley thought this was more like the Roper he knew; all he had to do now was to try and work out what all that meant.

"Could you run that past me again, only this time with subtitles?"

When Roper was in one of these moods it was like watching an old-style word-processor transform into to a super computer: A few lights would start flickering, then before you knew it the machine powered into life, all flowing lights and print-outs.

Roper said: "Quis custodiet ipsos custodes?"

He looked expectantly at Hooley who grinned as he recognised the phrase. "'Who watches the watchers?'" then he caught himself. "Actually, it should be "Who watches the watchmen?'. My Latin may not be up to your level, but along with 'Carpe Diem', that is one phrase I do know, as should every policeman."

He was quietly enjoying his triumph when he realised that Roper clearly expected more. He was confused, had he got the translation wrong? No, it wasn't that. So it was something about the phrase itself. Then realisation hit him. "The Ipsos. You think that the name of the boat is important."

Roper nodded. "I'm quite angry with myself for not picking up on it before but I can now see that I was right about disinformation. Someone made sure that the intelligence about the Somali pirate operation would come to my attention.

"Giving the boat the name Ipsos was a small gamble but I think they were relying on me overlooking the name. They knew I would be drawn by why such a powerful vessel had been purchased in the first place. I was far too busy thinking about how they might be using it to spot the obvious - the name. This was designed to keep my attention away from something else."

"But how did you know that the name was the clue?" His faith in Roper was so strong it hadn't occurred to him that he might be wrong. He was fascinated to hear how the younger man had worked it out. He thought this must be what it's like to spend time with a chess champion; someone who can see dozens of moves ahead.

"I went back to the beginning and noticed that the boat should have been given a Somali name. The moment I looked up Somali names on the net I instantly spotted that Ipsos was wrong. Then I worked it out.

"I now know that the name of the boat could have been altered by the person who is trying to manipulate me. If they can intercept all this information, then changing a detail like that would be easy.

"Again, this comes back to the way I use the Rainbow Spectrum. I have been placing too much emphasis on finding answers without thinking for myself. Once I understood that it all started to fall into place. That name was changed to make me think someone wants me to know they are watching me."

Hooley felt a sense of foreboding. "That sounds like a threat. I hadn't believed this was so personal; that someone has you in their sights."

32

Roper's conviction that he was the main target of a GCHQ mole seemed to cause little impact - at least on the surface. Hooley noted that while he had been thinking misinformation was a widespread GCHQ phenomenon, others were already wondering if it was Roper-specific.

He was surprised to learn the Cabinet Secretary had been informed. Sitting here in Cheltenham was a long way from the Corridors of Power. It showed how intense the spotlight on Roper was.

Once he had accepted Roper's logic, and he had no doubt he was right, the DCI had felt his mood lift. Here was something he could get his teeth into, and to which detective skills had a part to play.

The first thing he wanted to do was to talk to David Cotter in the neurodivergence team. He could have sent an email but decided he would stick to old fashioned methods: he would walk round and see if he was available. As he made the short journey he reflected this wasn't quite like the old days of wearing out shoe leather while going house to house but, if he didn't think about it too much, it did at least give him an impression that he was back on the beat and looking for answers to his questions.

His reverie was interrupted when he was forced to a standstill by what could only be described as a land train of young analysts who came tearing towards him and then shot past, forcing him to step to one side to avoid colliding with anyone. Arriving at the neurodivergence team's location, he went to walk in then checked carefully to make sure he wasn't about to be flattened by someone coming the other way.

Stepping inside the only person he could see was a woman in her mid-30s, with short black hair that crowned a pale face. He thought she was very pretty. She was engrossed in her computer screen like everyone here in Cheltenham - and didn't acknowledge him. He glanced around to make sure he hadn't missed Cotter, and then stepped over to stand in front of the woman's desk.

She looked up and smiled as he approached. Like everyone else she was wearing a t-shirt, although this one was plain and had no names on it, jeans and a pair of Converse trainers. This was a footwear label he was familiar with so he was mildly surprised that people here seemed to wear them.

"Brian Hooley, right?" she stood up and extended her hand, making Hooley realise she was about five feet, six inches tall and very slim; a bit too skinny for his taste. Not that he was an Adonis himself. "You're quite famous around here. The person that Jonathan Roper trusts, probably more than anyone else."

He wasn't sure how to react to that and ended up displaying a goofy grin that was only missing an 'Aw, shucks' caption bubble. He told himself to get a grip and managed to change the goofiness to what he hoped was a look of professional inquiry.

"You're right about me being Brian Hooley. What was it that gave me away? The grey hair, suit or the general sense of a man not quite knowing what's going on?"

The woman laughed, displaying a set of very white teeth. "None of those things. I was sent a picture of you, along with your file, when you joined the team here. And people do talk about you, but in a complimentary way.

Everyone knows Jonathan doesn't suffer fools so you must be pretty sharp for him to spend so much time with you.

"Anyway, my name is Helen; Helen Sharples. For my sins, I run the team here and had intended to meet you when you first arrived; it's why I had your file. But, as always, events took over. While we are based here there are a lot of other sites to cover.

"Plus, our field of study is going through a lot of change at the moment which means I encourage my team to go on as many refresher courses as they can. I like to think we bring the latest thinking to our job - so long as it's tried and tested of course. This is no place for random, experimental projects."

Hooley couldn't help but instinctively like the woman. She had a subtle self-confidence to her that was infectious without being overpowering. He became aware she was waiting patiently for him to reply to her question about how could she help.

"I came over to try and find David Cotter, but given I can't see him, and after what you have just said, I think I can guess what the answer is going to be."

She flashed her big smile again, making Hooley remind himself he was nearly twice her age.

She said: "He is out, but you're in luck. He's been on a tutorial in London with one of his former lecturers. He called me this morning to say he was coming back today and expected to be here around mid-afternoon."

"Fantastic," said the DCI, rubbing his hands together. "I can send him an email and try to book an appointment with him."

Sharples was suddenly very serious. "I think I can guess what this is about. You want to talk to him about who Roper has interacted with here at GCHQ? I could give you an overview but David is the man for all the details.

"Do send him a message and I will back it up as well. I'm here all day so I will see him when he gets here. She bent down to her desk and briefly tapped at her keyboard and then looked back at him. "I've sent you an email with David's mobile on it so you can send him a text message as well."

He thanked her. "I'm still finding my way around here and don't know how the etiquette works. If I was back at Scotland Yard I'd be chasing him until he responded, but you may do things differently. I didn't want to get his back up before I'd had a chance to ask my questions."

Sharples laughed out loud; she sounded quite raucous. "Don't worry about that at all. He'll recognise that it just means there is some urgency behind the request. This isn't a place to work if you don't like sudden spikes in pressure. The atmosphere may seem calm but you're only ever a short hop from a crisis somewhere in the world."

33

"I had so many people to talk to that we had to arrange a rota, where I met four people at a time and talked to them about the Rainbow Spectrum." Roper was recalling his first few weeks at GCHQ and the excitement that surrounded his arrival. "We'd allowed up to ninety minutes a time."

"Must have been pretty intense," said Hooley. "Were you OK dealing with so many new people all the time? I got the impression you were always happiest in one to one conversations with someone you were familiar with.

"That was a big advantage of having you sat in my office. You could be right at the heart of things but also in your own space. Julie Mayweather was worried that it would be me who wouldn't cope. She knows I'm not one for small talk. But it was fine. When you left to come down here it seemed very strange to be back on my own. I had quite got used to you being around."

Realising he was starting to drift off the point he pulled himself back to the start of the conversation. "Anyway, tell me how you got on down here? You must have done pretty well because we never heard anything."

Roper fiddled with his shirt sleeves which had risen inside the arms of his suit jacket. Looking down he said. "You have to remember it is different here. There are a lot of people who are neurodivergent so it's not as if people have a go at you for doing things differently. Sometimes ordinary people are in the minority.

"We are all careful not to put each other under pressure; that's one of things the team here is really good about. Just because we are similar doesn't necessarily mean we will get on or all think and want the same things.

"My sessions were carefully planned and everyone was briefed beforehand so that they had their own individual plans. Most of them went well. People understood what I was talking about and quickly went off to do their own versions. When I first came up with this, while I was working with you, people got cross when they couldn't understand the Rainbow Spectrum.

"At first, I was worried it would happen here, but it was OK. A few people decided it wasn't for them, most were fine. It took two weeks and I saw forty people altogether, with thirty-seven going off to do it themselves."

Listening to this Hooley was suddenly certain that it was the pressure of having to keep proving himself at the Yard that had led to Roper being suspended while he was working the child abuse case. It spoke volumes for his drive that he had stuck it out. That had been three years ago, long enough that he could enjoy the benefit of hindsight.

That would always be a problem with office situations. Inevitably, there was a pecking order and if the top dog was a bit of a dick, then the people on the bottom rungs suffered. Good managers could go a long way to combating the problem but it required constant attention, and that wasn't always a realistic possibility. If you had a bad manager, forget it.

Nowadays the Met worked hard at being inclusive - but there were always problems. Today they tried counselling; in his younger days Hooley hadn't been above giving a difficult colleague a slap, just to prove who was boss. He sighed. Looking back, he wasn't a fan of the old ways - in many ways they had been pretty awful - and he wasn't proud of his behaviour then. But huge strides had been made from when it was rife with corruption and people were routinely 'fitted-up'. There was still a long way to go but it was better.

In the 'good old days' someone like Roper, a brilliant analyst and detective, wouldn't have lasted five minutes. His mobile went off, surprising him with how loud the ring was. He picked it up sure he must have disturbed everyone within a hundred feet of where he was sitting, but no one seemed to notice, apart from Roper who was paying close attention.

He looked at the number and thought it looked like David Cotter's. He hadn't had time to input his details yet so it wouldn't show on the caller ID screen. He tapped the answer icon and pressed the phone to his right ear. At first, he could hear nothing then suddenly Cotter was through: it sounded like he was shouting at the phone.

"I'm in the car and should be with you in ten minutes." The next bit was drowned out by what sounded like running water and it was Hooley's turn to shout at the phone. Then Cotter was back on the line. "I said if anyone is going for a coffee can you make mine a Cappuccino with an extra shot. In fact, make that two extra shots. I've had a terrible day."

He must have had the volume set high because before he could respond Roper was on his way. By the time a flustered looking Cotter turned up a cup of strong coffee was waiting. It was cool enough for him to knock back in four large mouthfuls. The DCI noted that not only did everyone here walk round like they were in a race, there seemed to be a lot of people who liked to race their drinks.

Cotter put his cup down, giving it a round of applause. "That was fantastic and I'm willing to bet that you got it Jonathan." Roper gave him a thumbs up. "I reckon there were three extra shots in there, which actually worked really well. I've got to go to the loo so bear with me and we can get started."

Minutes later and Hooley had outlined his initial thoughts about contacting everyone who had direct contact over Roper's Rainbow Spectrum, then expanding out to speak to anyone who may have known about it.

"The first part is easy," said Cotter. "Jonathan and I jointly organised it and I also spoke to each of the individuals who wanted to get involved. I've still got those name in my files, which it may surprise you I have called Rainbow Spectrum. After that it is going to get a lot more involved. There were some people who were interested but didn't know Jonathan and were uncomfortable at the thought of having to deal with a stranger."

Hooley couldn't help glance over at Roper, something Cotter picked up on.

"Jonathan wasn't the least offended."

Roper was shaking his head and shrugging to display he was fine about it. He said. "David and I discussed it at the time but I understood. Sometimes I don't feel comfortable with people so if it's possible to avoid them then that makes it much easier for everyone. There's nothing worse than having to talk to people when you don't want to."

"Are you talking about other people on the autistic spectrum?" asked Hooley.

"Of course," came the reply. It was accompanied by one of Roper's looks that suggested just by asking the question Hooley had shown how out of touch he was.

Hooley smiled and held his hand up in mock surrender. "Sorry Jonathan, I'm just a mere mortal. Thanks for putting me right. Even at my advanced age you can still learn something new and interesting."

This triggered an unexpected response. "At your age, it is terribly important that you are in an environment where you exercise your brain; another important tool against dementia. The latest research is very clear on how vital it is to maintain brain fitness as well as body fitness." He paused and studied Hooley in a way that suggested he had a lot more to say.

Hooley cut him off. "Thanks for that Jonathan. You know I always treasure your advice but that is the second time you have drawn my attention to a dementia threat. A man could get paranoid."

He turned to Cotter for moral support and was dismayed to find the man had gone red from the effort of not laughing. The DCI tried to ignore him. "As I was saying, it would be good to know just how many people I need to speak to about the Rainbow Spectrum. We have to start somewhere and I would like to do so very quickly."

To his chagrin Cotter was now wiping his eyes with the back of his hand, at least he wasn't rolling around chortling. He finally pulled himself together.

"It's going to be a big number. To make it simple, let's take the first thirty people, even though not all of them developed their own ideas. Then you have the people involved in the second round. Just doubling that number, which is very conservative, takes us to sixty people. They will have talked to other people. We're looking at a minimum of one hundred and twenty, maybe as many as two hundred."

"In that case," said Hooley, refusing to be daunted. "Let's get started. Jonathan, you need to be involved, at least at the start."

34

The office was small and square, the walls free of any decoration and the carpet a metallic blue colour. The room was dominated by an oblong table that was big enough to allow four people to sit around in comfort. It was constructed from the sort of recycled plastic that made you think it was probably indestructible.

Sitting on top of the desk was a thermos flask of hot black coffee, one of hot water and a smaller one containing semi-skimmed milk. There was also a selection of tea bags, two large bottles of mineral water and a plate of assorted biscuits. The effect was neutral and unthreatening; just what David Cotter had ordered. He wanted to convey a simple message that this was strictly informal and people could leave at any moment.

The first four people had been spoken to: it hadn't taken long since it was a straightforward exercise in asking them to recall what they had done at the meeting with Roper, and how things had developed since then.

One young woman was prone to wandering off the point; she enjoyed picking up on different ideas and within minutes would have guided the conversation into unexpected areas had Cotter not made a number of deft interventions to bring her back on course.

Hooley had asked for a time-out: he was already starting to wonder if this was the best approach, at least from the point of view of using Roper's time. Maybe it would be better to use a different tactic.

"What do you think Jonathan?" he asked. "I appreciate it was my idea to have you here but I'm thinking that may not be the right call."

Roper had sat unmoving throughout the earlier discussions. He had positioned himself slightly to one side, and to a large extent had kept his head down, looking at a spot on the floor but not asking any direct questions or appearing to take much interest in the proceedings.

He looked up. "I did find it helpful. Although not in the way you might have been hoping. I wasn't sure how this was going to work but I thought it might turn out to be a general discussion about the Rainbow Spectrum. It's made it even more obvious to me that if you understand the spectrum then it tells you how I think about things. So, for that reason it has been useful, but I don't want to sit through much more of the same thing."

It wasn't exactly a ringing endorsement of his detective skills, thought Hooley, but it seemed that he had managed to avoid being rebuked by Roper. Given his recent warning that he was risking dementia he felt a sense of relief. What other medical horrors might have been mentioned? He knew he needed to lose more weight, but he was fitter than he had been a year ago, and had significantly cut back his drinking. Not all the way. Life was too short not to have the odd pint or decent glass of wine.

He turned to Cotter. "What do you think David? I'm inclined to agree with Jonathan: we are going to have to rethink our approach."

Cotter stood up to stretch. In this confined space Hooley noted for the first-time what good shape the man was in. Not especially muscle bound, but clearly fit. Even in his younger days the DCI's idea of a workout was standing at the bar for an evening session.

"I'm with you," said Cotter. "I don't want to sound big-headed, but I think the three of us might be a little too high-powered for what you are hoping to achieve. At least at this stage. What I can do is provide someone from my department to take my place. That will help to reassure people that this isn't some huge witch-hunt."

Hooley also stood up. "That's sounds sensible. You and Jonathan can get back to your own work, but I am going to stay with this for now. We need to keep pushing ahead with this and I think I can afford the time more than either of you."

"That makes sense," said Cotter. "It gives some continuity to what we are doing and allows my team to adapt to what we are looking for and then if you have had enough we get someone to take-over from you. Would you like me to get the ball rolling on that one? I can talk to the MoD police for you."

Hooley and Roper walked back to their work area, stopping off via the coffee shop for essential mid-morning supplies. Although Hooley avoided the rather delicious looking chocolate muffins, he thought it was bad form of Roper to bag the pair and then clearly enjoy every mouthful of them. To add insult to injury he would probably lose weight.

The DCI checked his watch. "I've got half-an-hour before the next round of interviews. Are you happy with these arrangements? I'll only be down the corridor if you need to speak to me urgently. Otherwise this isn't going to take up all my time so I will be popping back here for a decent chunk of the day."

35

Just after midday, Hooley returned to find Roper was having an early lunch, his food and drink carefully lined up. Two sandwiches at the head of the queue, followed by a pair of muffins and finally his coffee. All in a nice straight line. As a finishing touch, he'd moved his waste bin so that he could throw his rubbish away without moving from his seat.

He looked up, tugged at his left ear lobe and said. "I've been making quite a bit of progress. The answers are going to be in what I was looking at before. The way I failed to pick up on the boat being called the Ipsos has really opened my eyes."

Hooley's back protested as he eased himself back into his seat. He needed another visit to the osteopath. He didn't know how Jonathan spent so much time hunched over his screen without suffering any aches or pains.

"I wonder if the next bit will be that straightforward?" Hooley couldn't help sounding a note of caution. "It isn't often that terrorists leave cryptic clues lying around. Usually, it's a bit of internet posturing and dire threats, nothing as subtle as hiding information in plain sight."

"You're right, it is going to be difficult," said Roper. "The person doing this is very smart and wants to prove they are cleverer than me. I used to get this at school. Kids said I was just a nerd and kept challenging me.

"This gives me the same sort of feeling. Someone out there doesn't like me; they don't like me at all, and probably want to hurt me. It was just the same as school. I used to get hit all the time. I would pretend it didn't hurt but that didn't stop them."

Hooley was thinking Roper had just revealed a bit more about himself. He had no idea if this was a good or bad thing, only that it was a clear sign of how much pressure he was under to be delving back to his hated school days. He wished he could help but he shared Roper's view that time was running out.

"I'm interested that you keep saying it is one person doing this. You don't think it could be a group of people?"

Roper didn't hesitate "That's a very good question; one that I have been thinking about quite a lot. There is an overall approach, or master-plan, which has been created by one person. That much is obvious."

Hooley couldn't agree more, thinking that even he had worked that out. He looked expectantly at Roper, fascinated to hear what came next.

"But as I said, this is one person, and they want to destroy me. It's exactly like being back at school. I've had to dig down, more than I have ever done before, including overhauling my approach to the Rainbow Spectrum. It's allowed me to start pulling together details that had been closed off to me.

"Once I accepted this was entirely about me, rather than a plot to disrupt GCHQ with me as the means to an end, other things started to make sense. I asked myself how many people would be needed to work on the plan; again the obvious answer is one. It would have required a lot of thought but you don't need a team of people.

"So, the next thing is what evidence do I have? By doing a deep memory dive I could see that there was a clear pattern. First, I was 'prepped' to look at developments in a certain way. One example. Before I was given anything about the American situation, I was sent a lot of statistical information about contacts between far-right organisations.

"These were incredibly detailed, had been previously checked and approved by intelligence experts. Once I had absorbed it all there could be no doubt that there was a lot more activity and co-operation than previously believed. Social media has allowed anyone with an extreme view to find like-minded supporters.

"By the time I received the main briefing documents I was already convinced and looking for new links. It was why I jumped on the meeting in New York and read too much into it. But it was the way they exploited my Rainbow Spectrum which really got my attention. They spotted a weakness I hadn't been aware of."

Hooley took a drink of water to cover his astonishment. While he had never claimed to understand how Roper's Spectrum worked, he had come to view it as an amazing asset. It hadn't occurred to him that it could be a massive weakness as well. He was equally amazed at the way Roper was calmly deconstructing his own performance. Like a mechanic stripping an engine; but this engine was the brain.

When Hooley picked up the water cup Roper had broken off. Now he carried on. "The problem is simple. I was in the habit of assuming that using the Spectrum let me see the whole picture, and that is a big weakness.

"You actually brought it home to me with your observation about the weather. I realised I had stopped looking everywhere and was exclusively using the Spectrum to get my answers. After that it was easy for them. Just hold things back - like the weather report - and I would go off in the wrong direction. Now I know what has gone wrong I can do something about it."

36

Hooley had gone off for another of his group discussions, leaving Roper glad of the opportunity to spend time on his own. He wasn't uncomfortable with the DCI, but he desperately wanted to practice his unique form of meditating. Not because he wanted to relax. He was confident that all the answers were almost within reach; he had to find a way of bringing them closer.

Many years ago, he had discovered he could, with very little effort, slow his heart down. In the early days he had made himself pass out, but persisted until he got it just right. He was able to bring himself to a place where he hovered on the cusp of falling into a deep sleep while experiencing real clarity of mind.

He used sheets of paper, held in each hand, to achieve a state of 'mental lift-off.' A sense that for a brief moment his thoughts were free of their normal constraints, allowing him to find previously hidden answers. It was very similar to the Rainbow Spectrum.

When he had first arrived at GCHQ, he had worried the open plan nature of the building would stop him using this technique. With people being able to see in to his cubicle he was concerned that they might object. He needn't have worried. No one even remarked on it.

Taking a deep breath, he made himself comfortable and kicked off his shoes before placing his feet on the desk. He had experimented a bit and found that he needed to have about a foot of leg balanced on the table-top to feel totally secure that he wasn't going to shoot backwards on his chair castors.

Today the effect was fast and he felt a surge in energy of the type that made him feel strong and grounded. Now he could start to use his vivid imagination. He had once read about a hypnosis technique which asked people to imagine being on a beach.

He had tried it in his second year at university and was so successful he managed to burn his arm in the imaginary sunshine. He went online to read-up about this and was relieved to find various articles talking about the power of the mind, enough to make him realise that he wasn't the only person who could do it.

This afternoon he transported himself to the Indian Ocean, just off the Somali coast, and aboard the Ipsos. It was a sleek and powerful vessel capable of more than forty nautical miles per hour and carrying up to ten heavily armed men.

When he resurfaced he thought about his experience. He had learned that during his hypnotic state his subconscious mind would find ways of alerting him to problems. Maybe not the detail, but a warning that something was wrong. It would then be up to him to work out what that was.

This hard-won experience confirmed, beyond doubt, he had been misled with the information he was given. Although he had pretty much expected this answer, the final confirmation meant he could now focus on unravelling whatever this plot was about. He was so confident this was the case he didn't feel the need to try something similar with the Australian drugs gang or the US militias.

Towards mid-afternoon Hooley appeared and updated him. "We're making progress." The DCI made a rocking motion with his hand. "Nothing concrete yet, but I think we might get something. I don't want to get you involved too soon so I'll let you know the moment it starts getting interesting.

"All I really have are a lot of people telling me how clever you are and how they wished they could have thought of the Rainbow Spectrum themselves. I think you may have a bit of a cult following here. Especially among the ladies."

Roper blushed and looked startled. "Only teasing, Jonathan," Hooley assured him. "But a lot of the women clearly think you are a decent bloke." His attempts at deflecting the problem were making it worse. He swiftly changed the subject.

"My end will go on for a while - how about another trip to the curry house tonight? We haven't got any food in the flat and I don't fancy going shopping."

He knew Roper hated shopping. Give him any chance to avoid it and he would, especially in a supermarket. He hated the crowds, the bright lighting, the music and the overstuffed displays of food. Hooley wasn't a massive fan either. He had learned that the best time to go with Roper was either late at night or very early in the morning, when there were fewer people around.

As he suspected, presented with a choice of curry house versus Tesco, it was going to be the restaurant option every time. He turned to walk away, stopping mid-stride as his mobile went off. He pulled the phone out of his pocket and checked the number, it was caller ID blocked and he contemplated letting it go through to answer phone but he took it. It might have come through a police switch board.

As he listened to the voice at the other end he stiffened, thanked whoever it was, and angrily hit the off button.

"I've been broken into. That was the local cops, they say the front door has been forced. I am going to have to skip tonight because I need to get down there and see if anything has been taken. I'll call you when I know what's going on."

37

Mr. Roberts was reluctantly concluding that his memory problems were getting worse. He had the sense that from time to time he was really struggling, only for the problem to disappear, leaving him unable to remember what his concerns were. At one point, he had even had the odd sensation that he was flickering in and out of different realities, but that was too weird to think about.

He was sure something was going wrong even though there were quite long periods when he felt perfectly normal. He knew there was a way he could address the issue, but he didn't want to take that path just yet. It might open uncomfortable truths that he didn't feel ready to confront. At some point he would have to, but not right now.

He tried to convince himself it might not be that bad. He was keenly hoping there was some mundane issue that could easily be resolved. He was a man who had learned to take his brain for granted. Just a few days ago he had reeled off, from memory, a long list of facts about the life and times of Tom Bennett. It wasn't that he viewed this as a difficult task - it was yet another illustration of his superior mental abilities. His IQ of 180 was off the charts compared to 'normal' people.

One thought he was working very hard to keep suppressed was the strange feeling he had only recently gone through the same thing. He wondered if he might be suffering a form of selective amnesia, as if he had been given a drug that took away some recent memories but left others intact. It also seemed highly specific. Or maybe it was a concussion caused by hitting his head.

It wasn't down to lifestyle. He didn't drink, he never took drugs - not even an aspirin - and he ate healthily. He'd checked his blood pressure and found nothing to worry about there. He briefly wondered if someone was spiking his food in some way then dismissed the idea. That was just paranoia.

Perhaps he could start leaving himself notes. At first, he seized on this as a brilliant plan, but soon found a big hole in it. If he was having problems with his memory, all he would be doing was reminding himself of something he would then forget.

With plans coming to a head, it was frustrating that this was distracting him from a moment of triumph. He had another thought. Maybe he had picked up some sort of virus? That could explain his problems. He went back to medical websites to see if an answer could be found there.

After an hour, he gave up in frustration. All he had learned was that viruses could cause memory problems, but he needed far more detail than that. He came back to the idea of seeing a doctor, and ruled it out again. It wasn't an option, whichever way he looked at it.

He noticed the time, ten minutes to 2pm. Something about that troubled him. He knew it was important and found himself physically straining to try and recall what it was.

His memory started to surface - he was late for something and needed to be somewhere. He became aware there was a sort of mental barrier blocking the way forward. He pushed against it. Now he could remember what he was supposed to be doing - and he had left himself pushed for time.

He shrugged. It had been a close call but he was back on his game. Brian Hooley should be on his way back to

London, leaving Roper on his own for a couple of days. The DCI might be getting on a bit but he would be able to give a decent account of himself if there was trouble.

Not that the plan called for a confrontation, at least not tonight. This was more about keeping Roper off-balance for a little while longer. He had known that the man would eventually see through what was being done, but it was amusing to imagine him racing off in the wrong direction.

Mr. Roberts reviewed his plans. He decided they were just fine and allowed plenty of flexibility. He couldn't see anything that needed changing, although he did have a vague sense that there was something just on the edge of his recall. He shrugged. He wasn't going to stop now.

38

Hooley was unaware of what a tight grip he had on the steering wheel until he let go, triggering cramp in his fingers. With traffic at a standstill he flexed his hands to ease the discomfort. The journey from Cheltenham had been a headache inducing misery of jams and road-works. It had been teeth-grindingly slow-going, even the brief periods when he could put his foot down soon came to a stop. His mood wasn't enhanced by the tiny pool car he'd been lent by HQ, his own more comfortable one gathering dust in Pimlico. By the time he reached Hammersmith it was idling traffic as far as the eye could see.

At last, after as frustrating a journey as he could ever recall, he pulled up outside his flat. It was a luxury two-bed, two-bath conversion in an elegant late Georgian building. The cost would have been way beyond the price range of a divorced DCI, but his millionaire property developer brother had let him have it after the break-up of his marriage.

Hooley had loved it from the moment he'd moved in. It offered a refuge from the stresses of both work and the fall-out from his marriage. Not so small as to be cramped and not so large as to be a place he would rattle around in. He'd always wanted to live in central London but had never been able to afford it. He relished the freedom the location offered him and had even been known, on his days off, to walk over to South Kensington, to see how the other half lived, before making his way back to his own patch and the surprisingly good pubs it boasted.

On the drive down, he had heard from Roper, whom he had asked to remotely access the CCTV and the cameras covering the immediate entrance way. Surprisingly, since his front door had been forced open, nothing was caught on film and nothing had triggered the alarm. The apparent break-in had been picked up by local police who were keeping a watch on the outside of his home. Julie Mayweather had requested the checks when he had been assigned to GCHQ; she had argued he was potentially a high-profile target who needed a degree of protection.

Hooley had thought his boss was overreacting, but was glad she had decided to have his home checked. He parked and trotted up to the front door. As he climbed the steps he spotted someone approaching from his left and spun round. There must have been something in his expression that alarmed the man; he held up both hands to indicate he was no threat and introduced himself as working for his brother's company. He was smartly dressed in suit and tie, in his early twenties, and was clearly one of the bright young things his brother liked to employ.

"I've been waiting in my car," the man said, pointing vaguely at the blue Mondeo parked a few feet away. "Peter had your door fixed and asked me to meet you with the new key, and to see if there is anything else I can do to help you."

Realising he needed to make an effort at being polite, Hooley thanked the man profusely for waiting and sent him on his way. It turned out to be a good call. "It's my boy's second birthday today. The missus would have killed me if I'd been late," said the man, who all but ran as he took off. Hooley instantly dismissed him from his thoughts. He needed to concentrate on seeing what was inside.

He carefully studied the camera which covered the front door; no damage, or interference, as far as he could see, yet he was puzzled that Roper hadn't found anything when he'd remotely accessed the digital log. He inserted his new key, noting the slight stiffness, and pushed the door open; not making his way inside.

He was listening for sounds of intruders. His head told him he was being daft; his heart said, 'check everything'. He stepped through the door, enduring the unease that affects homeowners after a burglary. He made his way into the kitchen, he might have been broken into but he still had priorities. Had he left some beer in the fridge? He was going to need it shortly. He had. He had also left some milk which was past its sell by date. He was puzzled by this as he had a clear memory of emptying the last of the milk down the sink.

Shrugging, he made his way into the sitting room and his instincts started screaming something was wrong. At first, he couldn't place it, then he shivered involuntarily as he realised what had happened. Virtually all the contents of the room had been moved around. He'd brought himself a couple of cheap prints to liven up the room and these had swapped positions.

His gaze was drawn to a small office table he used for his printer and Wi-Fi gear. For some reason, this had been placed to face against the wall, rather than into the room. He glanced at his book case and felt a jolt of adrenaline.

While not the neatest person in the world, he was obsessed with placing books alphabetically, by author. Now that had been disrupted and his first novel was by Jack London and the last by Lee Child, with all the names in between in random order. To his ordered mind the placing made no sense.

A sudden thought struck him and he hurried into his bedroom. At first glance, nothing seemed to have changed.

His white duvet was neatly folded in half on the double-bed - he felt this allowed it to air while he was away - and the pillows appeared as he had left them.

But looking closer he saw towels had been placed under each of the pillows. His heart was pounding. He had the horrible sense that he was being watched. He checked his drawers. Opening the first, it should have contained his socks and pants. Now the space was occupied by printer paper.

In the cupboard, he found more bizarre changes. Someone had swapped all the trousers on his suits so that blue trousers were with grey jackets and the same thing but reversed. And on each of his shirts the intruder had hung a tie around the collar.

It made him feel deeply uncomfortable. Someone was clearly sending him a message and he had to sit on the edge of the bed for a moment to regain control of his breathing. He hated to admit it, but this was so creepy it was frightening. He felt clammy from sweat, even though it was cool in the flat.

The quiet was pierced by his front door bell. The sudden noise panicked him, making him leap to his feet. He could feel his heart thudding in his chest and stood panting for a moment until the bell went for a second time. He was badly spooked but he had to answer the door.

Making himself go slowly he approached and looked out through the spy hole; he had never been so pleased to see Julie Mayweather. He'd forgotten that they had arranged to meet. As he opened the door to let her in she stared at him. "You look like you've seen a ghost. Is everything alright?"

He waved her inside and then went straight to the kitchen to grab a bottle of cold lager. She followed him in, a concerned look on her face, as he took a deep swallow and then another. He put the bottle down carefully and looked at her.

"I think it's best if I show you. I'm not sure I can explain it properly."

By the time he showed her the shirts and ties she had her hand to her mouth; clearly as badly rattled as he was. She said. "I've never come across anything like this. It's the sort of thing you can imagine a stalker might do."

Her company, and the beer, was helping to restore his equilibrium.

"The only person who might want to stalk me is my ex-wife, but I think she'd just want to throw things at me. She wouldn't have the patience for this sort of weirdness. I think it's fair to say that someone is trying to get my attention. They've certainly done that even if I have no idea what the message might be."

Mayweather's resolve had also stiffened after the initial shock. "Until we know otherwise we are going to treat this is as a direct threat. Up to now I've had the locals doing a drive-by, but we'll step that up to a uniformed guard placed at the door here and talk to the Home Office liaison people about arranging the same down in Cheltenham.

"Talking of which, what about Jonathan? Whether this is related to what you're doing at GCHQ or something else is irrelevant for now. I'm not going to take any risks."

Hooley was pleased she was making the calls. While part of him never wanted to make a fuss - as he often said, police officers are going to make enemies - there was something about what had happened in his flat that was too weird for words.

There was something else he needed to tell her. "My CCTV system didn't pick up anyone coming into the flat. I was thinking it's because no one came in, just stayed outside but now, well they obviously were inside so how did they avoid getting caught on film?"

Mayweather's eyes narrowed, a sure sign something was bothering her. "The case we picked up just after you left for 'Spy Central,'" she mimed quote marks in the air before continuing. "It involves some pretty advanced surveillance equipment."

She was speaking quietly, almost to herself, and the DCI was straining to hear every word. She noticed the questioning expression on his face. "I'm wondering if we need to compare notes?" she said, then cut him off from replying. "Bear with me. I intend to brief you but give me a bit of space. There's a lot of sensitivity going around and I need to talk to the head of MI5 first. She needs to know about this as well."

She smiled apologetically. "I was going to buy you dinner tonight but I think this takes priority. I'll let you know when I have it sorted out. If I'm right we need to talk to Jonathan as well. Can you get hold of him and warn him he might need to come up to London?"

"Definitely," said the DCI. "If ever there was something shaping up to need his Rainbow Spectrum, then this is it."

He let his boss out and he turned back into the flat. The first thing he was going to do was get those books back in the right order, then the rest of the flat, then a glass of wine - he'd already checked his stash in the kitchen - then get food delivered. He was going nowhere tonight and would be double checking all the door and window locks.

39

For once Roper didn't mind being interrupted. He had been known to ignore his phone, but seeing Brian Hooley was on the end of the line he was more than happy to talk, especially as the work he had been doing was taking him nowhere. The lack of progress making him feel irritable and restless.

He grabbed his mobile, barked 'Roper' loudly, and waited for Hooley to speak. The DCI was so used to this abrupt form of greeting he didn't notice. He started talking straight away, also skipping a greeting. "Things get stranger and stranger. So much so that we may find ourselves working for the boss again, sooner rather than later. She's just gone off to talk to the head of MI5, and will be getting back to us after that."

"What and why?" asked Roper. On the phone, he hated using more words than he had to.

Hooley laughed. "Short and to the point, as usual. All I can tell you is she said she had to speak to the head of MI5 to get clearance to tell us what she is working on. Between ourselves, I heard the team is heading up the investigation into the awful murders involving the man the press are calling the Face Ripper."

If he had been hoping that Roper would be impressed by this, he was disappointed. The younger man could be remarkably disinterested in events that had no bearing on him, or where he could see no value in finding out about them.

The DCI decided to fill him in on the fact that someone had entered his flat, despite the CCTV showing nothing, and that his personal items had been moved to different positions.

He added. "It's a funny thing, but over the years I must have heard dozens of burglary victims talk about feeling violated by someone being in their home. This is the first time that I have totally understood what they meant."

To his surprise Roper cut him off with a curt "I will call you back in five minutes," then broke the connection. Hooley stared at the phone before putting it down. He couldn't help thinking Roper might have been a little more sympathetic.

Roper was back on the phone. "My Rainbow Spectrum says there is a clear link between what happened to you and what has been done to me. It is the same mind that has found ways to disrupt both of us."

Hooley's patience ran out. It had been a long drive. "I'm not sure you need a revolutionary way of thinking to work that one out. It's bloody obvious someone is trying to cause us problems. If you'd stayed on the phone a moment longer I would have told you that."

If Roper was troubled by the outburst, he didn't react. Instead, he carried on as if the DCI had said nothing. "For someone to go so far shows that there is something they are trying to hide. We just need to work out what it is."

Roper was fascinated by Hooley's account of someone going through his flat and moving things around. He wondered if it had been done in a random way, or there was some sort of pattern to it. He was also excited at the thought of working alongside Julie Mayweather again.

When Hooley rang off Roper decided to call it a day. He had been intending to have a toast feast tonight but the thought of curry intruded. He placed a take-away order, aiming to pick it up on his walk home. Half an hour later he was stepping through his own front door, a delicious smelling bag of food in his hand, when he froze. Someone had been into his flat. The door opened into the large living room and he could already see that the furniture had been moved.

It had all been pushed back against the walls and the leather chair from the third bedroom had been placed in the centre of the room: alongside it were two piles of paper. Whoever had done this knew quite a bit about him.

He was so absorbed in the scene that he didn't realise someone was there until he was shoved from behind. He shot forward, tripped, and sprawled over the floor, landing on top of the food containers. They burst open against his stomach, burning him painfully.

He struggled to his feet, spinning round to see who had attacked him, but there was no one in sight. He heard a fire door being pulled open and the sound of footsteps on the concrete staircase as the assailant vanished.

Becoming more aware of the burn from the take-away, he tore off his clothes. His stomach was red from the heat and he headed straight for a cold shower. He wanted to cool it down and get rid of the smell as quickly as possible. After five minutes, he turned the shower off.

The cold water had done the job and taken the edge off the damage caused by the hot food. Luckily, it was a short walk from the restaurant so the hot food had cooled a little. He doubted he would need to go to hospital.

He looked at the mess spread across the floor and was glad it was wooden. It would have been disastrous if all that curry had gone into carpet. He got some kitchen paper and was carefully mopping up when his phone rang again. It was Hooley.

The DCI was stunned as Roper outlined what had happened. He said. "Just make sure you lock yourself in. After what happened to me the boss said she wanted us given protection and she wasn't in the mood to argue about it. Fortunately, that means uniformed police are on their way to you anyway.

"I need to stay here this evening. In the meantime, I think you might want to let David Cotter know what's been happening. Tell him local police will be looking after you but he may want to involve the MoD police at GCHQ."

*

He was mopping up the last of the curry sauce when he heard someone running up the corridor. He'd left the front door open to help get rid of the smell of the food and now he realised he might have left himself vulnerable if his attacker had decided to come back.

Not being the most coordinated person, he slipped while trying to get back on his feet and then turned to grab at the door which he slammed shut just as the runner reached the door. He caught a glimpse of a man, probably wearing a suit, before the door slammed shut. Whoever was outside started shouting but the sound was muffled by the thickness of the door. Roper leaned against the wall, his fear was making it hard to breathe and he was panting heavily.

A short period of silence outside was followed by shouting. At one point the door shook as something hit it. Then more silence. Roper was terrified. He was trying to think of something to do when his mobile went off. He looked at the screen nervously; to his relief it was Hooley.

He started babbling. "Someone's trying to get in. I don't know what to do."

Hooley tried to inject calmness into his voice. "It's OK Jonathan. The local police are right outside your door now. They found someone outside so they didn't wait to ask questions, they just grabbed him. It sounds like they may have David Cotter there, but you need to open the door and check."

Roper sagged against the wall as the words sank in. He was safe. He pushed himself up to his feet and made his way unsteadily to the door. He paused to tell Hooley what he was doing, and then opened it to look out.

Standing there were two police officers, one looked very young, even to Roper, and the other was about Brian Hooley's age. It was a warm evening and they were dressed in standard issue white shirts. It was clear from their large shoulders that both men were more than capable of looking after themselves. They were either side of an embarrassed looking David Cotter, holding his arms in a grip which meant he would be going nowhere.

Despite the age gap it was the younger officer who took the lead. "Can you confirm who you are for me sir?"

The question threw Roper. Of course, he was who he was. Why did they need him to confirm that? As he dithered over his response the man added. "Could you tell me your name and it would be helpful if you had some photo ID on you."

Now he was on safer ground. "My name's Jonathan Roper, and just a tick. I will get my passport." A few seconds later the officer was studying it, before passing it to his colleague who looked first at Roper then at the picture, before shrugging and handing the passport back.

Returning it the younger officer said. "My colleague and I are part of the Special Support Team with Gloucestershire Police. We were sent to your address to provide protection for you when we found this gentleman banging on your door. He claims to work with you."

"Oh yes, that's David Cotter."

They let him go but he had to suffer a rebuke from the younger constable. "It might be a good idea to have some sort of ID on you at all times, sir. I'm surprised that a senior man at GCHQ would need reminding."

To Roper it looked as if the GCHQ man was visibly shrinking as he was rebuked. He managed a weak grin followed by a stuttering apology. The policemen ignored him, telling Roper they were here for the night and would be right outside.

Cotter followed Roper into the flat. "If you fancy making a cup of tea I could do with one to steady my nerves. I made a right prat of myself just now. After you told me what happened to you I got in a panic and raced down here. When those two arrived, I was trying to get you to open the door and they grabbed me.

"I was so surprised I would have taken a swing at them, not because I am big tough fighter; I was just frightened. Fortunately, they had a good hold of me so I couldn't move. I'd have been done for assaulting a police officer."

Roper had been listening while he made the tea and handed the drink to Cotter, who held it in his hands, obviously drawing comfort from the heat.

"You've gone quite pale; that'll be the shock," said Roper. "Would you like some sugar in that? It's very helpful when you've had a nasty surprise."

Cotter shuddered at the thought. He disliked sweet tea. "No thanks." He glanced around, as though trying to find something. "Look, I only came around to see if you were OK. You've got your own protection outside, so everything should be fine now."

He drained the last of his tea and held his hand out. "At least I've stopped shaking, thanks to your tea. I do have a nasty headache though. I'm not being much help; shall we get in touch tomorrow morning? I think we could all do with a nice lie down."

Roper was happy to see him go. He wanted nothing more than to shut the door and get the flat back to normal.

He was starving so rang the restaurant to discover they could deliver in half-an-hour. Just enough time to move stuff back where it belonged.

He had a thought and rang the restaurant back. "Tell your delivery man to make sure he has some ID on him."

40

Brian Hooley couldn't help laughing. A combination of Roper's deadpan delivery, and the thought of the apparently unflappable psychologist antagonising a couple of burly coppers, appealed to his sense of humour.

"Good job you were there to identify him. He'd have spent the night in the cells otherwise. He might even have been tasered. Those officers would have been briefed that there was a serious threat, so you couldn't have blamed them if they'd acted first and asked questions afterwards."

Despite having a couple of conversations with Roper over the course of the evening, he couldn't resist getting him to repeat it once more when he called early this morning. He had the phone on speaker and took a long swig of tea as he made an effort to be serious.

"Sounds like you are coming up here," he added, rubbing his hand through his hair. He'd had a long night getting his flat back to normal, sleeping badly and having horribly vivid dreams that someone was in the bedroom with him. With the first trace of dawn touching the sky, he got up and had a bath; the hot water soaking away his disquiet. A cup of strong instant coffee, to wash down two paracetamol tablets, and he felt close to normal.

Whilst he wouldn't say he was as fresh as a daisy, he was fit to face the world. Julie Mayweather, who was always awake early, had texted him at 6am with a simple update. "Looks like joint briefing on. Will need Jonathan there. Call after 9am with details."

It was this message that had triggered this morning's call to Roper. Like the DCI he'd also spent the evening putting things back where they belonged. As soon as he'd been told about the message from Mayweather he had wanted to get on the next train to London, but Hooley cautioned him to slow down.

"You've got a protection detail outside and nothing has changed about why they're there. Let me make a few calls and see how we should handle this. I suspect you will end up being driven up here but people need to know where you are and what's going on. If you race off it will start a big panic."

He broke the connection before Roper could say anything. He was very hungry and needed to get out for breakfast since he had nothing in the flat. He knew he had a little time before he heard anything and there was a coffee shop around the corner. An Americano with an extra shot, plus a bacon roll, would help restore him to full order. He could think about getting Roper to London after food.

The DCI had just returned from getting his breakfast when Julie Mayweather called back. She wanted to meet in the squad office at Victoria that afternoon. He needn't have worried about organising Roper. She'd already had him collected by car that was headed for Pimlico. She added. "I hope you don't mind, but we probably need him to spend some time in London so I assumed he would stay with you - like before."

Hooley smiled. "We seem to be becoming inseparable. I'm just surprised that people haven't started calling us the 'Odd Couple.' The pause went on a moment too long. "We are being called the Odd Couple, aren't we?"

He could almost sense Mayweather's embarrassment. If you put her on the spot she was hopeless at telling lies. Finally, she broke the silence. "It's all done with great affection you know. And I suppose you two are a most unlikely pairing when it comes to it."

Hooley shook his head. He'd been called a lot worse in the past, and that was just by his own side. "I take it you are having him dropped here and then we can make our way into Victoria for the meeting?"

"I thought that would be best. You will have time to get settled. It's going to be a long meeting. There's a huge amount to get through and I am anxious to hear what both of you have to say about the case we have been working while you were at GCHQ."

The DCI replied. "If the little I've read in the news is anything to go by, I can see it taking time. I think the best thing I can do is make sure our man has a decent lunch. A hungry Roper is never a good idea at the best of times. It seems to affect his concentration really badly."

Just after 10am Roper turned up. He was wearing his skinny black suit and holding a couple of overnight bags. Standing on the doorstep radiating energy and purpose he seemed to drain Hooley of what little energy he had after such a terrible night's sleep.

He made a snap decision. "Welcome back to Pimlico. You know where your room is so please make yourself at home. I barely slept last night so I'm going for a power nap. Probably best if you stay in for a while, so help yourself to the Wi-Fi and settle in."

41

The high-pitched alarm woke him with a start. He had gone out like a light the moment his head hit the pillow and now it was an hour later. As he came around he wondered if taking a nap would turn out to be a mistake. His head felt like it was stuffed full of cotton wool and his body felt numb, as though he hadn't moved a muscle since lying down. Keeping his eyes closed he made himself lie still and relax. It came to something when even lying in bed made you ache all over.

After a few minutes, he began to feel more normal so decided to risk getting up; he kicked his legs out while twisting his back to lever himself to a sitting position, finishing on the edge of the bed with his bare feet on the floor. An osteopath had urged him to try and get up more sedately to avoid putting his back under strain, but it was an ingrained habit. Without really noticing he rubbed at a point at the top of his left hip. He often felt sore there and wondered if he should get it looked at.

He glanced at his watch and saw there were still nearly four hours to go until the meeting. He briefly thought about going back to sleep and then dismissed it. He might not feel on top form now but was sure he would notice the benefit later on. The sun was pouring in through his window, lighting up a patch of cream carpet on his side of the double bed. He'd never seen that before, he was normally up and out long before the sun could reach that angle in the sky.

Feeling like he was ducking a day at work, he went off to have a shower.

The shower acted as the hoped-for kick-start. Feeling very much better he walked out of his bedroom to find Roper sat staring intently at his laptop.

"Found anything new?" he asked, heading for the kettle. First up he was going to have a cup of coffee.

Roper threw his hands in the air, a sure sign that things were not going to plan. "It's very strange not being able to access all the material we see at GCHQ, but there's no way they are going to allow me to look at that from outside the building. While you were asleep I've been catching up with news about Chelsea." He looked embarrassed at this admission that he hadn't been hard at work.

"You can look all you like but it won't make them play any better," scoffed Hooley as he reached the sink and turned on the tap to fill the kettle. "You fancy another cup?" he asked. He knew the answer. Roper rarely turned down a hot drink, or food.

He grabbed a couple of clean mugs, placing two heaped spoons of coffee granules, plus the same of sugar, for Roper. It was a drink that would have had Hooley trembling with a caffeine overdose; by the younger man's standards it was the minimum order.

Drink in hand he eyed Roper through the steam rising out of his mug. "Two options. We get lunch here, or we have lunch out. What do you fancy?"

"Can we look at a third option?" Hooley raised an eyebrow but said nothing as Roper carried on. "Is it going to be possible to get back into your office at Victoria? I mean the way things were arranged before I went to GCHQ?"

"No problem at all. I kept your desk in there because it never hurts to have extra workplaces, and, from time to time, team members need a bit of peace and quiet. The main office can get a bit hectic. It wouldn't surprise me to learn you are still logged on to the system."

"That's brilliant," said Roper, his eyes lighting up. "The point is that I will have far better access there than here. So, my third option: pick up lunch on the way in, we can go to that brilliant place nearby, then I can use the computer in your office."

Hooley was fine with the idea. If they were already at HQ, then there was no way they could be late, and he really wanted to know what Julie Mayweather had to tell them. He picked up various empty mugs and placed them in the dishwasher.

"Right, let's get going."

*

To Roper's enormous surprise everyone they met said hello and asked how he was. The last time he'd been at HQ he'd been used to people largely ignoring him. Something he preferred, since being the centre of attention was always stressful. Hooley explained his new-found attraction was partly because he hadn't been around, and partly because going to GCHQ had given him a certain status.

"You're a sort of Spook now," he said, then wished he hadn't. At one point in the ensuing discussion he found himself trying to explain why someone could be seen as a Spook but not actually be a Spook. At the end of that he wasn't entirely sure himself. "Let's leave it that people are quite pleased to see you back and looking so well."

Roper responded by stabbing at the keyboard as he sat down at his old desk. His name didn't come up automatically because so many others had signed on since he had last been here. He put in his old user name and got a prompt for his password. It failed. Twenty minutes later he was looking comically grumpy when a young guy from the IT department turned up to fix the problem.

Moments later Roper was back in and surfing away. He'd been so preoccupied he had ignored his lunch but now his two bacon and avocado sandwiches, and three blueberry muffins, were lined up and he was steadily demolishing them as he worked down the food line. Hooley was carefully unwrapping his solitary sandwich. Suffering a bout of health consciousness, he had asked for salad with his tuna mayonnaise, telling himself it would make a useful contribution to his five a day, but now, at the moment of truth, he was carefully picking it out. He was going to have his sandwich plain, the way he always did.

42

Twenty minutes before the scheduled meeting Mayweather arrived, greeted them both warmly, and rushed off to her own office, pleading an urgent phone call. She told them they would be joined by DI Cleverly. Hooley had picked the man out as a star in the making and was delighted he had been filling in while he was away at GCHQ.

With five minutes to go he coughed loudly until he drew Roper's attention, who looked up, clearly irritated at being interrupted. Hooley held out his hand in apology. "I know you've been getting stuck in to something but you need to put whatever it is to one side for now because we are seeing the boss in a few minutes."

This appeal got through as Roper's face cleared. "Good idea. I suppose now is as good a time as any to stop. What I've seen so far is more like a reminder of what I can't access. Although in a funny way that is quite helpful."

Hooley decided he didn't want to get involved in that one so jumped up and led the way over to Mayweather's office. When he walked in she gestured at the table on one side of the office. With four of them it wasn't going to be practical to sit in front of her desk. He and Roper were making themselves comfortable when a smiling Cleverly appeared, holding a jug of water and some plastic cups, which he set down in the middle.

Mayweather didn't waste any time, taking her place at the head of the table and bringing everyone to attention by the simple tactic of looking at them. Happy that she had their undivided attention she started talking.

"If I had a pound for every time that Brian Hooley has said to me he doesn't like coincidences, I'd have a lot of pound coins."

Hooley grinned. It was a cliché, and one that had been around a long time, but that didn't mean it wasn't valid. Sometimes people overlooked how useful a cliché was. It got everyone thinking about things in the same sort of way, and that could be invaluable.

"Norman will talk you through the highlights of what we have been working on in just a moment; but I want to start by telling you about what made me wonder if there were links between what we are investigating and what you are looking into at GCHQ."

Hooley glanced at Roper and saw he was staring unblinkingly at Mayweather, those intelligent eyes of his looking bright and alert as he waited for her to go on.

"Putting the details to one side, the thing that jumps out at me is the way that advanced electronic eavesdropping has cropped up in both lines of inquiry. And we are under the clear impression that two of our victims were actively working for the Ministry of Defense and quite possibly the intelligence services.

"I've been speaking to the head of MI5, Jennifer Cameron, and she agreed to give me some insights into what we may be dealing with. But - and it's an important but - we can only discuss this between ourselves and certain senior MI5 officials.

"What prompted me to go and talk to her was the fact that you both had your homes broken in to, both times apparently bypassing your home security systems. I was especially surprised that Brian's system had failed to record video footage of the intruders; that suggested it may have been compromised in some way."

Hooley nodded at this; it was really annoying him that his cameras had picked up nothing. "Why do I get the feeling that you are just about to tell us something amazing?"

"Your instincts are spot on, as usual. And yes, I do have some top-secret information to share with you. I'm not going to try and explain the technical details, but Jennifer Cameron has been incredibly helpful in explaining things in a simple way. Now, none of you here is going to like the sound of this, but they are working on something that sounds a lot like one of those computerised assistants. As Cameron herself put it. 'It's a Siri for burglars.'

"The MI5 version packs such a punch it can force most security systems to override their own programming."

All three men started talking at once, demanding more information about the technology that had been developed.

Mayweather held her hands up. "Bear in mind that this has me very much out of my comfort zone. But, as it was explained to me, this involves some sort of Artificial Intelligence. This kit can talk to security systems and play havoc with their protocols. Wiping a surveillance tape would be a prime example."

She glanced at Roper. "You will be receiving a detailed appraisal shortly. Not the full details - that is still restricted - but a bit more than I have given you. Something about machine learning? But the key point here is that no one is supposed to know about it and it certainly shouldn't be being used in routine burglaries."

She stopped and glanced round at the three men. Each was waiting patiently to hear what she had to say next.

She carried on. "The second thing for us to consider is that we discovered similarly advanced surveillance equipment had been used against two of our victims. Again, top-secret and only available to a highly restricted group of people. Or that was what they thought.

"This stuff is so advanced, no one likes to admit it exists. Now it is clear some of it has gone missing. That's causing a huge row and an even bigger panic.

"MI5 are wetting themselves. They were supposed to be overseeing this but had no idea what had happened until we started investigating brutal murders."

Mayweather took a small drink of water. "The third element for us to consider is that everything we are doing points towards GCHQ. Up to now we have been talking about MI5, but intelligence gathering is at the heart of what they do, and that's what goes on at Cheltenham."

Roper interrupted. "That might be more important than you think. GCHQ is already known to be using some pretty smart software to lift information from mobile calls and emails. Another application of AI is that it can be used to find and filter key messages from the billions that are out there.

"People tend to think of AI as being something that will appear as this big change but actually it is already here. You mentioned machine-learning a moment ago, well that is all part of it. You mentioned Siri. Well the version today is smarter than the original and getting smarter all the time. If GCHQ has reached a stage of being able to use a powerful AI program in intelligence gathering, they will be desperate to keep that quiet, and everyone else will want to get their hands on it."

Mayweather said: "That is incredibly useful to know, Jonathan. I think it explains why the stakes are so high. I also think we need to fill you and Brian in on our case so far. It's been brutal in places. Norman and I both agree that there is an element to the violence that is unlike anything we've come across before. I'll pass this briefing over to him now, but be prepared for some unpleasant details."

43

It took DI Cleverly the best part of an hour to run through the police investigation. Hooley found it gruesomely compelling, although the video of Tom Bennett's face being removed proved tough going. It had never occurred to him that anyone would do such a thing; especially disturbing was the skill being shown by the man wielding the knife.

While the film was playing he had also kept half an eye on Roper but reckoned he was taking it pretty well. He was probably dealing with it better than the DCI who was regretting having eaten that fish sandwich not long before. Halfway through the clip and his meal was starting to repeat on him, his stomach tight and full of wind.

Not wanting to draw attention he casually helped himself to a glass of water and gulped it down. He thought it might help but it had little effect on countering his indigestion. Trying to be discreet, he swallowed repeatedly in the hope it would stop him belching out loud. It really didn't help that the other three, while looking grim faced, were clearly not struggling as much as he was.

The clip ended and Mayweather commented. "That's the fourth time I've watched that and I can assure you, it doesn't get any easier."

They were all silent for a moment, then Hooley, who had made a heroic effort to recover, said. "So, it looks like we are trying to find a spy, probably a highly trained one, with a fondness for slicing people up and wearing their faces." He shuddered. He would never be able to understand why people wanted to mutilate a corpse.

Cleverly spoke up. "I'm very much in agreement with you, but I'd like to hear why you think this is someone who is highly trained?"

"To be honest, while I was listening to your briefing I couldn't imagine it being anybody other than a spy. It's almost got a touch of the James Bond about it, with our man a sort of anti-hero type villain. It would be hard to think of someone much worse. Yet everything says to me that he is very controlled. He doesn't hesitate when he uses that knife and I would say he has sent you the clip as a statement - a sort of 'look at me. I'm in control here.'

"I would also argue that the fact that he knew to send the email to you, proves two things. He is reinforcing his 'I'm in charge' message, but he is also letting you know that he has some sort of inside track. Only an insider could have known you and Julie were on this case at that stage of the investigation."

"What about the other killings? The ones where he hasn't tried to remove the faces?" Mayweather asked.

"Good question. I must admit there's something about them doesn't quite fit. The first two victims were taken and killed quickly, yet the second pair were kept alive, for a while at least. He even gave them food and water. Why were they treated differently?"

"Maybe there are two killers," Roper's sudden intervention made the other three start. Even though he was right there with them at the table; he had been so still that they had almost forgotten he was there.

Mayweather was the first to respond. Her troubled expression underlying the complexity of this brutal case. "We asked that same question, but can find no evidence of a second person. We don't have any finger prints at all, which is problematical."

Hooley butted in "It also suggests that out killer was wearing gloves, which is what a professional would do." He thought, then added. "Or anyone who watches TV crime shows."

Mayweather acknowledged the intervention. "If I'm quite honest, the fact that it may be just one person who is causing all of this is quite troubling. To my mind that certainly supports your view that we are dealing with a professional. It's especially troublesome if that person has got access to both the police and intelligence worlds."

She looked at Roper. "Is there anything else you would like to add Jonathan?"

Roper blinked a couple of times. "I asked if it was two people, but I think it probably is just one. I suspect he is trying, quite literally, to get inside the heads of his victims.

"By wearing their faces, he is saying he can be just like them and know everything about them. I can't think there could be any other reason. But he is also saying that he is better than them; that by killing them he has beaten them.

Mayweather took a breath. "From a layman's perspective, it is quite hard to argue with your view that it is about some form of control. It certainly fits with what the profiler told us. This is a trophy collecting exercise. He takes the faces away with him after the murders so must be keeping them somewhere safe and probably likes to inspect them.

"Worryingly, the profiler also reminded us that this is classic serial killer behaviour. He's already gone way beyond the norm so we can expect him to do something similar again. I suppose that means he will be targeting more people with intelligence links."

Hooley jumped in. "We've already said he couldn't be doing that without detailed knowledge of both worlds. Does that suggest we are looking at someone with a grudge? Maybe they were fired from MI5 and now they are out for revenge. Or maybe it is someone who had some sort of liaison role? There are a lot of jobs like that which have opened up in recent years with all the anti-terror initiatives. It may sound melodramatic, but you know what I mean."

"Not at all," said Cleverly. "It is something we were about to consider and now you have raised it as well I think we should make it a priority to find out if there is someone who fits that profile." He glanced at Mayweather who nodded her agreement.

She stood up. "Let's get that rolling, Norman, and say meet here again in an hour's time? Then Jonathan and Brian can run us through what they have been doing."

Roper dashed out of the door. Hooley wasn't surprised he was heading for the toilets. He'd drunk most of the jug of water. He seemed to get extra thirsty when he was thinking hard.

44

Hooley volunteered to get the coffee. He didn't just need the caffeine; he wanted to go for a walk. What they had seen and listened to was right up there in the list of terrible things human beings can do. It was always tempting to look for reasons why crimes were committed. If you could find a reason then maybe you could stop something happening again. This felt like one of those awful cases which couldn't be explained because there was no reason.

This case was different again. The violence was almost cinematic. The killer always had the intention of murdering the victims and removing their faces. That was never good. It was like some people were happy to flaunt their cruelty, entirely unconstrained by any need to follow the rules. People like that were always the ones to be truly frightened of.

He wandered aimlessly for twenty minutes, taking comfort from seeing so many people going about their day, blissfully unaware of the problems he was now confronting, too busy with their own lives to imagine these horrors could be possible. He was glad that not everyone had to worry about such dark issues.

He made his way to the coffee shop, ordering a couple of drinks, and was about to leave when he decided Jonathan was bound to be hungry again. He added a couple of blueberry muffins to the two Americanos. When he walked back into the office, the look of delight on Roper's face told him he had made the right call. The day Roper turned down food would be the day to get worried.

He glanced at his watch. It was almost time to get back to the session. He rapped on his desk to attract Roper's attention. "I've been thinking about the best way to brief Julie and Norman. What we've been doing is a bit hard to explain. What do you think about this for a plan? If I take us through the background, from the moment you were seconded up to the present. That will give them the outline. Then you can talk about how you have been interpreting it and explain why you now believe it is you specifically who is the target."

When Roper didn't protest he took that as yes.

Mayweather had already taken her place, clearly eager to get things moving again. They watched as DI Cleverly bustled in. Hooley took his cue from Mayweather who was already holding a pen to take notes. He launched in without preamble. With questions, he was in the spotlight for fifty minutes then handed over to Roper.

Until now the younger man had sat impassively. At one-point Mayweather had studied him and noted he had barely moved a muscle, just an occasional slow blink. On previous occasions she had noted he was in almost perpetual motion, shuffling in his seat as though he was unable to get comfortable. This stillness was quite different; she hoped it was a sign that he was fully engaged.

He started speaking and within minutes she felt that familiar sense of fascination as she heard him describing things from his perspective. It wasn't so much that he was incredibly intelligent, although that was the case, but it was the way he noticed the tiniest details and could then accurately recall them.

He rattled through his original thoughts about the information he had been sent, followed by his subsequent difficulties. He described the arrival of Brian Hooley and his hope that this would get him back on track. But nothing seemed to work.

While he had been talking he had kept both hands flat on the surface of the table. Now he folded them into his lap and stared down at the floor for a brief moment.

He said. "It turned out I was totally wrong and it was because I didn't factor in that someone could turn the Rainbow Spectrum against me."

Hooley was anxious to prevent him taking too much responsibility. "You can't take the blame for this Jonathan. As you explained it to me, you now understand that you were being actively targeted for a disinformation campaign.

"That tells me there is an argument that GCHQ is at fault. Maybe this could have been anticipated and you could have been helped to avoid exactly this sort of problem from emerging in the first place."

To his relief Roper seemed, at least partially, to agree with this argument. "I was cross with myself, but there was a system in place to double check my work and maybe that should have worked better."

Mayweather steered the discussion back on track. "Do you think that the case that DI Cleverly and myself are working on, and what you have been checking out at GCHQ are connected?"

"I do. No question." he said, placing both hands back on the table and looking at all three of them. "I had been speculating there must be a link. It always seemed unlikely that you would end up investigating murders at firms with military connections at the same time we were at GCHQ.

"As you just heard, I've already told Brian that I believe I was targeted from the moment I arrived at Cheltenham. It is my strong opinion that someone wants to prove they are better than me and that person is also responsible for the murders you are investigating.

"It feels like a cleverly constructed trap to keep us all busy. But I think the overall intention has always been to make it look like I had no idea what was going on. Which they very nearly succeeded in doing. Although I think there is more I haven't worked out yet.

"But going back to your question, the clincher for me was when you revealed secret AI technology had been stolen."

For just a moment Julie Mayweather broke the habit of a lifetime and gave herself a silent pat on the back. She had started out unsure if her theory was right, but convinced it had to be explored, and then listened to the discussions in the growing certainty she was correct.

But there was something special about hearing it from Roper. It might not immediately get them to the answers but at least she was moving in the right direction.

She could still vividly recall the conversation she'd had had with the head of MI5. Jennifer Cameron had listened patiently, giving none of her feelings away, while the policewoman argued that the barriers between them needed to be pulled down. She had agreed, but with a clear warning that she had better not be wrong.

"Your reputation precedes you Julie, and I say that as a very positive thing. Anyone else and I might be tempted to dismiss this as a conspiracy theory, but you're not like that." Mayweather had gone to thank her, but Cameron had held her hand up. "If you are wrong, so be it. You're tough enough to survive, probably, but if you are right," she paused. "Don't lose sight that there are those who will never forgive you for pointing out that we have a traitor in our midst. Not everyone appreciates it when the sunshine gets in.

"At the same time, there will be plenty of people who would see it as a career opportunity, the chance to remove a few senior people; maybe even step up to our jobs. So, my advice; if you do find something smelly, don't let your guard down for a moment."

She came back to the moment and became aware that the three men were waiting for her to react first.

"Right," she said, standing up and brushing down her blouse with a graceful sweeping motion of her hand. "I'm going to leave you three to work out who is behind all this. I need to go and play office politics."

She would have preferred to stay but took comfort from knowing the trio were as good as she could hope for and didn't need her help. She also knew that Roper would never have said there was a link unless he was totally confident. That was good enough for her; now they could work on the answers.

She had to deal with the big beasts further up the food chain, that way her team would be free to get on with detective work. She went over to her desk and picked up the phone, tapping in the direct number for the MI5 chief. The woman had already proved she was a friend by agreeing to back Mayweather's hunch. She would be pleased and alarmed, in equal measure, to hear that Roper agreed.

45

"Why don't you start with your take on why everything here is linked?" said Hooley. He thought he probably knew the answers but wanted to listen to the answers.

Roper was good to go. "I agree with Julie Mayweather. The use of classified surveillance technology is too much of a coincidence. Another element stands out to me. This is starting to feel like peeling an onion. Each layer is linked to the next but that connection is hidden until the top layer is pulled back.

"You see, first, there was the material at GCHQ which I got very excited about, but which turned out to be a way of manipulating my thinking. Now I know I was wrong in my first assessment. So why was that?

"I've spent a lot of time thinking about it. I am sure it was designed to do two things. As I told Brian, the person responsible wants to prove they can beat me, and they would have done without Brian's help. I had completely lost my way.

"I was assuming the second motive was to keep my attention away from something but I couldn't think what that might be. After hearing the briefing today, I am wondering if the secret surveillance equipment was what was being hidden.

"But going back to the onion layers. What if that is another bluff? If we start to think it is all about top secret equipment then are we missing a third point?"

Hooley glanced over at Cleverly. The DI wore an expression he recognised. It was the first time he had heard a complicated debrief from Roper and the unique way he had of setting out problems and potential solutions.

He smiled sympathetically. "If it's any consolation he's very good at answering questions. I tend to let him go through it his own way and then go back over the many bits I can't quite follow." The DI grinned, his relief obvious.

Hooley turned back to Roper. "Can I ask what you think the third point might be?"

Roper shook his head and shrugged. "Not exactly. But I am starting to think that one of the ideas is to kill you, Brian."

Hooley blinked back his shock. "You've already talked about this person wanting to hurt you, but murder me? What makes you think that? And why have you only just mentioned it?"

Roper ineffectually tugged at his hair. Hooley knew that little quirk; it was about to get complicated. He hoped it wasn't going to be like the time he had tried to explain quantum computing.

As if he had read his mind Roper said. "It does get a bit involved but let me finish and it should make sense. Once I knew the Rainbow Spectrum was compromised, I have been trying to focus on what is really happening.

"The clue was right there in front of me all the time, I just didn't see it. I was far too busy thinking about everything else. Which is exactly what this person wants to happen? They want us looking everywhere but the right place.

"Last night I saw I had made another mistake. All along the person behind this has had a very detailed knowledge of me and what I'm like. Good enough to totally throw me off the scent and use my own creation against me.

"The clue is what happened next. I went to David Cotter and he suggested that I needed your help to find my way back. Until I had to work on my own I hadn't really understood how much I have come to rely on you."

Hooley was caught between anxiety at being identified as a murder candidate and being moved at the trust Roper placed in him. "I knew we worked together well but I'm honoured to hear you say that I really help you."

"You do, but that is what placed you in danger. A perfect way of hurting me would be to kill you. I would lose your support and feel guilty for not spotting the biggest clue of all. At some point, I was going to ask for your help, which would have been anticipated."

"Like I said at the start, I did think last night that your death might be a possibility, but I wasn't sure and didn't want to set off in another wrong direction. It was seeing that video which convinced me that I was probably right. It was the mutilation of the body. This person sends out strong messages designed to shock and cause distress."

Hooley's thoughts finally stopped racing round his head. "Are you thinking that the strange attacks on where we live were all part of a bigger plan? That this person wanted one of us, in this case Julie herself, to make a connection between the killings and what was happening at GCHQ?"

"I do. But if you remember I said that there was more to the plan than just killing you and hurting me. I'm still trying to work out what that might be. But I will."

Hooley was keen to bring the discussion round to practical concerns. "We need to start coming up with some ideas of who is behind this. I know they've started their own investigation at GCHQ but I think we need a separate police operation."

Cleverly chipped in. "Listening to you two I think we need to establish a list of people who could have had access to the material you were looking at, and I'd like to know how they could have manipulated the flow of intelligence material; I thought that was impossible?"

"Not impossible," said Roper. "But very difficult. You'd need to be a genius really, if you were going to cover your tracks successfully. Even then the chances are that you will get caught eventually. Someone might manage to disguise what they are doing in the short run, but eventually anomalies are going to stand out. So that means someone is thinking quite short term."

He went quite still. Cleverly went to speak but Hooley put his finger to his lips to stop him speaking. Roper came out of his reverie.

"There's another clue I'm missing - this is coming to a head. That's why this was always a short-term plan. Whatever the final goal is, it is very close, or may even be happening now."

Hooley said. "When you say short term, what do you mean?"

"I'm thinking that whoever this is, will be off the moment you have been eliminated."

That made Hooley sit back while Cleverly jumped up. "I don't think either of you can expect to say goodbye to your police guards any time soon. In fact, I expect they will be doubled and given guns."

46

The meeting broke up shortly before 6pm. Most of the time had been spent liaising with the security team at GCHQ to set up interviews that needed to be done as soon as possible. Cleverly decided to send a team of detectives to be based in Cheltenham to speed things up.

Roper announced he had changed his mind about staying with Hooley, arguing he needed to see his flat near Tower Bridge. He hadn't visited the top-floor, three-bedroomed apartment since heading to Cheltenham and was determined to spend a night there.

The DCI realised Roper needed some time alone. He said. "I don't mind you going back to your place, but while I know you have identified me as a Prime Target, DI Cleverly needs to make sure your security is stepped up as well. It won't take long."

Roper was adamant that he wasn't waiting. Once the idea of returning to a favourite routine had entered his brain, it wasn't going away. "I'll even take a route I have never used before, that way no one could possibly anticipate where to mount an ambush. You can get someone to make sure it's all clear outside the building here, and I can be on my way."

The argument went back and forth for a short while, but Hooley was finally persuaded when the word came through that the protection team would be on site at his flat from 6.30pm, shortly before Roper would arrive on foot. Despite still feeling unsure he relented, arranging to meet back at Victoria at 6.30am. "Your turn to get the coffee and food this time," said Hooley. "I can't keep on subsidising your eating habits."

Roper set off at a brisk pace. His plan was to cross the Thames as quickly as possible and then follow the Embankment to his home. He knew he was risking getting a soaking but was happy to chance the warnings of heavy rain. He almost got away with it, reaching Blackfriars Bridge just as the heavens opened. By the time he arrived at his building he was totally sodden and looking forward to having a hot shower and getting into dry clothes.

Card key in hand, he was just opening the door to the building entrance when he heard a voice calling his name. He looked over his shoulder and to his surprise saw David Cotter, hurrying towards him, using a newspaper as a shield against the rain. Dashing up he reached past Roper to push open the door. "Need to get out of that rain; what a nightmare." The two men were standing in the lobby, water pooling on the floor as it dripped off them on to the marble flooring. With his inherited wealth Roper had been able to move into a prime building with fabulous views over the River Thames.

"I've been waiting half an hour for you so was delighted when I saw you emerge just now. Brian Hooley told me you were heading here so I thought I might as well come and wait. Hadn't bargained on such bad weather though."

Roper took in that Cotter was looking as equally bedraggled, but where Roper was in his standard black suit and black tie, the GCHQ man was wearing jeans and a casual shirt. "Why didn't you call me? I'd have got Fred over there to let you in to the lobby of the building. At least you'd have been out of the rain. He nodded at the counter where the security guard, a whippet-thin man, in his mid-twenties, wearing a dark blue uniform with a logo on the right breast, was seated behind an imposing desk. Cotter pulled a wry expression. "Trust me. I have been trying to call but I couldn't get any signal. I know this rain is bad but I hadn't thought it would knock out mobile signals as well."

"A bit of heavy rain shouldn't cause that," said Roper, pulling his own phone out of his pocket and looking at the screen. He grunted in surprise. "That's odd. I've got no signal at all, yet normally this is one of the best areas for reception."

He looked over at the security guard. "What about you, Fred? Have you got a signal? I'm on a different provider to you, maybe your signal is OK."

Fred was shaking his head even before Roper finished. "Nah, I've got nothing at all. I was talking to the wife about 20 minutes ago and she was just about to give me a list of stuff to pick up on the way home when she was gone." A small smile appeared. "Divine intervention, some might say. But I haven't been able to get through since so she'll be doing her nut. I'm bound to get a bollocking, even though it's not my fault.

"The weird thing is that the landline is down as well." He picked up a handset and waggled it in Roper's direction. "I can't get any ring tone on it. And I've had quite a few residents coming down to ask what's going on because they can't use their phones either. It's not the power though, all the lights are on and the lifts are working."

"What about broadband service. Can you still get online?"

"That's gone as well. It's the same for all the residents. People have had to actually come and talk to me because they can't send emails or get an internet connection. Even TV is off at the moment."

"This is terrible. Have you managed to get hold of building services?"

Fred rolled his eyes. "I have spoken to them. They said they knew nothing about it and have promised that they will look into it. If I was you, though, I wouldn't be holding my breath. I got the impression that they won't be doing anything until tomorrow."

He rummaged around in a drawer and pulled out a selection of business cards. He spread them out on his desk and pulled one from the middle of the pack. Looking pleased with himself he stood and offered the card to Roper.

"This is their number, it might be worth you giving them a call as well, they might take a bit more notice of a resident. It says they operate a twenty-four-hour service, but I reckon that just means they have an answer phone that's switched on all the time. I bet they only do stuff during the day."

Roper's face was darkening. The lack of a phone connection troubled him far less than the idea the internet was beyond reach. He couldn't remember the last time that had happened to him. He had to go back to his hated school days to recall it. Feeling seriously disgruntled he marched over to the lift and hit the call button. The lift was already there and he stepped inside as the doors opened.

He tuned to hit the button for the third floor and suddenly remembered David Cotter was with him. The psychologist was standing half-in and half-out of the lift, stopping the door closing by leaning against it with is right shoulder. It was gently battering against the human obstacle as it tried to shut.

"Room for a little one?" he asked with a smile.

Roper shook himself. "I'd forgotten you were there," he said, and then stepped back to make room.

If Cotter was put out by being overlooked he wasn't showing it. Instead he stepped into the lift and stood in the corner, watching Roper closely as the doors gently closed.

47

Roper didn't go in for casual clothes. At home, he slopped around in a towelling robe, or comfortable pyjamas. Otherwise, it was his suits and shirts. And none of his stuff was in Cotter's size. But he did have a spare robe and a tumble dryer which could deal with the sodden clothing.

He'd left Cotter to his own devices. Roper explained he had come home because it was the most comfortable place for him to access his Rainbow Spectrum. After a long-hot shower to get himself in the right frame of mind, he was going to be in his spare room, the one set-up with a comfortable chair and 'flapping' paper to send him into one of his light trances.

Cotter was fine with that. He'd been running around a lot recently and welcomed the chance to put his feet up for a while and just think. He was in the living room and sitting on the black leather settee. The place was bereft of decoration. Roper had muttered something about it being a 'minimalist' decor; Cotter thought it looked empty.

What it did have was a magnificent view across the river, or he would have had if it wasn't raining so hard. To the right he should have been able to enjoy a splendid view of the buildings at Canary Wharf, lights blazing, but the gathering gloom ruled that out.

He was staring into space when the beeping of the dryer alerted him that his clothes were dry. He realised he must have been sitting there for half-an-hour and was surprised the time had gone by without him noticing. He stood up gingerly, wincing at a sharp muscle pull in his lower back.

He ignored it and went to get his clothes. By the time he had pulled them on he was feeling bright and alert and the pain was receding.

He'd left his phone on the side in the kitchen, along with a few odds and ends from his pockets and a small black-leather bag he had been carrying. Picking up the mobile he checked that the signal was still down. The new technology that could create localised 'black holes' in the digital world was quite remarkable. Then he unzipped the bag and pulled out a pouch, opening it to extract a small syringe that fitted neatly into the palm of his hand. He carefully loaded it with a clear fluid from a small bottle marked with a blue label. He didn't bother to check for air bubbles, he wasn't bothered about that, but he did double check that he had used the right bottle to fill the syringe.

Satisfied, he carefully closed the bag and let himself out, taking care to leave the door on the latch. He took the lift downstairs and stepped out cautiously, making sure nobody was around apart from the security guard. He produced an apologetic smile. "Hi Fred. Just wondered if you had any news about us getting reconnected?"

He kept smiling and walking so that by the time Fred started to reply he was right in front of him. Before the guard could finish his sentence Cotter suddenly pantomimed horror as he stared at a spot just behind the security man's right shoulder. Fred couldn't resist turning to see and as he did so exposed the left side of his neck; without hesitating Cotter leaned forward, expertly hitting the carotid artery and emptied the syringe. It was fast acting stuff and Fred could make no sense of what was happening before he was slumping in his chair.

Cotter walked round and shoved the body out of sight under the desk. He figured that even if one of the residents noticed he wasn't there, none would come and look for him. He had received a lethal dose of heroin so would be dead very soon.

Pleased with his work he walked back to the lift and headed back up to deal with Roper. Time the man understood he was a long way from being as clever as everyone seemed to think he was. In the flat Cotter went to his little bag and pulled out another vial of clear liquid. This was LSD and it was going to take Roper on the ride of his life.

He walked purposefully to the third bedroom and opened the door. Roper was clearly deep in a meditative trance. He was leaning back in a single leather chair, his feet up on a leather foot-stool and his hands hanging loose at his sides. Pieces of paper were lying in piles either side of the chair.

Cotter paused to study him and sneered. This was the man who was going to be transforming the way things were done, was he? Well, good luck with that. Cotter was sure that his interventions at GCHQ must have raised many questions marks about Roper's abilities, making him look a lot less clever than his supporters had claimed.

He walked over and plunged the newly loaded syringe into his carotid artery - he was getting good at this - and watched as Roper opened his eyes in shock. Cotter held him down and within moments was delighted to see his eyelids fluttering closed. If he'd got it right then he would be out for about an hour and then wake up to a world gone mad. It was time to get him out of the flat and into somewhere where they wouldn't be disturbed. His flat near the Elephant and Castle was ideal, and it wasn't far away.

He needed to get his van, it was parked ten minutes' walk away. He could park outside, collect Roper, bring him down in the lift and then carry him to the vehicle. If anyone saw he'd say the man had drunk too much. He bent and scooped Roper up. As he had anticipated, he was so skinny he weighed very little. Moving him would be easy.

He looked out of the window and noted the torrential rain showed little sign of stopping. Looked like fate was on his side. The foul weather would provide him with cover for getting Roper out of the building. From that point on he would be totally in control.

The dose he had given him was very large and he couldn't predict how Roper would react to it. If he survived he might experience flash backs for months. Not that he cared. He'd set out with three objectives. The first was simple: to prove he was better than Roper. He reckoned he had passed that test with flying colours, outmaneuvering him at every stage. Even when Roper had realised he was being duped over the intelligence briefings he still hadn't worked out what it was really all about.

The second objective was to get more of an insight into how his mind worked, especially his annoying Rainbow Spectrum; the thing that had made him so famous and captured the imagination of those fools at GCHQ. To be fair, it showed that Roper wasn't entirely stupid as it was quite a clever idea, one that no one had come up with before. But maybe he had just got lucky.

Well, if Roper was going to give up any secrets then this might be the way to do it. He hoped it worked, but of course it may be that it was too much for him. Bad luck if that proved to be the case. In fact, it would save him from worrying about the third objective. Once he had extracted Roper's secrets he was going to kill him.

48

A sense of dread had dropped so hard that Hooley almost staggered. Arriving at his Pimlico flat he had instantly realised there had been a horrifying mix-up. Roper's protection team was outside his flat. Roper was out there alone.

He'd immediately tried calling him on mobile and landline, but all he could get was a message saying, 'number not responding.' He didn't wait. He ordered the armed officers to take him to Roper's flat. With the blue lights and sirens, they battered their way through the rush-hour but even that couldn't defeat the log-jam at Blackfriars caused by the sudden downpour.

He kept trying the phone with no luck. He looked around at the stationary vehicles and was about to get out and run when they started moving again. His sense of anxiety transmitted itself to the driver who pushed it to the limit.

Finally, they were there, he hammered on the door to be let in, but there was no sign of the guard and no response from Roper's flat. He hit every number on the call pad until someone buzzed him inside. He was heading to the lift, with officers behind him, when an instinct made him turn to the desk.

He ran over, looked behind, and nearly fell over with shock. The bedraggled body proving beyond doubt that they had all under-estimated the danger they were in. For a moment, he was filled with rage but quickly got himself back under control and headed back of the lift, leaving one of the officers to guard the body.

It didn't take long before bad news became catastrophic. The door to Roper's flat was firmly shut and there was no response to ringing the bell. It had taken agonising minutes before a specialist team arrived, equipped with the tools to smash open a reinforced door. Inside there was no sign of him. If he needed any further clues, the CCTV system had been smashed to pieces. Just as he was giving into despair Mayweather turned up to take command.

A long slow night finally gave way to morning. It was coming up on 5am and still no news about Roper. Hooley was standing impatiently outside the penthouse as scenes of crime people made a careful sweep through the apartment. They found his mobile inside the flat. There were no signs of a struggle. The last time he had been seen was leaving Victoria.

For about the hundredth time Hooley studied the door to see if he could detect any signs of a break-in. His knew there was nothing. It just gave him something to do while he beat himself up for allowing Roper to leave unprotected.

When he'd first arrived at the building he was so agitated he had tried to kick the door in, to no effect other than to bruise his foot. Panic had lured him into a daft stunt that only worked on TV. He'd wasted more energy by slapping the door and then resigned himself to waiting. He'd kept trying Roper's number, pressing his ear to the door and thought he could hear it, but it was very faint and he wondered if it was his imagination.

The waiting shredded his nerves. Good police officers don't make assumptions, but Hooley knew this was related to the GCHQ investigation. He couldn't stop himself thinking about the potential danger Roper was in. There were far too many bodies already. He instinctively felt time was running out. Finally, the specialist team arrived.

That had been almost eleven hours ago. He was downstairs in the lobby, so lost in worry that he nearly jumped out of his skin when Julie Mayweather spoke from behind him.

"I've just had an update from Cheltenham and there's no news there either. It's as though he's just vanished. Any hints from here yet?"

Hooley didn't bother trying to hide his worry. "Nothing at all. He was clearly here early in the evening because there are soaking wet towels in the shower. I'm guessing that would fit with the terrible rain we had last night and him wanting to clean up and change.

"But otherwise all the building security cameras are out so we can't see him coming or going. The odd thing is that residents are complaining that they lost all connections to the outside world last night. Internet, wi-fi and landlines. They couldn't even get television. It all came back on about 9pm but they were out for several hours.

"I've had uniforms canvassing other buildings, but so far they are coming up fine. This 'outage' seems confined to Roper's building. Normally I'd say that was odd, now I think it's very suspicious."

Mayweather gently rubbed her eyes. It had been a long night and she was feeling badly in need of a cup of coffee and a chance to sit down for a while. But all that would have to wait. She said. "I bet I can guess what you are thinking. This must have something to do with secret technology belonging to MI5." He nodded and she looked around at all the people in sight.

"I'll check, but not here. I'll make the call from my car. The trouble is that while we would both like to know what is going on, I'm not sure that it will take us any closer to finding Jonathan."

49

Roper was dreaming he was lying in a beautiful meadow on a warm summer's evening. He knew that various animals were coming out to feed but also understood that they were nervous and trying to keep out of sight. He blinked and made an amazing discovery; he could see more clearly, as though he was looking through a pair of binoculars.

He blinked several times in a row and the edges of the meadow started coming into focus and he could see several deer nibbling delicately at green shoots. A few more blinks brought his sight into ever greater focus. Now he could make out much smaller animals and birds also feeding quietly.

The colours were vivid, the sun was warm and it felt as though he was in a magical world, even his hearing had improved to the point where he could make out the smallest animals munching on blades of grass.

It was the most natural thing he had ever seen, until the world lurched. He could see the heads of the hunters, but they weren't tracking the other animals, they were looking at him. A golden-coloured stoat sat up, its haughty features making it look cruel and majestic. Its face was turned towards him. It was rocking gently from side-to-side.

It began to move, slowly at first, then all flowing movements as it raced across the meadow, getting bigger and bigger as it approached. By the time it reached him it had turned into a huge creature and its mighty jaws ripped into his puny body. He looked down to see his blood flowing out onto the earth.

Roper was locked into this fantasy, totally unaware that his true location was rather more mundane. He was in a flat near the Elephant and Castle, tied to a bed and being monitored by David Cotter, who noted with disgust that a few moments ago, his victim had emptied his bladder. The smell making it obvious.

The transfer from Roper's own place had gone smoothly but he had been waiting more than an hour before Roper showed some signs of life; moaning and thrashing against his restraints. Cotter was getting frustrated because he wanted him to wake up and start answering questions. He had tried talking to him but to no avail, his words were not getting through.

A few minutes later and he noted that Roper was starting to sweat and soon his face was running with it. Then he was shivering violently, apparently going from extreme heat to extreme cold. Cotter wondered if he might be about to die but Roper surprised him by opening his eyes.

He looked around and at first seemed to ignore his captor then he looked directly at him and smiled. "David, good to see you. Do you have some water? my mouth is very dry." His manner was matter of fact, as if he wasn't truly aware of his position. He debated the request, he didn't want Roper getting too comfortable, but pragmatism won out. Maybe having a drink would help him answer questions.

He fetched a glass of water from the kitchen tap and held it to Roper's lips. In the event he only managed a couple of sips before falling back, apparently exhausted. He lay there with his eyes closed, breathing shallowly. After a few minutes Cotter gave up in disgust. He had been warned that LSD was an unpredictable drug, but he still hadn't expected this. At the same time, he was forced to admit that he wouldn't complain if the drugs killed Roper. He didn't like to admit it, but killing him was not a task he was looking forward to.

He had been experiencing quite violent mood swings all day. One moment calm, the next angry. Now he was overwhelmed with a ravenous hunger, he felt faint from lack of food. He had no idea when he had last eaten. It might have been the previous day, or the day before that. He looked out of the window and noticed that the rain had eased off so he might as well go out for a short while. Roper was going nowhere and seemed in no state to talk. If he left him a bit longer he might get the prefect result. Roper would come around just enough to answer questions then slump unconscious once more.

The thought of food was driving him mad. He needed something now. Something hot, fatty and salty. He was in an area where fast food was king. He shouldn't have a problem. As he walked out he stopped in the door way and looked down. Roper looked almost peaceful. As Cotter stared down at him he felt a sense of disquiet, something about this situation was worrying him, but he couldn't pin the thought down, like one of those dreams that slithers away as you come awake.

He exited and went outside to call the lift. There was a decent chippy nearby; a bag of chips would make him feel better. Twenty minutes later Mr. Roberts opened the front door and walked in. The first thing he noticed was the smell of urine. He followed it to the source and was amazed to see Jonathan Roper lying on one of the beds.

He was unmoving, his features relaxed. Mr. Roberts wondered if he was dead and even finding a pulse could not stop the sudden panic grip him. What was going on? Yet again he was coming back to find people tied to the bed. He must have brought Roper here, but he had no recollection of having done so.

He was forced to admit that those gaps in his memory were getting worse, not better. The strangeness of the situation began to play on his already taut nerves. Roper being here, coupled with his memory loss were threatening to overwhelm him. He had to get out of the flat.

He ran out, taking the stairs at full pelt, unconcerned he might miss a step. He emerged into the deserted lobby and bolted straight outside into a wall of rain which had chosen that moment to start falling again.

Mr. Roberts ignored it. He made straight for the pub on the corner, the Red Lion. It was a large, cavernous place, typical of the area. He burst through the door and marched straight up to the bar. "Pint of lager mate," he said to the barman, not bothering to see if the man was ready to take his order.

The bar tender was normally talkative but not this time. There was something about this customer that suggested it would be unwise to engage him in conversation. He silently placed the drink and stepped back. Mr. Roberts snatched it up and drained it in one. The empty was thumped down hard enough to make the barman wince and Mr. Roberts spun on his heel and left without a word. He hadn't paid and the barman decided he wasn't going to make an issue of it. It was best to let some people go; even better if they never came back. He regretted that the money would probably come out of his wages, but sometimes it was better to be safe than sorry. That man was the type you could imagine ramming a broken glass into someone's face.

Outside it was still raining heavily. As he stood in the pub entrance, with the first effects of the alcohol starting to kick in, David Cotter looked around with a startled expression. "What on earth am I doing out here?" he thought to himself. He could taste the lager in his mouth and turned around and pushed back through the door. He walked towards the bar and stopped, frozen by the way the barman, who obviously recognised him, shrank back in fear. He needed to get out of here and back to the flat. He didn't want to know why the man was scared. He'd lost all track of time and couldn't recall how long he'd left Roper alone.

Back at the flat he paused outside the front door, listening carefully, but could hear nothing. Not that he really expected to, the door was reinforced, designed to resist burglars, which also gave it excellent sound insulation. Inserting his key into the lock he stepped inside.

As the door swung shut behind him he felt a sense of deja vu that was so powerful it was almost a physical sensation. It made him shiver and he started to wonder if he had accidentally ingested some of the LSD as well. That would explain the odd things that were happening. He shook his head, he'd been too careful of that. He walked in to the bedroom and studied Roper, standing there for five minutes while he waited to see if the man would come around.

This short vigil did nothing to clear his mind. Roper was still out for the count and he was having doubts about his plan. Ever since he had brought Roper here he had been feeling very strange. If anything, the feeling was getting worse by the moment.

He began to wonder if his subconscious was trying to tell him something. Being realistic, why was he doing this? He'd already made his point. What more could he wring out of Roper that he had not already extracted through their numerous sessions in Cheltenham? The fool had been so innocent, happy to try and answer all and every question put to him. And that was the key; he had answered a lot of questions and provided an awful lot of answers. Just as importantly, his other plans were coming nicely to fruition,

Maybe he was fixating on Roper - hold that thought - he was fixating on him. Perhaps the best thing was to just finish him off. He leaned in closer and listened to his shallow breathing. It would be the easiest thing in the world to place a pillow over his face and suffocate him.

No sooner had that thought surfaced than it was chased by another. The problem with killing him was that he would lose the only adversary he had ever felt was truly worthy of his attention. Surely it would be better to let him live, with both of them knowing that the better man had won?

50

Cotter stood over Roper, the pillow he was holding just inches from his face. He'd decided to give him one more minute and then that would be it. He was counting the seconds off in his head; now he was in the final countdown.

Five...four...three...two...one... he pressed down on the apparently unconscious form. At first there was no response then Roper began to struggle. Cotter hadn't thought he would fight back. In his mind, it was all going to be over quickly and quietly. Instead the victim was struggling more violently. Showing surprising strength Roper managed to force the pillow off his face.

He took in an enormous breath of air as he pushed hard against the pillow, making Cotter stumble backwards. Roper's eyes were wide open. He'd gone from being out cold to looking very alert.

"I was right. It was you." said Roper. Unlike earlier he was obviously awake and alert. "You were the one person who had all the access needed. I checked with our security people and they said you had the clearance to work on undercover operations. That's how you were able to get your hands on the top-secret surveillance equipment. With your training, I bet it was easy to get people to tell you far more than they intended."

He lay back on the bed, the simple statement leaving him exhausted. "What did you give me? I know it was some sort of hallucinogen."

Cotter had got over his shock at Roper suddenly waking up. He realised he was quite pleased - it meant they could talk, which would mean that Roper would be forced to acknowledge he had lost out to the better man.

"It was LSD I've given you. Now, tell me, you're such a smarty pants, have you worked it all out?"

"Most of it; I even know why you have got gaps in your memory."

Cotter felt that comment like a blow to the stomach. "What do you mean? What gaps in my memory? That's absurd."

As he was talking he was going red in the face and starting to jerk around like a puppet on a string. Roper's comments had triggered a bout of uncontrollable rage and he started raining blows down on the helpless man. His fists pummeled Roper's face and body. In his already weakened condition he lapsed back into unconsciousness. As quickly as it had come the rage left and Cotter looked down at his bloodied victim.

For the second time he experienced anger, but this was against himself. He started hitting his head, beating so hard he could see stars. He fell to his knees besides the bed and started shaking the unconscious Roper.

"Wake up, damn you, wake up. You need to tell me what you meant."

He was in torment. This wasn't how it was supposed to go down. He should have been goading Roper over his failures. Instead, the man had woken from a drug induced coma and immediately turned the tables by coming out with the one thing that was absolutely terrifying him.

How could he possibly know about his memory problems? Surely that was impossible? Yes, he had his famous Rainbow Spectrum, but that was it. He knew how that worked. Surely, he couldn't have found out anything through that?

Another thought hit him. What if Roper had shared this information with other people, especially that annoying plod Hooley? He liked to call the DCI a plod but had quickly worked out the man was not to be underestimated. He might not have a string of qualifications to his name but he was as sharp as they came. It was a good job he had a plan for disappearing.

That made him rush off to check his documents. He was going to need his fake passport. He'd intended to bring it with him when he'd come up from Cheltenham but recently he kept forgetting everything. Just leaving his home to go to work was a nightmare as he nearly always left something vital behind, like his security pass. He got on well with the Military Police guards, but not that well, and was constantly having to go home to pick it up so he could get into the building.

To his intense relief he had managed to remember it. He put it down, then thought better and picked it up and stuffed it into the back pocket of his jeans. At least he knew he had it with him. He also had a French identity card as a back-up and this he also put into his back pocket.

Sorting out the documents made him feel calmer and he had an idea. He filled up a glass with cold water and made his way back to the bedroom. He could tell from the already prominent swelling that Roper was going to have a pretty good black eye and he was bleeding from cuts to his mouth and ear. Cotter stood over him and poured half the contents of the glass over his face.

It worked and Roper spluttered back to life. This time he looked a little warily at Cotter and said nothing. Silently, the psychologist held the glass angled to his mouth so that he could get a drink of water and the rest of the glass was quickly drained. Roper sat back, panting heavily.

"Why did you attack me? There is nothing I can do to you, especially when you've got me tied to the bed. I doubt I would be a match for you at any time, least of all now."

Cotter was still feeling rattled but determined to put on a front. He produced an unpleasant sneer, which was meant to be a chilling smile, at least in his own head. He said. "You're never going to be a match for me at anything and its best you remember that. You forgot yourself a moment ago and that's why I had to teach you a lesson."

His eyes were darting around and there was a sheen of sweat on his forehead. It was quite a change. Cotter had always seemed so laid back and relaxed. He was one of those people who made sure to give Roper some space. A lot of people didn't understand that even standing a few feet away could make him feel uncomfortable.

Yet here he was looming over Roper, bending down and getting so close he could feel the man's breath on his face, smell the lingering aroma of chips combined with beer. If he hadn't been tied so securely he would have shied away from being in such close proximity. Ever since the night he had almost been arrested at Roper's flat something had changed in his behaviour. As Cotter backed out of the room, wiping furiously at his eyes, he was convinced he had a good idea what might be causing the problem.

51

Brian Hooley's phone beeped to indicate an email had just arrived. He was back in Roper's flat now that the forensics team were done. He hoped the message was something important; not just the telephone company offering the chance to buy tickets to an already sold-out event. He was tempted to leave it, but professionalism got the better of him. It might be a message he needed.

His phone was wedged into the inside left pocket of his suit jacket. Getting it out proved harder than he would have liked. He had big hands, with thick fingers to match, and as he reached to grab his mobile he couldn't get a proper grip on it. Instead he pushed it on to its side, making it stick in the lining. Frustrated, he forced his hand in harder, feeling the fabric tear slightly as he managed to envelop the phone in his oversized hand.

He pulled it sharply. At first it resisted then it suddenly came free, making him yank it out too quickly, losing his grip at the last minute. He cursed as it gently flew through the air, reaching a peak height about a foot above his head and then gravity took over, pulling it back towards the ground. Although it felt like it was happening in slow-motion he could do nothing apart from will it to reach the safety of the soft, black-leather, sofa rather than the unforgiving wooden-floor.

To his relief it did, bouncing once before settling back against the covers. He was puffing a sigh of relief as he walked over, picked it up and checked who the email was from, nearly dropping the phone again when he saw it was from Roper.

The email read, "Brian, I am writing this last night, while you, me and Cleverly worked in Julie's office. I have set this to go out on a timer, if you do get this then I have made a bad miscalculation. I believe David Cotter is behind everything and he has double-bluffed me. I was so certain that you were the one he was going to kill, but it was me all along.

"I started having doubts about him a few days ago, he just fitted the profile of the person we were looking for. He has a high security clearance because of who he has to deal with and the freedom to come and go to different sites around the country.

"But what really got me interested was looking into his past. He used to work with Prof Roland Penrose at London University. In simple terms, he was the pioneer behind Artificial Intelligence, a man way ahead of his time. Then there was a tragic accident at his lab and he died. But his assistant was David Cotter. His PhD student. By an 'amazing' stroke of luck he was away, applying for the post at GCHQ, so escaped.

"Penrose was working on ways of enhancing the human brain. I think Cotter may have stolen that work and used it on himself. I had suspicions that this was causing problems for Cotter and when we discussed the murder cases it fell into place. How could there be one killer but two methods of killing people? Easy if there were two people in the same body. You need to get that chased up.

"I don't know if I will survive. Cotter is deeply unstable, and may have multiple personalities because of what he has done to himself. Just in case I don't make it, you need to get someone trawling the Dark Web. They'll need to look for items made by the companies where the murder victims worked. I believe Cotter's plan also involves selling secret equipment to the highest bidder. Being at GCHQ allowed him access to two companies making the equipment and that led to the chain of murders, to cover up his theft.

"My only hope is that soon you should be able to get a GPS signal with my location. That is if I have been successful at swallowing one of the new personal tracking devices. It starts working when the coating is dissolved by my stomach acid. It can take longer for some people than others so it needs monitoring. The security team at GCHQ know I have got this so will be able to help you if you call them. I don't know how long the tracker will work for, but hopefully it does. Best wishes. Jonathan."

Hooley felt a profound mix of emotions. Some of it relief and some of it intense anxiety. He thought only Roper could put "best wishes" at the bottom of a note like that. He rushed off to find Julie Mayweather, charging down the stairs and out in to the bright morning sunshine. He looked around for her car. He couldn't see it and realised he was panicking. Then he spotted it.

She saw him walking towards her and clambered out of the rear of the black Jaguar XF. When Hooley reached her he didn't say anything, just passed her his phone with the message on display. She read it quickly, her eyes widening as she took in who it was from.

She looked up, her face a mix of hope that they could rescue him, astonishment that he had found a way to communicate and frustration at his unorthodox behaviour. "I wish he'd told us, we could have had him surrounded by armed guards."

Hooley held up his hands in a 'what can you do' gesture. "He'll have had his reasons for keeping it quiet. You and I may not understand them, but that's Jonathan for you."

She handed his phone back, her face assuming her ubiquitous 'business as normal' expression. She called over to DI Cleverly who was talking quietly to one of the scenes of crime team. Hooley handed him his phone and they waited while he read it. He looked up expectantly.

Mayweather issued instructions. "Norman, you need to co-ordinate the search for Cotter, making sure you cover Cheltenham, his flat up there, and talk to anyone and everyone who knows him and might be able to throw some light on where he's got Roper." This was standard police work that hardly needed spelling out, but her words were influenced by her concern. Cleverly understood this and didn't bridle at being told how to do his job.

Mayweather added. "I'll deal with the MI5 end and make sure they know to talk to you."

Hooley chipped in. "Cotter's boss is called Helen Sharples. I know her a little bit so why don't I talk to her and see if she can throw any light on this?"

Cleverly gave a thumbs-up as he started backing away to get his part of the hunt underway, making for a command vehicle that had found a space on the embankment walkway. Morning joggers were looking disgruntled as they discovered their normal route closed off.

Hooley leaned against the boot of the Jaguar and started scrolling through his contacts list. He was sure he had made a note of Sharples' direct line number. He knew he could have sent an email but this was urgent and he wanted to hear her voice rather than sending messages into the ether.

To his relief the number was there and seconds later she was answering, sounding bright and breezy. Hooley took his time. What he had to say was both fantastic and complicated and he needed to get her to understand as quickly as possible. Which she did. Minutes later he had details of Cotter's parents, former girlfriends and a previous address in London. It was a flat close to the Elephant and Castle, not far from where he was standing.

She ended the call promising to light a fire under everyone she could think of at GCHQ and saying she would also speak to the security people. "I'm not supposed to know this, and you didn't hear this from me, but they do carry out sweeps on people.

"Don't take this the wrong way, but your Jonathan Roper may well have been a target after you were brought in. It's not that they would have thought he was guilty of anything, but they are trained to pick up on behaviour change"

"I can believe that," said Hooley. "there is something else which is very urgent that I want to ask you, if you don't mind?" He heard her murmur yes and carried on. "This is all a bit Sci-Fi to me, but Roper says he has swallowed a tracking device that will switch on when his stomach acid dissolves some sort of coating on it.

"He says he got it from security and I need to know how to track this device straight away. I don't know how he managed to get his hands on it, although somebody must have broken the rules, so there may be some reluctance to admit anything. But we need to get over that, I just need the info about how the device works. Would you be willing to go and talk to them directly?"

"Of course. I'll go now and call you once I have what you need." He could tell from the tone of her voice that she would not allow herself to be deterred. Hooley ended the call. He would have smiled if he could have seen Sharples's determined expression as she raced off to the security team. She liked Roper and hated the thought that something might happen to him.

Ten minutes later and she was on the phone to the DCI, sounding slightly breathless. "They can monitor the device from here. It hasn't come on yet but they are keeping a constant watch, the moment they have anything they will contact your team and transmit the data."

She stopped and he could hear her catching her breath. "As you suspected, he persuaded one of the younger guys here to give him one of the devices so he could inspect it. He told him it was just for an experiment to do with his Rainbow Protocol.

"It was quite clever of him actually. He made it sound like there was concern over safety protocols and that he had been asked to check it out. He even managed to produce an email from me saying that I was part of a larger group involved in the check-up and had given my consent to him having it. My security rating is high enough to authorise something like that."

There was a pause. "I know it's not a priority, but when you get him back, I wouldn't mind finding out how he accessed my email."

52

The man who walked into the room looked like David Cotter - but he wasn't. There was something very different about him and Roper realised his recent suspicions were correct. But it was also dawning on him that he had placed himself in enormous danger. The attack by Cotter could prove to be the least of it.

While he was hopeless at reading body language, he understood some people were dangerous, and there was something about this man that was very disturbing. At boarding school, he had run into problems with two types of bullies. There were those who were frightened of being bullied themselves, so were glad to have someone else to pick on; they seemed to think that if they had a go at Roper then they might escape their own issues.

It was the second type that scared him. Those were the boys who were bigger, stronger and nastier than the others. They liked to hurt people and being able to pick on the 'weirdo' like Roper was just an added bonus, because it provided entertainment for their fellow pupils.

Fortunately, there weren't as many of the latter type. He had also learned that if you took your beating without making a fuss then there was a chance you would be left alone for a bit. These were the boys who didn't care about 'fairness', they just hurt you. Roper knew he was looking at someone like that.

This person was standing quietly in the doorway. His eyes were hooded and there was a faint smile on his face, as if he was listening to some private joke. His hands hung down by his sides. Where the David Cotter personality had been clenching and unclenching his fists, this one kept his hands quite still.

He had been looking at Roper for almost a minute. He stepped further into the room until he was close enough to reach out and touch Roper's face. He reached behind him and produced a knife that he must have had tucked into his belt.

He stood there for a while longer. The knife was in his right hand, the blade unwavering. That strange smile was in place but, if Roper had been able to read such things, it never reached his eyes. They remained cold and calculating, the pupils unnaturally dilated to make it look as though he had black holes in the centre of his eyes.

Roper was very frightened. His mouth had gone dry, for some reason his bladder was hurting, and his heart was thumping. He had read about people knowing when they were about to die and wondered if this was what it felt like. With blinding speed, the knife moved towards him. He closed his eyes then shouted in pain as the blade entered his body.

He felt a burning sensation as the knife withdrew. He opened his eyes and saw the weapon had gone into his palm. Blood was pumping out. It hurt but he daren't shout out again.

He was panting with the effort to keep his equilibrium but recovered enough to look at his tormentor. The man was disturbingly calm.

Roper wondered what to do but eventuality his powerful sense of curiosity managed to override the pain and fear. He said. "You're not David Cotter, are you?"

To his surprise the man laughed out loud. "That little wimp. No, I'm not him. Although he likes to think he can tell me what to do. The little coward has disappeared. Just as well really; when I get hold of him we are going to have a nice little chat."

Anybody else might have found the conversation almost impossible to deal with; especially since the David Cotter look-alike was brandishing a bloodied knife he had just stabbed you with.

Roper was different, he really wanted to know. "Would you mind telling me who you are? I've got a theory but first, if you don't mind, I need the answers to a couple of questions."

The man who said he wasn't Cotter looked at his knife and then shrugged as if to say, 'why not.' He said. "You can call me Mr. Roberts. Now go ahead, ask your questions."

His hand was really hurting now but his need to know helped him overcome the pain. He used his mind to screen it away where it couldn't do so much harm.

"The murders of Tom Bennett and Harry Jordan. Were you behind that?"

Roberts grinned, showing a row of brilliant white teeth. "Yes, that was me. Cotter put me up to it, he didn't have the balls to do it himself so got my help. But he whined like a little girl when I did it my way. He told me I had got it all wrong so I had to warn him."

No more was forthcoming, so Roper asked. "I'm guessing he didn't like the fact that you cut their faces off, or sent that video to the police?"

"You could say that. He went potty about that. But stuff him. I wanted to know what it would be like wearing their faces. I thought it might make me feel like them." All the time he was talking his expression hadn't changed, although he now sat down on the edge of the bed. He went on. "It didn't work though. I still felt like me. But at least I knew what was what."

He'd been looking at his knife but now he said. "Your turn again."

"I'm interested in how you talked to each other. I mean you've never actually met, have you?

Mr. Roberts gave him an appeasing look. "Sounds like you already know the answer. So why don't you tell me." he waved the knife at him.

"I think you've always known what each other is up to. At first, it must have felt like you were leaving messages for each other, but later it got more confusing. Somethings you knew, somethings you didn't.

"The problem is that you have never been able to meet up and speak directly. That might have helped, or not. You might not like each other. I'm thinking that things really started going wrong with the murders of Peter Knight and Sandra Hall."

Roberts studied him intently. "Cotter likes to make out that you're not as sharp as people say, but how did you know that?" He leaned forward, letting the sharp blade run gently across Roper's forehead. It was all he could do not to scream. It wasn't painful, but it was truly terrifying; it made him think of having his face cut off. Once again, he forced the fear down. He had to know the truth: that was the most important thing.

Roberts was back on his feet. He was losing some of his detachment, swaying on his feet. "I admit that things got odd. I started getting strange memory lapses. After I'd taken the pair of them I couldn't remember if Cotter had asked me to do it, or it was something I'd done myself. I was so confused I didn't leave myself enough time to take their faces.

"If I'm honest it gets worse. Sometimes I can't even remember where I've been for a couple of hours. It was a real shock to find you here when I walked into the flat. I didn't know if I had brought you here, or it was him."

He started hitting his head with the palm of his hand, the hard blows making his skin redden.

"Sometimes I think my mind is going altogether. My memory seems to be in little pieces, none of it is connected and some of it is disappearing, it's like something is eating away at my brain."

The blows were landing harder, Roberts was starting to make himself bleed as the skin around his eyes swelled and burst under the onslaught. He lurched out of sight and Roper heard the front door open and close.

All was quiet, then the door burst open and a wild-eyed Roberts - he was sure it was Roberts - burst back into the room. "You know what's going on. You have to tell me."

53

It took almost an hour to assemble the hit team but finally they were ready to go. Hooley was waiting outside in the street as the officers prepared to force their way into the flat registered in David Cotter's name.

But even before they had got inside doubts were growing. The hit team had deployed a mini-drone to point its cameras inside. There was nothing to be seen. They needed to get inside to be sure but it wasn't looking hopeful.

Even so, the Inspector in charge was taking no chances. Hooley's request to come in with the first wave had been emphatically rebuffed. He would wait out in the street until he was told it was safe.

He made a furious protest, insisting that if Roper was being held captive he would need to see a friendly face. The Inspector wasn't having it. "We'd all like to see a friendly face but if you go in there you are just going to get in the way. Best case, that slows us down, worst case, you, or one of my team, gets shot."

The DCI had given up at that point; he knew the argument was over and prolonging it just wasted time. Now, over the radio link, he could hear the team calling in that the flat was empty and there were no signs of life. He dashed upstairs, determined to see for himself, but even an eagle-eyed inspection could find nothing. The place was coated in a thick layer of dust, indicating it hadn't been occupied for a very long time.

He'd almost made it back to the temporary command centre near Roper's penthouse when the call came in from GCHQ. Roper's tracking device had just turned itself on. They would have a location in a few minutes. His car pulled up and he sprinted to the Control van. They had big screens which would be better for displaying the information when it came through.

Opening the door, he found Mayweather was already in position. She said. "We should have the information any second now."

Hooley had one urgent question. "Does this mean he's still alive?"

The answer chilled him. "Not necessarily. The device doesn't need him to be living to turn itself on."

He was stood in the door, holding it open so that light flooded in. The space was surprisingly large, allowing two sets of desks on either side with space to walk down the centre.

An operative stepped forward and held out her hand to encourage him in, pointing at the door as she did so. He noticed the natural light was disturbing everyone and hurriedly pulled the door behind him. He went and stood by Mayweather. Nobody spoke. They just had to wait.

"Got it." The voice appeared to float out of the gloom. "I should have full contact in a few seconds."

Hooley was grinding his teeth so hard he was surprised no one had complained about the noise. "Come on, come on, come on." His voice was playing in his head on a continuous loop.

The technician started talking again, reeling off GPS details which the operative next to Mayweather fed into an online map. Hooley leaned forward and was stunned to see it appeared to be exactly where he had just come from. Then he did a double take. It was the Elephant and Castle but a different building. At last some good news. They already had a team in place.

He was about to dash out when Mayweather held his arm. "Let the team there get on with what they're good at. You and I can travel together. He's going to be alright. I can feel it."

By the time they turned up at the new address the hit team were almost ready to go in again. The drone had been in action once more and this time they had captured something. The inspector was replaying the film on a lap top.

"We only had a quick look, I didn't want to tip anyone off that we're outside, but there is something. I think we have your man and Cotter, and I'm hoping you can confirm."

The picture quality was surprisingly good and suddenly they were looking through a window into a bedroom where the familiar figure of Roper appeared to be tied to a bed. Also in the room was David Cotter.

Hooley's sense of relief to find him still alive was immediately squashed when he saw the knife in Cotter's hand.

The inspector spoke "Did you notice the blood all over Mr. Roper's hand? I think he has been stabbed. We are going to be ready to go any minute and we shan't be hanging around. Your man is clearly in danger. Do I have your permission to use lethal force once we gain access?"

This last request was directed at Mayweather, who didn't hesitate "You are authorised to use lethal force." she replied. Spelling it out for the record.

54

"Have you ever heard of Professor Roland Penrose? Or maybe Neuromorphic Computing?"

Roberts shook his head. "What have they got to do with me?"

"Let me explain," said Roper. He felt surprisingly calm and alert. "The idea of Neuromorphic Computing has been around for quite a while. More than 30 years, and Professor Penrose was one of the leading figures in the field.

"The idea is simple, the reality is very complex; maybe it will never happen. But it started out as the thought that you might be able to create computer chips that would mimic functions of the brain. From that there were all sorts of theories.

"Some people started talking about the ability to create super-soldiers or super-learners. People with neuromorphic chips in their brains who would be able to do things that no one else could. That theory got a flurry of mention in the media, then it went quiet once it was more widely understood how difficult that is to do.

"There has been progress on creating neuromorphic computer systems, but these are highly specialised and only available in the most advanced institutions or companies on the cutting edge of Artificial Intelligence. But no one has yet worked out how to make the most of these advances so they remain a sort of fantasy."

The burst of talking had tired him out and he shut his eyes for a moment as he gathered his thoughts for the next bit. Sitting in front of his own screen this had seemed very easy, but out here it was proving harder to pin down. When he opened his eyes again he was surprised to see Roberts holding a glass of water. He raised his head to accept the offer, gulping down water while half of it ran down his chin.

"Thanks for that. I was thirsty." He swallowed and carried on. "The problem of trying to link people to computer chips is that chips are very hard and brains are very soft. So, they're not the most compatible material. But things changed a few years ago.

"A new material was developed that could, in theory, be implanted in a brain. Body heat would then allow it to gently firm up and start working. This is still a very complex field and Professor Penrose was one of the leaders in it. He was also working on a much easier way of implanting the chips that did away with the need for major surgery."

"You keep mentioning this guy and saying he 'was'; I take it he died? If so, what on earth has that got to do with me?" While Roper couldn't read it, he was looking anxious, as though dormant thoughts were coming to life.

"Professor Penrose did die, two-years-ago. There was an explosion and a fire at his lab in London and all his research was reported missing. But there was one lucky survivor, David Cotter, who in fact had a cast iron alibi because he was being interviewed for a post at GCHQ. He told the interviewing panel that the work with Professor Penrose was getting nowhere and he wanted a change."

"Go on," said Roberts. His voice low and wary.

"I think David Cotter caused the fire and stole the advanced work. I believe Penrose had a new chip ready to implant and this is what Cotter got his hands on. I think he wanted to turn himself into a super being with an extraordinarily high IQ and strength, but he wanted to keep it secret so that's why he sabotaged the lab, killing Professor Penrose in the process.

"Moving to GCHQ was a key part of his plan. It gave him access to military secrets and diplomatic intelligence, things he could exploit by selling to the highest bidder. There are plenty of people out there who pay top dollar to get an advantage over their rivals.

"From the moment he inserted the new chip he gave himself a huge increase in brain power - the trouble is he also created you at the same time. Not that he realised. You and he are one and the same. I suppose you are like a modern Jekyll and Hyde. Something about the chip went wrong and made two personalities.

"I think that may have something to do with him implanting the chip in the wrong place. Our knowledge of the mind may be growing, but there is a long way to go. I suspect that in reality, having two personalities is just too much for the mind to process, and that is probably why you started to develop memory problems. The two of you fighting for the same space just succeed in erasing small bits of each other."

Roberts made a growling noise, like an enraged dog. "Are you saying that I'm some sort of freak? Who else knows this?"

"I wouldn't say freak, but no one else knows all the details. But it won't take them long to find out though."

Roberts stood up. "Well let's slow that process down a little bit by getting rid of you. He raised the knife, his face becoming a mask of menace. At that moment, there was an ear-splitting bang and a dazzling light. The room seemed to shake from the incredible noises.

Totally blinded, Roper missed Roberts spinning round and falling as masked men ran in and shot him. The effects of the flash-bang grenade detonated by the rescuers had rendered him helpless.

He was still suffering deafness, and temporary blindness, as he was cut free and rushed straight out of the flat and down the stairs to the next floor where a make-shift field hospital had been set up. Hooley and Mayweather looked on anxiously as Roper was laid out on a stretcher.

A doctor swiftly checked him and pronounced him in reasonable condition. "We can fix the wound in his hand but it will be a little while longer before his hearing and sight return. Some people are more sensitive to that than others. What we need now is to get him into hospital so that we can do a full job on him."

Mayweather thanked him. "You go with him Brian. He's used to you turning up when he's had a bit of a going over so we might as well keep things in the normal routine."

She watched him being stretchered into the lift and wiped at her eyes. "How come it has to be Jonathan who ends up on the wrong side of a beating, every time?"

Hooley said. "I've come to the conclusion that where trouble is concerned he's like a magnet. There's no other way to describe it. I'll call you from the hospital. I'm rather hoping that Cotter survived. I'd quite like to know what was going on in there."

55

Forty-eight hours later.

After two days on a drip and some antibiotics, Roper had been cleared to leave the hospital. He had declined pain killers, telling the doctor he would use mental control against the pain. The consultant had shrugged and warned him to expect some lingering after effects.

He told Hooley and Mayweather. "For anyone else, the dose of LSD he received might have been fatal. Not your man. Mr. Roper has a unique strategy where he just ignores any side-effects. And do you know what? It seems to work brilliantly. I'm happy for him to go home."

The police officers had smiled and nodded, entirely unsurprised to learn Roper was defying conventional medical wisdom.

Also present was Helen Sharples. She gave Roper a wry smile. "You must talk me through this technique of yours. I can see it being very useful to lots of other people. I suppose you could call it a sort of placebo effect - do nothing and get better."

Roper, who was lying in bed in a private room at Guy's Hospital, levered himself up on his pillows and went to reply. She held up a hand. "Just one more thing. While you're explaining to me how that works; you can also explain how you managed to get hold of my email details and trick some poor young chap in security to handing over top-secret technology? Some people might call that espionage."

Roper looked so crest-fallen she felt sorry for him. "Actually, don't worry about the espionage bit. The view is that since we almost got you murdered, then the least we can do is overlook a small problem of miscommunication."

Mayweather gave her a quizzical look. Sharples picked up on the expression. She glanced around and closed the door.

"I got a head's up on part of the 'official' response last night. The feeling is that not only did we let Mr. Roper down, but it was a good job he took things into his own hands and sorted it out. Otherwise who knows what would have happened. I gather there is going to be some sort of briefing at Downing Street later today."

Mayweather nodded. She had received her invitation to the 'top-secret' briefing just that morning. She said. "What about Cotter or Mr. Roberts? What's happening there?"

"The pair of them are going to make it," said Sharples. "The bullet only just grazed a shoulder so they're going to live. They're in a secure facility near Cheltenham. I've been to see them and it's not good news.

"There are two fully formed personalities in there and they are fighting for control. The Cotter character is quite lucid and has confirmed Jonathan's theory. He did implant the chip in his own head and at first it seemed to work. His cognitive function improved massively and that is when he got the idea of challenging Roper to a sort of duel, without telling him he was taking part in one.

"But now I have had a chance to talk to him, it is clear the man is a psychopath. His plan to steal the chip was extraordinary for both its daring and the fact that he was indifferent to murdering his mentor.

"With the chip in place his aggressive side started to assert itself. That's when he came up with his crazy plan to not only prove he was better than Roper, but to actually kill him." She looked at Hooley. "He says you were next in line because he needed to make sure Jonathan hadn't left any secrets with you." The DCI looked rueful.

"Back to the plan to kill Jonathan. As far as I can tell that is the point at which the Mr. Roberts character appeared. At first neither knew about the other, but now they do. It has made Roberts become psychotic in his determination to get at Cotter, and Cotter is terrified he will.

"It's quite a horrific thought, but he is being hunted by himself. I have no idea if they will ever be able to confront each other, but Mr. Roberts wants Cotter dead. Heaven knows what will happen if he succeeds.

"What is fascinating, is that there are genuinely two people in there, that sort of thing is incredibly rare, and, if I dare say it, incredibly interesting." She noticed the stares she was getting. "Speaking as a psychologist and doctor, finding new conditions is always rewarding."

Hooley had been listening closely. "I have enough trouble with me. I'd hate to think there was a worse version of me in there as well." He tapped his forehead. "I wouldn't wish that on my worst enemy, although Cotter does seem to have brought it on himself. What's going to happen long term?"

"Well, I think that will be talked about at the meeting this afternoon, but I don't think they can just close this down because there are too many murder victims. Those families need some sort of closure from this."

"They're looking at some sort of secret trial at the Old Bailey," said Mayweather. "The families can know some of what happened, at least that Cotter is the killer, but not much more. Cotter or Mr. Roberts, is clearly not fit to stand trial and will be sent to a secure hospital."

Roper piped up, his voice still sounding weak. "Was I right in thinking Cotter was stealing industrial and military secrets?"

"You were bang on the money. He had stolen some especially valuable software programs that are worth millions. Not that I can tell you that.

"The Cotter character also revealed that poor Tom Bennett had his own invention used against him. He has told us where to find all the surveillance tech he hid around the man's home.

"He was able to manipulate his position at GCHQ to do that, but should never have been able to. That also allowed him to hack Scotland Yard computers, so he could keep an eye on you and your team." This last statement was aimed at Mayweather.

Sharples added. "It's caused quite a stir in the security section. The head man is off to spend more 'time with his family' and his deputy has taken over. So hopefully the next madman won't get so far."

She turned back to Roper and fixed him with a warm smile. "As you can imagine, Jonathan, with all that on their plates, the decision to let you off for a bit of email hacking was quite easy. So now you're home free. What are you going to do? If you'd like to start again at GCHQ you'd be welcomed with open arms, but maybe you'd like a break?"

Hooley intervened. "Before you decide that I'm guessing you will be coming back to my place for a few days? Give yourself a chance to recover. I've already got enough food in to feed a football team. Should last a couple of days."

Mayweather looked over at Roper. "We've all been talking about you. The view is that after what you've been through it might be best if you came back to the Yard for a little while. That way Brian and I can keep an eye on you." She stopped. "Does that sound OK to you?"

Roper could only nod. He seemed to have got something in his eye.

THE END

Thank you for reading the third novel in the Jonathan Roper Investigates series.

I wanted to create a character who was a little bit different and I think Roper fits that bill. His autism and lack of social skills provide him with both insights and problems. My sense that Roper would be an interesting fit for the modern world was influenced by my autistic son. He is non-verbal but despite this it has been heart-warming to see him develop; partly down to the brilliant support of so many carers, but also because of his own determination. This determination is a trait he shares with Roper. It was always my intention that the Roper series should be regarded as series of "page turning thrillers", each one capable of being read alone. While it offers some small insights into the autistic world, I also wanted to show some of the unexpected side of autism. There can be humour there and I hope that my portrayal of the relationship between Roper and his long-suffering boss, Brian Hooley, demonstrates that.

I am a self-published author and would really be grateful if you could leave me a review on Amazon. The number of reviews a book accumulates on a daily basis has a direct impact on sales. So just leaving a review, no matter how short, helps make it possible for me to continue to do what I love... writing.

For more information on upcoming launches please like me on my Facebook page, Jonathan Roper Investigates or send me an email at hello@michael-leese.com – I always enjoy reading your comments and thoughts about Roper, Hooley and Mayweather, and do my best to respond to all correspondence.

HERE ARE A COUPLE
OF CHAPTERS OF THE
NEXT JONATHAN
ROPER BOOK

The Long
Reach

1

City Airport, London.

His client, Maxine Dubois, was focusing on her iPad. Her expression, normally impossible to read, was rapt. She'd run the ten-minute clip twice, leaning forward each time she reached a favourite part, the tip of her tongue emerging between her lips as if tasting the air. Dubois went in for the third time. The Courier relaxed a little as he allowed his mind to wander back to the moment he'd first met the pair who had put together this special performance.

He needed something different, and when he discovered their work he found a way to be introduced. At their initial meeting, a year ago, the Courier had known they would be right. Like him, they would only do something if they could do it perfectly.

They were a contrasting pair. The knife specialist was short and pixie-like, with a mischievous smile that lit up her face. The Courier noticed it didn't reach her eyes. The camera user was tall and thin with a faintly quizzical air, as if she had missed a turn and found herself in the wrong place. Many were the victims who had died puzzling over how they had misread the pair so badly.

He'd met them for drinks at a pub in Blackfriars, the pixie soon making him splutter into his beer. Size really matters, she told him: the bigger the better. Laughing at his reaction, she had tapped her forehead. It was the size of what was between the ears that was important. In her opinion this was an area where a lot of men were poorly equipped.

Evidently, he had passed some sort of test; at least on the mental side. As for anything else, even if he had been offered he would have declined. Business could be a pleasure, but you never mixed the two.

Elegant and frosty, the French woman had a mind like a trap and not a trace of sentimentality. Those attributes had helped her create a global business from the failing family concern she had inherited at just 22 years old. Within a decade Dubois had created a conglomerate that spanned shipping and digital media to luxury hotels and high fashion. Not only did she have an unerring ability to pick out a company with potential - she had a gift for identifying talented executives to run the businesses for her. It was a wonderfully successful formula, and she had elevated her role to the point where there was little for her to do, apart from removing the odd senior manager to "encourager les autres".

But Dubois was bored, and heard through a friend of a contact that the Courier was a man who could provide "entertainment". At their first meeting she had immediately thrown down a challenge, affecting boredom and indicating she might leave at any moment. The Courier had seen through that act, understanding that this client was hiding a keen sense of anticipation. Through patient questioning he had learned that, while Dubois had her own ideas, she expected him to provide her with alternatives. As the discussions became more detailed, Dubois had specified that she did not want to have any sort of connection to the victims. That had surprised him since her earlier behaviour led him to think she was driven by a desire for revenge, maybe against a business rival or a former lover.

The revelation led the Courier to what she truly wanted - to take someone who had led an ordinary life, one who would be intensely missed by her circle of loved ones.

He was impressed. Not many people thought in such a simple and direct manner.

He had found the victim quicker than he had expected. Anne Hudson was a young woman who volunteered at her local church to help raise money for impoverished families in the UK and abroad. The Courier found her picture on a charity website. She was standing at one end of a five-woman line-up with a shy smile that suggested she hated attention. She had the sort of prettiness that is particular to healthy young women, especially ones that are blooming from pregnancy, without being truly beautiful. It took his team a day to find her.

The picture was taken outside a church in Worcester Park, south London, so that was where they started. A talkative cleaner provided her name and one phone call provided her address. Then it was just a case of doorstepping her home and waiting for her to come out. Which she did, although this time with a baby in a pushchair; the website picture had been months old. They had taken their own pictures and even shot a short clip of video, which had been edited into the package that his client was going through now.

Dubois was still enjoying the video clip, allowing him to study her closely. He was confident she was buying into his plan. What he needed now was for her to agree to the final price. If she wanted what he could provide then she was going to have to pay up.

2

Tower Bridge, London.

Detective Chief Inspector Brian Hooley was wearing his "divorce" outfit: a pair of dark blue jeans, blue cotton shirt and light grey jacket that he had bought the day after his marriage had officially ended. If pushed, he might have admitted to being influenced by the sartorial style of a middle-aged TV presenter who fronted a motoring programme.

His clothes suited his burly six-foot frame, but his tenuous hold on a large bunch of flowers and box of chocolates was doing less for his image. He looked as though he might drop them at any moment as he tried to maintain his hold while looking at his watch. He was 15 minutes early and in a dilemma. Could he turn up before the agreed time?

He decided to wait a little longer but his need for the bathroom was becoming urgent. He thought about sneaking into a nearby restaurant but was put off because it appeared to be full of serving staff waiting to pounce on the first customers of the day. There was no way he could sneak in unobserved.

Although it was a warm day, the wind blowing off the river Thames felt cold, making him shiver. He combined a sigh with a shrug as he reached a decision - he was going to be early. He had been repeatedly warned about being late, even by a few seconds. An attempted joke about sudden death as a cause of lateness had earned him a hard stare.

He hustled over to his destination: an upscale apartment block on the south side of the river. It boasted fabulous views over London's financial district to the east and the London Eye to the west. He caught the eye of the security guard, who grinned in recognition.

Buzzing him inside, he indicated the visitors' book with a nod of his head and watched as the Met detective filled out his name and time of arrival. Writing as slowly as he could had shaved a few more seconds off, so now he was just eight minutes early.

"That's all good, Chief Inspector. Do you want me to buzz up and let him know you're here?"

Hooley returned the smile. "No thanks, Dave; let's make it a surprise."

Since the terrible events of 12 months ago, when a guard had been murdered by a man who had come to kill Jonathan Roper, the area where he sat was now protected by security glass and conversations were through a two-way microphone.

Roper had personally paid for the improvements and also made a substantial payment to the widow, ensuring she could buy a small property near her mother and leaving a little over as well. Although no one blamed him, he insisted and with the money he had inherited from his parents he could afford it.

Hooley pressed the elevator call button. The car was waiting, and the door opened straight away. He stepped inside and went up to the top floor - the third - where Roper owned the three-bedroom penthouse. He glanced at his watch: just five minutes early. Still just managing to hold on to his gifts he pressed the door-bell.

He thought he could hear shouting, but then the door opened, and Roper was there, a strange smile - almost a grimace - on his face. The Detective Chief Inspector was thinking his colleague's thick black hair looked more unruly than usual before he was dragged sideways. In his place appeared a smaller, female version of Roper, who, at five feet two inches in her bare feet, was a foot shorter than the man she had replaced.

This had to be Samantha, or Sam, he assumed. Like Roper she was very pale, her colouring contrasting with her jet-black hair and dark eyes. She had her hands on her hips and was glaring at him with such a fierce expression he took an involuntary step backwards.

"Why are you here now?" she demanded. Her voice was amazingly deep for someone who shared Roper's extremely slim physique, and there was a huskiness to it he would normally associate with a smoker, but he doubted that was true as Roper couldn't abide the smell of cigarettes.

"I'm Brian Hooley. Jonathan invited…"

She cut him off. "I know exactly who you are. I asked you why you are here now."

This doorstep interrogation was scrambling his brain. He froze, his mouth half-open. Time slowed and then Roper reappeared, looked apologetic and slammed the door shut. The DCI pressed his ear against the door. He could make out a fierce argument, and it was Sam's voice that was dominating.

The apartment went silent and he pulled his head back just in time as the door swung open. Roper was back. "Could you knock again in exactly five minutes?"

The door started to swing shut but Hooley managed to jam his shoe in the door. He handed over his gifts and said, "When you finally let me in I will need to go to the loo."

The presents were snatched away. Some people might have taken exception to such a bizarre greeting. Hooley took a steadying breath and set the timer on his phone for four minutes and fifty seconds. At least this was happening away from prying eyes.

Not for the first time, he wondered at how life with Roper could quite suddenly take on a surreal quality with activities measured in precise amounts of time that left no margin for human error. He tried to remember the last time arriving somewhere had caused such a furore. A long-buried memory surfaced of the day he had accidentally arrived an hour early at a girlfriend's home, only to bump into the boy leaving. He'd quite forgotten about that and wondered what the girl was doing now. Probably dreaming about the days when boys were throwing themselves at her feet.

But all this over a few minutes? Roper had told him it was important he arrived on time. Now he knew that meant don't be early as well as don't be late. He couldn't help smiling; the lunch they had planned was going to be interesting, especially if Roper's girlfriend was going to remain upset with him.

The alarm made him jump, but he counted to three and pressed the bell. Roper opened the door instantly. The DCI suspected he had been waiting there the whole time. He was beyond being polite. "I'll be with you in a minute," he said, shoving past and heading for the guest bathroom. He'd been to the flat many times, but never when Roper had a girlfriend.

He emerged to find Roper and Sam waiting in the living room. Before he could say hello again she nudged Roper sharply in the ribs and nodded.

"Sorry," said Roper, rubbing at his side - it had been a hard dig - "Sam's flight has been altered and she's leaving earlier than she thought. She's only got fifteen minutes before she has to go so we thought coffee here and then she can head for Heathrow and you and I can go on for lunch."

"Don't you want to go with her and see her off? You should have rung me and cancelled. I'd have totally understood."

Sam spoke. "We've done all that here. Much more comfortable, if you know what I mean." She gave Hooley a surprisingly frank expression and he felt his face warm slightly.

"Er, yes. I think I do." He supposed that anyone who went out with Roper was bound to be a little out there. The man himself was a one-off. Loyal, passionate and capable of making breathtakingly brusque personal comments, totally oblivious to the impact they might have.

Only last week, in the course of work, they had needed to talk to a new forensic scientist. At the end of the interview Roper had said to the woman: "You look a lot older than the picture you've put online."

Shock, rage and embarrassment flashed over her face, to be replaced by misery as she looked as though she was about to burst into tears. Hooley had frog-marched Roper away before he could do any more damage.

Outside in the corridor he had hissed, "How many times do I need to tell you that people get distressed if you criticise their appearance, especially if you have never met them before? That very nice lady you just upset probably likes that photograph and imagines she still looks like that. It's just a small vanity thing and certainly doesn't need you wading in with your size-tens."

"It's size-elevens, actually." Roper had that mulish expression on his face which meant he thought everyone else was being ridiculous and there was no way he was going to climb down. The DCI, worried that the woman would appear at any moment, had grabbed the younger man by the arm and pulled him towards the stairs. "Come on, let's go and get a cup of coffee." The episode exemplified Roper. It wasn't that his observations were wrong, but the way he pointed them out left a lot to be desired.

He came back to the present as he realised Roper was holding up a tempting looking bottle of lager. A drink was a very good idea, and he gave the younger man a quick thumbs up. As he took a swig he risked a quick glance at Samantha. She was still looking at him through narrowed eyes, but he thought she looked less angry.

Holding his hands up in an apologetic gesture he said. "My bad. I realise I should have arrived at the right time. I expect I threw all your preparations out, which must have been very annoying."

In truth he regarded the idea of a few minutes either way as inconsequential, but with Roper he knew that details that could cause the most intense issue. A couple of weeks ago he hadn't been paying attention when it was his turn to get the coffee.

Instead of a latte he'd given his colleague a cappuccino. Roper had reacted as if he was being handed a cup of poison, refusing to accept it. It had taken the rest of the day before they were back on speaking terms.

So he was relieved as Sam broke out a wicked grin.

"There's no need to pretend you really understand. From what Jonathan has told me, you are more relaxed than most neurotypicals. A lot of people would have complained that I was overreacting and not given me the chance to calm down. What they can never get their heads around is that someone like me experiences a physical sensation when someone is late or early. It's not as bad as a nettle sting but a bit more than an itch."

"Sounds like me when someone is slow getting their round in down at the pub." He was pleased with that but noticed from her stony response that she wasn't.

"You've been working in America, Jonathan tells me," he added quickly.

"I have, or in fact I am. I've been working with the NSA for the last six months and it's gone well, so they've offered me a two-year contract based in Washington - and you know what I love most about it, apart from the work itself?"

She didn't wait for him to respond. "You should see the food trucks that arrive for lunch; from every type of burger you can imagine to ceviche, creole and vegan. I love the food trucks. You can eat food from a different part of the world every day."

"I can imagine that Jonathan might like that, especially trying to find his favourite dish. But you two haven't had much time together; how are you coping with that?"

She shrugged. "It's not as hard as people say. We both have busy working lives and then you can always talk on Skype, or whatever. I don't suppose someone like yourself has ever tried anything other than talking, but you would be surprised by all the things you can do on a video call."

He had a horrible feeling she might just be about to go into detail and decided that was too much information. He jumped in quickly. "What I really meant was that you had barely got to know each other before you had to leave. That can be difficult."

"Not really - you just have to be disciplined, like doing some research. I think he's the one for me and I thought that very quickly. I told him we should see how things go and then maybe in another six months, when he comes out, we can talk some more and decide what we are going to do about it. We should have the data we need by then."

Data or no data, he was having trouble with how quickly this conversation had become so personal but didn't want to say anything that might antagonise her; then she said something that made him feel like she was reading his mind. "I totally trust Jonathan and he totally trusts you, so that makes you one of the good guys. In fact, it makes you one of the very few good guys at all."

He was very touched, but before he could reply the phone rang. It was the guard to say Sam's Uber had arrived. She and Jonathan disappeared into the bedroom, emerging with two huge suitcases and two smaller ones for her carry-on luggage. They squeezed into the lift and made their way down, ferrying the bags out to the car where they were stowed away.

"You can see why I needed a ride to the airport. I couldn't decide what to take to Washington, so I think I've packed too much, but best to be on the safe side."

She walked over to Roper and reached up to kiss him goodbye, then clambered into the back of the car which took off straight away. Only as the car vanished from sight did Hooley realise she hadn't said goodbye to him.

He looked at Roper, who was staring at the spot where the car had turned left and disappeared from view.

He patted his arm. "Come on, let's get you something to eat."

3

The Courier was sitting in the expensively upholstered interior of Maxine Dubois' Gulfstream G650. One of the fastest private jets you could buy, it was capable of just under the speed of sound. At around $70 million, only the seriously wealthy could opt to buy one, let alone afford the murderously expensive cost of running it.

He'd been sitting here for half an hour after joining his client at London City airport. He'd been told the plane would be departing again forty-five minutes later so, with just fifteen minutes to go, he hoped she would speak to him soon.

Dubois had chosen dark grey leather to cover the seats and the Courier thought he blended in well since he had chosen one of his many handmade grey pinstripe suits for the meeting. As he waited he looked down and admired the brilliant shine on his shoes that had been applied by the Savoy's service staff overnight. The watch with which he was keeping track of the time with was an antique gold Cartier with a brown leather strap. It was one of his favourites and he always wore it on important days.

It wasn't vanity that made him spend so much effort on his appearance; it was part of the way he sought to blend in and not stand out. Today he wanted to look like any of the bankers who swarmed through City Airport on a daily basis.

When he'd boarded the aircraft, Dubois was sat towards the rear of the cabin with her back to him and her right hand held up in a mockery of greeting. He walked forward and handed over the iPad he'd taken out of a leather carry case.

While she settled to watching the video clip he moved back to the front of the plane and sat where he could keep an eye on events - but especially on Dubois. With less than two minutes to go she was done. Her steward went over to her and bent down so he could hear what she said. Then he took the iPad and returned it to the Courier.

"Madame congratulates you on your choice."

Even though he had been expecting the outcome he had to resist the urge to sigh with relief. He had really wanted this to work and he wanted the money even more. A taste for high-stakes gambling meant he needed fuel for his addiction.

Walking down the steps he turned his mind away from quite how much had been riding on today. Instead he congratulated himself on having the foresight to set up a lucrative business that saw clients hand him eye-watering sums of money, in return for the opportunity to indulge dark fantasies.

For Dubois that meant the chance to get away with murder, literally. She would soon be enjoying a drama of her own devising as she watched from a ringside seat. She wasn't one for actually doing the deed, but she loved being in control.

He'd begun his criminal career as an arms smuggler ferrying weapons into the UK, making decent money - but he wanted more. The drugs business was too difficult to break into, protected as it was by ruthless gangsters, but there was still a niche space for people trafficking.

As London had grown ever larger and richer, he had spotted that demand would rise and since his rivals were hampered by being too large to change quickly he had made even more money.

His new fortune allowed him to indulge a long ignored creative side. Some people referred to what he provided as "snuff movies", but he knew there was more to it than that. Where else could people get to act out their dreams, even if the price was a nightmare for the victims?

Made in the USA
Middletown, DE
08 April 2019